Praise for *Dry Land*

"In precise, elegant prose, Pladek has given us a story set over a hundred years ago but with startling resonance for today. *Dry Land* is a deeply original novel that deserves attention. I can't remember reading anything quite like it."—Ken Harvey, author of *The Book of Casey Adair*

"*Dry Land* scouts the no-man's-land between heroism and humility. A heart-wrenching, heart-warming novel about all the ways we strive, fail, and learn to find grace."—Lara Elena Donnelly, author of the Amberlough Dossier

"If any man can make you long for a swamp, it is Pladek and his Rand, that unforgettable character whose perceptiveness extends to everything and everyone except himself. *Dry Land*'s settings are alive and living, fantastic only because they are so clearly seen, so deeply loved. Nobody writes nature like Pladek."—Natalia Theodoridou, winner of the World Fantasy Award

"*Dry Land* is vibrantly alive, achingly intimate, and rich in natural beauty. The characters' searing self-awareness and the author's astute attention to both historical and emotional detail speak of a maturity of craft that most debut writers can only aspire to. Pladek is a rare talent."—Isabel Cañas, author of *The Hacienda*

"*Dry Land* quickly transported me to the depths of the best walks through the northwoods, as sweet and familiar as fresh maple syrup in the springtime. I was captivated by the hero Rand, whose green journey through the woods of the Midwest, and much farther away still, sings beautifully of the tense and bitter pangs that come to us boys ill-adept at navigating nature and male camaraderie. Reading Pladek's descriptions of Wisconsin's northwoods conjured the familiar feeling of visiting one of Minnesota's oldest tracts of untouched lumber, the ephemeral pain of knowing what greatness was taken from the world."—Dennis Staples, author of *This Town Sleeps*

"Pladek has brought to life the marshes and woodlands of America. Through the protagonist, Rand, he explores queerness, masculinity, and the relationship of self to power and nature. This is a novel for anyone who is interested in the natural world and a human's place within it."—Alex Myers, author of *The Story of Silence*

Dry Land

B. Pladek

THE UNIVERSITY OF WISCONSIN PRESS

Publication of this book has been made possible, in part,
through support from the Brittingham Trust.

The University of Wisconsin Press
728 State Street, Suite 443
Madison, Wisconsin 53706
uwpress.wisc.edu

Gray's Inn House, 127 Clerkenwell Road
London EC1R 5DB, United Kingdom
eurospanbookstore.com

Printed in the United States of America
This book may be available in a digital edition.

Library of Congress Cataloging-in-Publication Data
Names: Pladek, B., author.
Title: Dry land / B. Pladek.
Description: Madison, Wisconsin : The University of Wisconsin Press, 2023.
Identifiers: LCCN 2023006023 | ISBN 9780299343941 (paperback)
Subjects: LCGFT: Fiction. | Novels.
Classification: LCC PS3616.L335 D79 2023 | DDC 813/.6—dc23/
eng/20230425
LC record available at https://lccn.loc.gov/2023006023

This is a work of fiction. Names, characters, places, and incidents either
are the product of the author's imagination or are used fictitiously,
and any resemblance to actual persons living or dead, businesses,
companies, events, or locales is entirely coincidental.

They wanted to blossom,
and blossoming is being beautiful. But we want to ripen,
and this means being dark and taking pains.

—Rainer Maria Rilke, "In the Drawing Room,"
trans. Edward Snow

Dry Land

Chapter 1

SURVEY JOURNAL: JUNE 21, 1917

Dawn chorus opened by robin, 3.30. Katydids calling,
10 p.m.?—forgot to check watch . . .

The woods had been logged, then logged again. Tall stands of maple
and basswood, chopped and floated downriver to La Crosse forty years
ago, had given way to pale thickets of aspen. These in turn had been
mown for pulp. Twenty years later they'd regrown. Rand imagined how
the forest's color had changed. Beneath their June canopy, open maple
woods were as green as ink, and nearly blue in the shadows. But here
the crowded aspens cast a sage-gray dusk. The pulpers had done a rush
job: as Rand's survey team shoved through the brush, he had to step
high to avoid tripping over the barrows of fallen poles the lumbermen
had missed.

Ahead of him along the chain, Gabriel was kicking black muck from
his boots. The motion sent a clicking shiver down the steel tape. Rand
shook back. Gabriel felt it, turned, and smiled over his shoulder. As
the team's chainers, they came last in the six-man survey train, and beyond the sight line hacked by the axemen, the understory was thick.
No one saw.

Farther ahead, Rand's ranger called a stop to consult his map. He
shouted back. The axemen called the instructions down to Gabriel, who
announced to Rand, "Turning west! Maybe we'll finally escape this mud."
For the last three weeks, Gabriel had been railing genially at *this boggy*

3

hellhole and longing for the dry, sweet pinewoods of his home in the southwest. His grudge against the damp was by now an old joke among the team. Rand tried not to take it personally. Few men loved swamps, especially when they had to trudge through them with chain and compass. It was stupid to want Gabriel to care for the soggy northwoods as much as he did. Liking Rand's home state was not necessary to their arrangement.

Talking was not either, though they sometimes did it anyway. Rand flexed his fingers on the chain. Their tips tingled. He had spent the day debating whether he could confide in Gabriel, and once again decided no. His secret was still too new, too unbelievable. He was afraid he did not deserve it.

The team pivoted west. Three weeks into their survey of cutover lands south of the Mondeaux, they had covered very little ground. Rand did not understand how they were expected to map hundreds of square miles at this snail's pace, chain-measuring every acre like a jealous farmer bordering his woodlot. Nor did his ranger understand, but as he'd told Rand, those were his orders and he followed them. Rand could not confide in him, either.

He squinted ahead along the line. The thick aspens knit together like a mottled green wall, effacing depth, hiding the ground's contours. As Gabriel drew the chain out again, Rand heard him curse. "Where did this hill come from?" A needle of fear touched Rand's stomach. He had thought they'd passed north of the esker, but an incline sharp enough to surprise Gabriel must be glacial, and on that miraculous evening Rand had been too startled to mark his location carefully. Pulse jumping, he fastened the chain to a pin and jogged forward. The mottled wall rustled, parted. As he passed Gabriel, Rand craned his neck to see the esker's slope sweep up, eighty feet high. The flagman already stood near its brow. To his left along its snaking crest, Rand could just see a flurry of unseasonable white.

"Weston!" he called. "Weston!" The ranger turned, looking nonplussed; Rand knew Weston thought him deferential, despite his education. As Rand halted beside him, he regretted that he would have to lean on that education to keep the team from the esker's white crest.

"I'm sorry, but this isn't proper. At the Forest School, when measuring glacial landscapes, we're to . . ." His explanation was half nonsense, and he suspected Weston knew it. But Weston only nodded. Hailing the flagman, he pointed him back down the slope.

The team bent like a hairpin, turning north to hug the esker's boggy flank. As the axemen pushed by, grumbling at their wasted work, Rand's nerves drained out in tremors down his legs. Gabriel passed him with a questioning look. He shook his head. Maybe the redirection had not been necessary. But if he was overcautious, it was because he was a bad liar. His face would have blared his guilt, even though there was no way his ranger or anyone on the team could have guessed that the esker's fresh white foam of trillium, a spring bloom flowering improbably in summer woods, had anything to do with him.

Thankfully the men asked no more questions. Rand returned to camp that night having turned the survey safely northeast. By the time he struck the fire, the axemen were too busy swatting blackflies to remember their irritation. Still, he sought to make amends. Layering the team's last salt side in the pan, he skimmed off the grease. Then he brought it around for his teammates to anoint themselves. "For the flies," he said. Better wards existed, but Rand had not been able to bring himself to snap the few white pine saplings he'd seen for their juice. All new growth seemed more sacred now, since his secret.

"Thanks," said Gabriel, nose wrinkling as Rand held out the cup of fat. More fastidious than the rest of the team, he always rubbed it in like aftershave, almost too thorough to be effective. One night, flushed and stupid, Rand had joked he liked him smelling of bacon. Gabriel had barked with laughter.

Greased, the team ate. Afterward Rand gathered the dishes. As he went he hurriedly chewed his own small portion. In the past week he had not been able to eat much. Wrapped up in himself, he could not tell if the men had noticed his distraction. He hoped not. Once the pan was cool, he scoured it with sand, then thrust the knives and forks into the earth before washing them. Moving to the fire, he noticed Gabriel had already rebuilt it. He nodded his thanks and got another smile; Gabriel was bolder than he before their teammates.

At last he strung up the pan, and his cook's duties were over. He retreated to the far end of their camp clearing. Propping his roll of tarpaulined blankets against a hemlock's knees, he drew paper and pencil from his kit.

Since last week he had tried several times to write to Jonna. She would not receive the letter for weeks; he would have to drop it with the postmaster in Merrill. But she was the only person to whom he could write honestly. Jonna believed the order of the world could be changed, the kings and bosses destroyed, the people restored to their rights. His secret was no more fanciful. Besides, they'd been friends for long enough that she would know he was not joking, or driven mad by the blackflies. As she'd said in a letter earlier that spring, since the war broke out, she could believe in anything senseless.

Dear Jonna,

You must promise you will not share what I am about to tell you. It will sound impossible, but it is real, and you must believe me. If I am right, it could change everything.

I will try to explain. Do you remember the story I told you, about when I was young, & Clearwater Marsh

A shadow fell across his paper. He looked up to see Gabriel leaning against the hemlock. "So unsociable tonight. I was hoping you'd care to explain that long detour you took us on—" Seeing Rand's paper, he stopped. "Ah, letters home? I'll leave you be. I'm off to play. Tell me if you'd care to sing, later." He held his eyes to be sure Rand understood, then turned back toward the fire.

In his wake, heat seeped down Rand's stomach. The letter on his knees seemed suddenly ridiculous.

He stared again at its final lines, and the scene returned with all the sharpness of shame. He saw himself at fifteen, standing in an airless room before a state subcommittee, clutching a sweaty petition he'd spent months compiling. Its hundreds of student signatures called for the preservation of Clearwater Marsh, that great mirror etched with birds Rand had loved since age ten. That year his father, anxious about his son's aimless rambles through the bogs behind their woodlot, had tried to focus his outdoorsmanship by taking him duck hunting. They'd ridden the train northeast from their home in the state's dry center, booked a room in a shooting club, and risen the next morning to an autumn fog silver with the peals of grebes. To his father's dismay, Rand had shot nothing. His heart was too full.

Eleven years later the marsh had been bled dry, parceled and drained for muck farming. Developers from Illinois had ignored rulings handed down by that same subcommittee, who had shaken their heads and told Rand gently that they were very sorry, but there was nothing they could do.

He set down his pencil. Right now, miles to the south, Clearwater's dried peat was burning. Perhaps he could have convinced the senators it would, if he had spent more time gathering support. The shooting clubs had opposed the drainage, as had inhabitants of nearby towns, who grew marsh hay and ran hotels for wealthy sportsmen from Chicago. But he had been fifteen, hasty and arrogant. He had just discovered the writings of John Muir and learned the difference between conservation and preservation. The latter concept had rung him like a bell. His shock that it was not the standard policy toward places like Clearwater was so powerful he trusted that feeling would move others, too. For the petition he had cut school, irritated his parents and sisters, and endangered his chances at university. He had given so much. He had never thought it would not be enough.

Slowly, Rand spread the letter across his knees and rubbed the words with an eraser until all that remained was *Dear Jonna.*

Four weeks remained in his team's surveying trip, enough time to determine whether his secret warranted the flame of hope that burned in his throat. If it did, only then would he tell Weston, who would inform the Forest Service. And then—Rand imagined pressing his fingers to the scarred peat of Clearwater. The flame rose, brightened. He bit his lip to stifle it.

He erased *Dear Jonna* as well. To write anything and omit it would be deceptive, and he could never lie to her. Until diligence had earned him a truer picture of his situation, he would forgo the comfort of her correspondence. Resolved, he tucked the paper back into his bedroll. Distantly he felt his stomach rumble. He ignored the discomfort.

From beside the campfire he heard a whistle, then an answering note from a violin. He looked up to see Gabriel perched on a log, adjusting the pegs. The rest of the team had arranged themselves about him. As Rand rose to reseat himself, Gabriel gave him a mock salute with his bow.

Their arrangement still surprised him. Not the mechanics—he'd gathered they were both old hands at secrecy—but Gabriel's interest. If Rand was the greenest member of the team, Gabriel was among its most competent. He could shoot as well as Weston, and ride better. The son of a wealthy ranching family south of Santa Fe, he had spent weeks as a boy in the high country, guarding the flocks from wolves.

Yet he rarely mentioned this history. It was not from false humility, Rand thought, but because it was somehow not how Gabriel saw himself. What he did see Rand only suspected, from glimpses he caught some mornings. While the rules of their nights had at first excluded conversation, night had lately been slipping into sunrise. On the first day they'd heard the dawn chorus together, Rand had given up on sleep, and after returning to camp had withdrawn again, bearing a lantern and a letter from his younger sister Greta. He was startled when Gabriel joined him, violin in one hand, folded paper in the other. Smiling, Gabriel had explained that he liked to practice in the morning after writing to his sisters. When Rand had held up his own letter, he'd laughed. "How many?" he'd asked. "Two," replied Rand. "Four," said Gabriel. "Maybe we should finish sooner."

After, their mornings became routine. Rand lit a lantern by which they wrote until the birds started, then sat back to listen, eyes closed. When the light grew, he built the breakfast fire while Gabriel played softly, not the campfire songs he fiddled for the men but breathless solos, some of which Rand recognized from his mother's piano versions of Bach and Mozart. Gabriel's whole body focused like a lens around the music. Almost more than he wondered what Gabriel saw in him, Rand wondered how a violinist of his talent had ended up on a poorly funded exploratory survey of a landscape he disliked, so far from home.

Now he wondered it again, watching Gabriel strike up "Ragtime Cowboy Joe" and the team follow. Rand's secret would alter their late nights, quiet mornings. Such pleasures were an appropriate first offering to its promise. But as he sat by the fire, following Gabriel's fingers over the strings, the thought of losing them sat heavy in his stomach.

When the singing was over, the men prepared their beds, blanket cocoons tented between tarpaulins to keep out the damp—two men to a set, since the service had only paid for three tarps.

"Well?" said Gabriel as Rand shed his boots. Leaning up, he snaked a finger beneath Rand's belt.

Rand hesitated, then removed his hand. "I have a lot to think about tonight."

Gabriel laughed ruefully. "A man who schedules his thoughts? Very diligent. Well, if you promise to be in the mood tomorrow night, I'll shoot you a prairie chicken for dinner."

Rand smiled as he slid beneath the blankets. "Woods are too thick for chickens here."

"A rabbit, then."

"Sure."

"It's a deal." He felt Gabriel turn over. Carefully, Rand tucked himself against his back, so his nose just touched the warm skin at the base of his neck. He listened to Gabriel's breathing slow.

Then he closed his eyes and, as he had every night for the past week, relived the moment he'd discovered his gift.

He supposed he should be grateful to Gabriel. That afternoon on the line he'd been playfully abusing Wisconsin after losing a sock to a kettle's swampy verge. Rand took it harder than he should have. As he did not want to be irritated with Gabriel before nightfall, that evening, instead of returning with the team to camp, he said he would gather mushrooms for supper. He struck off up the esker to the west, toward the drooping hemlocks lining its ridge.

Sliding down against a bole, he let his head rest against the red bark and watched sunset string shadows across the understory. The hemlocks were the only big trees left in this forty, snubbed by loggers because they made poor board wood. Beneath their shadows, the ground was mostly bare. Further down the esker the brush thickened. Around the old stumps of maple and basswood, needles of third-growth aspen flashed in the slanting sun. Chopping through them for sight lines was scratchy, tedious work, made worse by the mud. It was a broken landscape, hard to survey, harder to love. He should not have taken it so hard.

He curled his fingers into the soil and tried to let everything drain out of him: Gabriel's laugh, the draft card he'd signed three weeks ago, the hope and fear wound always about his throat at this, his first real Forest Service post. To focus he closed his eyes, remembering that he was here not for what these woods were now, but for what—with time and care—they could be. He imagined this forest as it might look in fifty years, if their survey convinced the Department of Agriculture to purchase and preserve it. He replaced the aspens with sugar maple and yellow birch, the churned mud with ephemeral pools, the brown Aprils with flowers: yellow trout lily, purple liverleaf, white trillium.

When he opened his eyes again, the ridge was a sea of snow.

He sat up sharply. Hundreds of trilliums unfurled across what had been bare ground beneath the hemlocks. Their three-pointed flowers nodded at him from dark-green shields.

For a long moment he could not think. He blinked, shook his head, wondering if he had misremembered the landscape. But he had just stared down the length of this esker, and knew no trillium grew there.

He looked down at his hands. Between each finger a flower sprouted. He looked up. The mat of trilliums was a perfect circle, and he was its center.

At his graduation from Yale's Forest School that May, its former dean, the Forest Service's chief, had spoken to their class. "Remember," said the chief, fixing them with keen eyes, "there are no mysteries, only phenomena. You are stewards of this nation's woodlands, but you are also its scientists. Never stop asking questions, and never rule out answers because they seem impossible."

Rand laid his fingers to the soil and thought of large-flowered trillium. He did not know much, save their Latin name and their cheery appearance each April during the second wave of spring blooms. Yet as he concentrated, he could feel something warm and bright flowing out of him, touching like a hidden spring the rhizomes buried below the hemlocks.

As he watched, at the tips of his fingers two green nubs pushed up. Their buds opened like white stars.

Trembling, Rand shifted his hands to the bole's far side. Touching the soil again, he drew up another trillium, then another, pausing between each to touch their leaves, stems, sepals. Slowly, deliberately, he grew flower after flower, testing their reality and his own sanity as evening fell around him and he tried to swallow the fire rising in his chest. Only when the hemlocks had gone gray and shadowless did he stumble back down the esker, his body lit with joy, his feet dragging through the field of darkened stars.

Now beside him, he felt Gabriel settle finally into sleep. Above, the night wind had risen, beating the tarp's slack sail. It rattled the aspens like breath through clenched teeth. Rand pictured it rolling through the nave of a mature forest. He saw himself raising beech and sugar maple here, tall, well-spaced. The air would sing between their columned trunks, and the canopy lift its green hands in praise.

The vision hovered in him for a moment; then he caught himself, and called it back down. Before he knew his gift better, he would not indulge useless dreaming. As Jonna always said, no revolution came without struggle. Wriggling a hand beyond the blankets, he touched his pack, within which lay his worn copy of Muir's *My First Summer in the Sierra*. Before the writings that would preserve Yosemite, Muir had spent years in the mountains, weathering snow from the heavens and mockery from his detractors. He'd earned the love that made him famous. Surely Rand could weather a few weeks of solitary study in service of his own.

Quietly he untucked himself from Gabriel, then slid out of the blankets. His legs felt watery; he forced them to work. This was only his fifth night of secret testing. He would not give in to exhaustion so soon.

He looked at the moon. By its position, midnight had not yet passed. If he walked quickly, he could slip south along the line they'd already surveyed. Three miles back he'd seen a white pine sapling old enough to produce cones. Some of last year's fallen scales might still contain seeds.

Chapter 2

Understory of alder thicket: red dogwood, white meadowsweet (pungent!), clump of black currant, many bedstraw sp. . . .

On the holiday morning, Rand woke late. Last night the team had sat up around the fire, singing and passing Weston's flask. He was grateful for the lie-in. As a boy he had foregone sleep easily, leading Greta on midnight expeditions behind the family woodlot to the creek where the raccoons fished, sharing secrets as they tramped, until the age came when he saw he was responsible for her, and both excursions and confidences stopped. She had resented him then. He wished she could see him now. Though Greta was not vengeful, she'd be amused by how pathetically he clawed from his bedroll in full daylight. His body had sucked at sleep like a parched man at a river.

He had not expected how challenging it would be to overlay his days with a new, secret pattern. The Forest Service kept a trim schedule. Between June and July, Rand's team was tasked with mapping thousands of acres of cutover between Taylor and Lincoln counties for a prospective national forest. The task had recently become urgent, since two years ago the governor had nullified Wisconsin's state forests and proclaimed their conservation a federal, not local, concern.

The thought that he might help salvage the northwoods sustained him through the days' grueling pace. Each day after Rand made breakfast, the team followed Weston out into the woods. Consulting the compass, the ranger sent the flagman ahead to mark the line. The axemen followed, hacking a path clear. Last, Rand and Gabriel strung out the thirty-three-foot chain, dropping pins to mark distance. Then the whole team moved forward to repeat the procedure. They stopped only for lunch and the occasional smoke.

As the team's only graduate of the Forest School, Rand's mathematical skills meant he was inevitably assigned to chaining; as what Weston laughingly called a "natural, natural philosopher," he acted as record-keeper, compiling an official list of landforms and timber composition alongside his more idiosyncratic private notebook. But he was camp cook because he'd asked to be. Save Gabriel, Rand was not close with his teammates. Perhaps they sensed the woods meant more to him than they did, or mistook his absorption for a college man's disdain. Rand had never tried to correct their impressions. Concealing his nights with Gabriel only increased his reserve. Cooking was his compromise, a sign of his care for the team that did not demand their friendship.

At least it meant they did not ask questions. Between all his tasks, it was difficult to step away to mark places where he could return at night. It was even harder to find them again in the dark. Those nights he did not spend with Gabriel, he made his excuses, waited until he was reasonably sure he was asleep, then crept away by starlight to the spot he'd memorized. Some nights he barely made it back before dawn.

His days grew stumbling. He yawned into his elbow and shouted the wrong signals to Gabriel, who frowned, though he said nothing.

But his nights were transcendent. The dark woods blossomed beneath his fingers. With each test he pushed himself harder. Despite his growing collection of pine scales, maple keys, and basswood nuts, he had started small, with whatever bulbs lay already dormant in the earth. After two nights of flowers he advanced to shrubs, raspberry canes and stalks of red dogwood; finally, in another three, to trees. His first spindly sugar maple took such a concentration of energy that he fainted briefly against it.

Though he tried to discipline his hopes, when he awoke beneath the maple stretching like a young god above the stumps, he could not suppress the visions that rose alongside it. His childhood had been spent wandering beloved landscapes, trying to imagine what they had once been. After his failure at Clearwater, he had applied to Yale at his parents' urging. Only in the Forest Service might his dreaming become useful. Pining away in swamps was not man's work, his father had scolded— and besides, added his mother, it would not save the places he loved.

What would it mean to save them, immediately and completely? The purple quartzite hills near his home in Inselberg were scarred with abandoned pastures, treeless save for the occasional old windbreaker. He saw himself as Johnny Appleseed, striding the farms with a satchel of acorns. Bur oaks blazed up behind him like flags.

Bolder dreams followed. He remembered his last year at university, when to hide from the pain of Jonna's gentle *no* and his fear of the European war, which had not ended by Christmas as everyone had said, he had followed the Hetch Hetchy dam construction with single-minded focus. He'd scoured the California papers for news of the timber speculators rushing in to strip the valley before it was drowned. Gazing up through the leaves of his first maple, he imagined himself standing before Congress and lifting a palmful of soil. To their hushed faces he pled the valley's cause, as from his hand a pine sapling sprung, symbol of what he could heal if they'd let him.

Angrily he shook away the vision. How arrogant, to believe he could succeed where Muir had failed. Against his heart, still fluttering with possibility, he pressed the heavy memory of Clearwater.

A wooly gray was daubing the dark horizon. He sat up, rubbing his eyes, and opened his notebook.

Over the next week he began to learn the rules of his gift. He found he could not grow from nothing. Prairie species would not sprout in the deep woods where their seeds had never fallen. Cultivars would not sprout at all. But if he pocketed a mayapple and buried it where none grew, he could coax its spreading umbrella into the air. Certain transplanted roots could also be coaxed to growth, though they required more effort.

Trees of any sort took more effort still. Rand did not know how the energy transfer worked, what warm brilliance bled through his fingers when he raised a sapling from the soil. He only knew that he must take care when growing trees, lest he pass out for too long and be found missing. He took pride in these fainting spells, as he explained to Jonna in the letter he finally felt comfortable beginning. They were small, tangible proofs of his devotion.

> I am calling it a *gift*, by the way, and not a power. That way I'll remind myself that it has been given me & I must earn it.

Jonna would understand. She took nothing for granted. Like Rand, she was from Wisconsin, the only daughter of an Iron County union boss and a Minneapolis suffragette. Both had died early, leaving Jonna savings and a mandate to improve herself. Rand had met her in college. She'd chosen Yale's art school as much for its proximity to New York as for its rare admission of women. After graduation she'd stayed out east, cartooning for the workers' dailies. In the past year she'd begun scheming ways to get herself to Paris. Still, a portion of all Rand's letters to her were given to portraits of the lakes and woods she missed dearly. She had requested this of him soon after he'd moved back west.

In a letter that spring, he had asked her why her dream was to migrate to a foreign city with no lakes, whose language she barely spoke. Her answer, tucked at the end of a rant about the Boy Mayor, was a single line: *Because I belong there.* Missing the northwoods was the price she'd chosen to pay. Rand respected her clear-sightedness. He hoped he could learn to accept whatever his gift cost.

> July is hot and still. Even the chipmunks are panting. The sky is thick as cream, and the aspens are a green kaleidoscope. They shift with the smallest wind . . .

Writing to Jonna also helped dull the sting of his teammates' increasing distance. Too tired for campfire chat, Rand fixed meals in bleary silence, then retreated to a trunk to catch a few minutes of sleep. The flagman and axemen began to avoid him. Only Gabriel still attempted to talk, in their shared mornings before breakfast, or as they stole out of camp once the fire had died. Rand's efforts to reciprocate were sleepy, conversational and otherwise.

If his ranger noticed Rand's exhaustion, he did not discipline him for it. But on the second Sunday after Rand had discovered his gift, when Weston announced they would move camp twenty miles northwest, he stared at Rand for a long time. "I hope you've said your goodbyes, Brandt."

"Sir?"

Weston did not elaborate. The hike was long. Rand lagged beside the mule, panting, wondering how long his body could sustain this pretense. Ahead of him at her bridle, Gabriel leaned back and asked, "You all right?"

He searched for a response that was not a lie. At last he said, "I'm very tired."

Their new camp lay beside a small kame overlooking a marsh. Beavers had clogged one end with drowned birches, packing them into a nibbled palisade. Behind its wall stretched a curve of open, tea-colored water. Rand's pulse quickened. The marsh would allow him to test his gift on many water species.

He awaited nightfall with a burst of fresh energy. Frying potatoes with juniper in the dutch oven, he even whistled.

When they were all beneath their blankets and Gabriel's breathing had gone easy beside him, he slipped out and made for the marsh.

His excitement quickly deserted him. The reedbed was surrounded by a wide, close thicket of young alder. During the day he would have found it beautiful, but at night the muck sucked his boots and the alders' nails scored his face. To save energy, he struck out east of the marsh and into the deeper woods, trying to keep the glimmer of open water on his left. After what seemed only a short time, his eyes dropped. He felt his feet stumbling mechanically for clearer ground.

He stopped. With an effort he wrenched his head upright, unsure of how long he had been walking.

Above, clouds hid the moon. He crouched to peer along the line of his own footsteps, but the brush was too thick. No slope was palpable beneath his feet that would direct him downhill, toward water.

Kneeling, he folded his arms across an old stump and cycled through his Forest School lessons on what to do when lost. Most required daylight, stars, or a compass. Yawning into his elbows, he tried to summon the energy for planning, or at least self-recrimination. But his head only swam. It circled around and around, and down finally into silence.

In the darkness a door opened, and he saw his parents, bent over the lathe in his father's old workshop. Rand held out wet hands to them. He had plucked marsh marigolds, the muddy stems dangling through his fingers. His mother took her yellow blooms with a faint smile. His father set his aside, then wiped his palms on his apron. Rand knew then that there was something more he should have brought them, something crucial he had failed to give, but it was too late to change it or repair his mistake.

When he woke, gray light was in the trees.

He pushed to his feet, reeling. The panic sleep had defeated now swept him like nausea. In an hour he must begin breakfast. He shook the dream away. Crouching, he searched for signs of his prior passage.

He was retracing his own mucky footprints when he heard a whistle—not the waking birds, but a steady, directed melody. He stopped to listen. When it repeated, he recognized it as the song he had been whistling at dinner, Schubert's "Gute Nacht."

Relief flooded his chest, alongside a familiar tightness. At dinner he had given no thought to the song; it had been thrown up out of his exhaustion. But now he remembered when he'd last heard it: at the hotel in Stevens Point, where the survey team had gathered in late May before taking the spur line north. Rand had disembarked from the same Madison train as Gabriel, and they'd shared a beer at the hotel's dingy taproom. At first their conversation had been guarded. But when Gabriel removed his violin to check its condition after the journey, he'd asked if German songs were still tolerated here, and if Rand knew any Schubert. Though Rand had a weak voice, when he saw Gabriel tuck the instrument beneath his chin and arch the strong line of his shoulders, he had met his eyes and said yes. Together they'd moved through as many lieder as they both remembered, Gabriel playing arrangements Rand guessed he'd composed himself. He had not seemed to mind how frequently

Rand fell off-key, or how one drink became several. Stumbling upstairs, Rand had not realized he'd given Gabriel the number of his room until later that night, when Gabriel had appeared at the door, asking if he'd waited long enough.

Now through the summer woods, Gabriel whistled "Gute Nacht" a third time. Moving toward the sound, Rand whistled back.

In less than five minutes he saw Gabriel's compact body picking through the trees. A thin sweat shone on his brown cheeks, and his mustache was unbrushed, wiry with sleep. A lantern swung from one hand. When he saw Rand he raised it to wave, and the light touched his tired face and eyes.

The tightness in Rand's chest reached up to close his throat. "Thank you," he said. "I'm sorry. Thank you."

"Well, you're welcome," came the yawning answer. "I guessed you'd gotten lost, since you weren't back by the usual time. Bold of you, on our first night at a new camp."

Rand looked up. "The usual time? So you've noticed?"

"Did you really think I hadn't?"

His expression was wry, and a little exasperated. Rand nodded, embarrassed.

Gabriel laughed. "So it's true, all your attention *is* reserved for birds and plants and things. Look, I'll admit I'm impressed. I don't know many men who can keep up this kind of schedule. But you should take some nights off. I don't even mind if they're my nights."

Rand was so exhausted it took him a moment to understand. When he did, he winced. Yet it was a good alibi. They'd shared enough of their histories to know that neither had qualms about other lovers. Gabriel need never discover Rand had lied to him. In this way he would be like every other member of Rand's team, who held him at arm's length and did not seek his trust.

Rand's heart sank. He tried to guess how Jonna might advise him. But his letter to her still sat in his pack. Lying was not wrong if his intentions were good, he reassured himself—even if Gabriel had wanted to know, and even if Rand wanted to confide in him, with a longing that surprised him. If only he weren't so tired.

Gabriel was watching him curiously now, his face unguarded. "Don't look so ruined," he said. "I thought we'd gone over this? You don't have to tell me anything."

In the gray depths of his fatigue, something jerked. As if from a distance, Rand watched himself sink to the ground. Faintly he heard Gabriel's shout of concern. He ignored it. Reeling, he splayed his fingers on the earth. Then he squeezed his eyes shut, and thought, *Trillium.*

When he woke again he was lying on his side. New leaves brushed his cheeks. Overhead, Gabriel was swearing softly in Spanish. He must have noticed Rand move, because a moment later he knelt and offered him an arm. Threading his elbow through, Rand pulled himself to his knees. A sea of trilliums surrounded them.

"Weston owes me a nickel. He'd bet on a farmwife." Behind the joke, Gabriel's voice was spooked. "What the hell is this?"

"I don't really know." He knew he should reproach himself, but he felt only a deep, liquid relief. "I've been trying to learn. I'd wanted to know more before I told anyone."

"But why would you hide something like this?"

"So I don't bungle it. So it's enough."

"Enough for what? This is a miracle." With his free hand, Gabriel ruffled the bobbing flowers, as if afraid they might dissolve. "Is it just flowers you can make?"

"No. Shrubs, trees. Anything that grows, if I have the right seed."

"Anything." Through their linked arms, Rand felt Gabriel's body tense.

"I think so. It's like a muscle I can work. I'm getting better at it."

Gabriel's voice was taut in a way Rand had never heard before. "What you could do with this kind of power—what you could save."

The same joy that had lit Rand's body on the day he'd made his first trillium was returning, spreading through his limbs as inevitably as the dawn. "Yes!" he said. "So many places. These woods, even. Imagine what they used to be. I could heal them, regrow the wilderness."

"Regrow it," Gabriel echoed.

Beyond where they crouched, in the distant marsh, dawn was threading through the mist. Gabriel's shock seemed to speak for all the visions Rand had not allowed himself. With a bright shiver he imagined filling the ratty alders with pinewoods, deep and fragrant. Perhaps he had been wrong to hesitate, waiting for proof that he deserved this gift before revealing it to others. Perhaps he was already enough; perhaps the gift itself proved it. His chest burned with light.

He thought of a different marsh farther south, burning too.

Twisting around, he looked east, which he could now mark by a paleness through the alders. "We should go. I want to tell Weston, before breakfast. I should have done it a week ago." He breathed deep, then turned to Gabriel. "Thank you again for finding me."

Gabriel stood slowly, pulling Rand up with him. He seemed lost in thought. "It's nothing."

As they walked back through the trilliums' spill of white stars, Rand felt like a constellation, grand and predestined, leaving night behind.

Chapter 3

Full bloom: orange jewelweed, evening primrose (on old logging road) . . .

Dear Jonna,

I know you have probably not yet received my first letter, but I wanted to tell you how things have been.

I have more time to write now. After Weston rode to Merrill to wire Washington (wire!), he has given me half days to practice the gift. He has also sworn me to silence, but I know I can trust you.

Beside him there was a scuffle, and Rand looked down in time to see an ovenbird pick its way behind a fallen tree. "What are you doing in such broken woods?" he murmured. "Not nesting, surely?"

In the pause he wondered, as he had often over the past week, if he had been too quick to tell Weston. Gabriel's awe was a powerful drug. Rand's haze of joy had dulled his usual caution. In the moment after he'd confessed, he realized he had not even considered what the Forest Service might want with his gift. Certainly he'd been foolish to hope he'd remain in Wisconsin. Weston's instructions implied they would put him to work at once—reforesting the White Mountains, maybe, or one of the national forests scarred by logging. He avoided guessing how soon he would have to say goodbye to the northwoods, and Gabriel.

Shaking his head, he returned to the letter.

Weston says I should focus on growing timber, as much as I can, & as fast. No sense for the forest's personality, just fleets of oak & white pine. But what else could I expect from an old lumberman? So I grow trees, but I plant flowers between them. Yesterday I made a blueberry bush for Gabriel, and found I could even ripen the berries.

He paused again, feeling his face warm. Writing to Jonna about Gabriel felt intrusive in ways for which he had no words. When they were at university together, Jonna had helped Rand understand certain things about himself; these included, eventually, how he felt about her. What she felt he had not understood until too late. His proposal, delivered with a bouquet of daffodils on a warm spring night, was the only time he could ever remember seriously embarrassing her. She had been very kind about it. Still, their friendship had tumbled back to its rocky base. They'd reascended slowly, cautious as any climbers who have fallen badly once. Though it was now two years since Rand had asked the fatal question, it did not feel fair to plunge her back into his feelings. Instead he asked:

How goes your quest to find work as a war correspondent? I am still surprised you are so adamant about it. Is getting to Paris really worth "burnishing the gold on the coffin lids," as you say? You hate this bankers' war, & it will be dangerous, even for lady artists behind the front. Please be careful. Right! Now I have said it once.

If Jonna balked at being courted, she hated being patronized more. She never described her living arrangements in the city, he guessed, because he might offer her some of his salary. She'd be annoyed at his warning, but he could not bring himself to erase it. He shook away the image of Jonna in no-man's-land, her face gaunt and smeared with blood.

Let me tell you about the woods. Today dawn was tranquil. The chorus opened with the robin, who normally begins a half hour before the light, & then the other thrushes . . .

As he listed the birds for Jonna, Rand recalled how that morning Gabriel had said something similar about Paris. After their return to camp, he'd seemed restless. At first Rand had attributed it to worry: since the trillium dawn they'd been less careful, lingering longer, returning later. Though Rand was not close enough with the team to sense shifts in lenience, Gabriel was. Rand wondered if they had finally grown suspicious. But as he gathered kindling, Gabriel had not seemed concerned with the men, still rolled like pill bugs in their blankets. Instead of opening his letters, he had risen to pace. Rand had followed.

Gabriel's calloused hands fidgeted, pressing ghostly chords. In an effort to cheer him, Rand began naming the birds as they sang. He kept his voice light, even as he remembered they would not have many more of these mornings.

"That falling double spiral," he said, "that's a veery. They're shy. And that buzzy trill—a palm warbler? Slowpoke, what are you still doing down here in July?"

"You talk about them like family." Gabriel sounded wistful. "Do you know all the birds in these woods?"

"Just about. I grew up farther south, but we get all these species during migration. There's a yellowthroat," Rand said, pointing to the bright song hidden in the reeds.

Gabriel cocked his head. "You mean the little wobbler between G and G-flat?"

"You can tell the pitch?"

"I have a good ear."

Rand knew that musicians found inspiration in birdsong, but he had never heard of one tuning the dawn chorus. He stopped walking to watch Gabriel tilt his face to the trees. "E, A-flat, C-sharp, D." Beneath his heavy curls, his eyes were pained. Rand remembered, with a small start, that he tuned his violin to his own whistle.

If this really was one of their last mornings, he would not get another chance. He might as well try. Quietly he asked, "Gabriel, why are you here? In the Forest Service, I mean."

Gabriel's shoulders stiffened. Rand feared he'd crossed their unspoken line. But after a moment, Gabriel said, "Our family's range is overgrazed.

I'm here to learn about damaged land, so I can manage our ranch when I'm older."

"But you're a violinist."

"I'm a first son."

Rand knew from his tone that he should not press further. For a minute he stood, watching Gabriel listen to the birds. Gabriel's eyes had closed and he swayed slightly, as if imagining his body somewhere else. "If you could go anywhere," Rand said. "Anywhere you wanted. Where would it be?"

Gabriel gave a startled, bitter laugh, and again Rand regretted his question. But he waited. When Gabriel spoke again, his voice was softer. "There's a violinist named Peeters. He's called the Tsar. They say he plays the moderns with the heart of a romantic. He's Belgian, so he's fled Brussels, and now he's teaching in the Conservatoire. I would give anything to hear him."

Rand had never heard of Peeters, but the Conservatoire was famous. "Paris?"

"You said anywhere. Though I'd take any place with a proper symphony. And don't mistake me, that's not just Europe, whatever the snobs say. Montreal, Mexico City, Chicago . . ." He nodded at the singing trees. "Not that your chorus isn't charming."

"Is that why you took a job up here, so far from home? Because we're close to Chicago?"

Gabriel gave him a long look, then turned back toward the birds. "If you like."

Rand looked down at his hands. Through them his gift pulsed, warm proof of his life's purpose. Then he looked at Gabriel, whose eyes had closed again as he listened to a wren trill from across the marsh. "Bravura," he murmured.

Carefully, Rand stepped forward and laid a hand to Gabriel's back. Gabriel did not turn, but leaned into the touch. Rand braced a portion of his weight, wondering what his burden was, if he'd ever learn. Gabriel said nothing. They stood that way for a long time.

Then the sun rose, and we went to work. Rand folded the letter and tucked it in his pocket. *Take care, Jonna. I'll write more soon.*

To keep the team from accidentally discovering Rand's gift, Weston had instructed him to practice far from the area of their survey. Every afternoon following lunch, he struck off on his own, blazing trees with a hand axe to remember his route. For caution's sake, he never practiced in the same area twice. Sometimes he came across a homestead of Norse settlers doggedly uprooting stumps from a field. More often, he was alone.

He did not mind. Knowing he must leave them soon, he took pleasure in the weedy, stubbled woods, learning their contours as if studying the slope of a lover's chin. With a half day of leisure to practice and test, he fell into a rhythm familiar from his high school days, when he had skipped class to roam the hollows around Inselberg. Having chosen his testing spot, he sat to knead the duff and smell its wet, fragrant quilt of leaves. Sometimes he rolled over to watch the brush lace the light, in patterns as minutely alive as the contractions of an iris. Then he rolled back and unhooked the trowel from his belt. He dug in his satchel for an acorn.

As in his youth, his ramblings were sunlit with dreams. But these dreams were real. He recalled the drawings he'd seen of the Peshtigo fire forty years ago, a million acres of ash sweeping up both coasts of Green Bay. Now if he buried the acorn in loam and concentrated, a white oak rose from it like a column.

He thought of his fifteen-year-old self, marching from the statehouse with red eyes. If only he could have told that crying boy that in seven years he would be calculating how long he might take to replant the northwoods, alone. The hope nearly requited his fear that he might spend years away from Wisconsin, doing yeoman's work for the service. He breathed slow, to soothe his nerves. Wherever he served, it would be in the cause of wilderness. That he could never regret.

Leaning back against his oak, he felt a trickle of joy. When he rose to move on, he swept a hand across its roots. Between them, the dry earth bloomed.

At sunset, as he followed his blazed trees back toward camp, he saw he was just east of where, a week ago, Gabriel had found him. He smiled. He would like to see those trilliums again.

No other large white blooms grew beneath new woods in July; he imagined his bed should be visible from a distance. But as he neared, no stars gleamed from the shadows. Instead, he saw a great, fetid tangle of plant matter, sprawling like rusted wire from the stump where he had slept.

The trilliums were dead. The whole mat had withered, shrunken like pulled weeds on the compost. Above, the heavy July brush had withered too. About the whole area hung a curious smell, both ripe and sterile.

A cold hollow opened in Rand's chest. Shaking, he drew his notebook from his pocket and walked slowly around the dead zone. Perhaps something had rotted here, or one of the nearby farmers used the spot for dumping. Dutifully he recorded these possibilities, already knowing they were wrong. *Setback*, he wrote, then crossed it out. *Failure.* He could not hear the woods around him above the hammering of his heart.

Looking up, he judged he had two hours of daylight left. If he went quickly, he could revisit one or two of his sites and still find his way back before supper. He was a scientist. Before he jumped to conclusions, he must have more data.

Shoving his notebook in his pocket, he ran.

Two hours later, as color drained from the sky, he trudged the last mile back to camp. Sweat gummed his shirt to his body.

He had visited three of his previous sites. Everywhere it was the same. His trees still stood, their bark firm, though an ominous pool of brown leaves surrounded one maple. His flowers were all dead. Worse, at one site, the ground cover about them had shriveled too, turning a sick yellow, as if touched by poison.

His mind was so numb as he stumbled into camp that he did not notice the evening fire had not been lit. His four teammates were clumped in a semicircle near the mule, whispering. Their eyes turned toward the edge of the camp, where a lathered horse was tied. Beside it stood Weston and a second man, whose back was turned.

As Rand approached, Gabriel broke away from the group and jogged up to him. "About time you're back. He wants to see you."

"He?"

Gabriel clapped a hand on his shoulder. "Gather yourself. It's Gray."

A wave of nausea gripped Rand's stomach. He swayed, and was grateful for Gabriel's hand. He had only met the chief forester once, at his graduation. But like all of the service's recruits, he knew Harry N. Gray's legend, his piercing eyes and uncompromising standards.

Quickly he counted: the fastest Limited from Washington to Chicago took one day; the local from Chicago to Madison, another; the ride up through the gutted woods to their camp, two more at least. It had only been a week since Weston had wired. Gray must have left immediately.

He thought of his flowers, dying in the woods.

"Recovered?" Gabriel asked. "You won't want to keep him waiting."

Looking up, Rand saw Weston waving him over.

"Randolf Brandt," said Gray, extending a hand. "The Swamp Boy."

Rand shook, trying to keep his grip steady. The nickname had been bestowed on him by the Milwaukee *Journal*, whose reporters found his youthful failure at Clearwater a charming feature story. He had not heard it for years. "You know, sir?" he asked.

"When I am told an outrageous story about a man in my service, I am going to find out as much about him as I can. I'm glad you care for wild places, Mr. Brandt. You must be overjoyed, if what Ranger Weston says about you is true. He has risked his entire career on you, you know. If he is lying, he is fired. Now," he continued, without giving Rand a chance to reply, "I would like a demonstration."

Rand stared at Weston. "Sir, I have something important—"

"Yet you made time to talk to Losada. Whatever it is can wait," said Weston, and lit a lantern. "Come on, sir," he told Gray. "I've chosen a spot."

He led them a mile away from camp, following the lamplit compass into the thickety woods. They walked in silence. Gray trailed Weston too closely for Rand to address him. The numbness had not released his mind. His thoughts were dark and wordless, as if he were watching himself sink in freezing water.

When Weston stopped and pointed, Rand knelt and stared at the ground.

"Well?" asked Gray.

"Grow something," urged Weston.

Rand could not look at them. "What do you want, sir?"

"We are in the northwoods of Wisconsin," said Gray drily, "and you are a graduate of the Forest School. You should not have to ask."

Rand nodded. Slowly, he reached into his satchel and withdrew a pine cone. Snapping a scale off, he laid it on the ground.

White pine, he thought.

He was sapped from running and hunger and panic, atop a full day of surveying and growing other trees. As the pine's taproot needled down into the gray soil, he felt his hands going cold. He fought for consciousness, pumping all the warm energy of his body into the swelling trunk.

When he finally blacked out, he did not know how large the pine had grown, only that he could no longer see Weston's lantern behind its shadow.

He awoke seated, to the smell of whiskey. Gray was waving an opened flask beneath his nose. Beside him Weston crouched, looking relieved.

Gray's own face was drawn. "Mr. Brandt," he said. "I see I owe you and Ranger Weston an apology. Please, have a drink."

Rand tipped his head back for a swig and realized he was leaning against his own pine's trunk. He glanced down among the roots, but it was too dark to see what had happened to the ground cover. The drink he immediately regretted: he was revived but dizzy.

"Your ranger has told me that you don't really know what this power is, but that you've been growing trees. That's good. He's also told me he's ordered you not to tell anyone else. That's good too." Gray turned to Weston. "I hate to ask this question so bluntly, but this is Wisconsin, and his name . . . Are his loyalties in the right place?"

Rand watched Weston's brows lower. "We are not traitors, sir. And I voted for La Follette. Sir."

"Steady, Weston. Just making sure." Gray turned back to Rand. "Mr. Brandt, have you signed a draft card?"

Rand nodded. Through his dizziness, a trickle of panic returned.

"Good," said Gray. "Now. I am not in the habit of exaggerating. But your power is—well, I would not have believed it, had I not seen it for myself. I know you are a preservationist. Weston tells me you read Muir. We may not wholly agree on how this nation's forests should be used, but I am sure we can agree that they must be sustained. Powers like yours are not awarded randomly by the universe. You have a duty." He took a breath. "And when the war is over, you will have any assignment in the service you please."

Despite his sickness, Rand pushed upright. His head throbbed with red light. "The war?"

"Our troops need timber. At the end of the summer I'll be leading a regiment of American lumbermen to France to supply our front lines. I don't know how closely you've been following the news, but this war will be won by supplies, not guns. With a ready supply of good timber, we can end it faster. I think we can all agree that's a good thing, no matter who we voted for." He glanced at Weston, then back to Rand. "Conservation within our borders is vital, but right now, winning the war is the Forest Service's top priority. You can help us do that. What do you say?"

Gray's gaze held his in the lamplight. Behind Rand's eyes, the red glare beat. Like many uneasy pacifists, he had signed his card to avoid trouble. Like most foresters, he'd prayed the importance of his work might spare him. To refuse the draft was to risk prison. His stomach lurched. He was not Jonna; he had never been brave.

Above him, his pine seemed to spin. From its wheeling branches hung a coil of brown dead things, trillium and alder, smoke from burning peat, distant guns.

After a minute of waiting, Gray's voice hardened. "Your country needs you, Mr. Brandt. What do you say?"

Rand whispered, "I'll do my best, sir."

Then he folded over and vomited.

Dimly he felt a hand on his back, and heard Gray say, "That's a good man. Now, Weston, let's talk arrangements. This is a stroke of luck for the service, in more ways than one."

Back at camp, the team eyed him but asked no questions. They clustered solicitously around Gray, currying his horse, roping their tarps over his sleeping space. They barely noticed Rand haul his kit to the edge of camp and fall, queasy, into his blankets. At one point he heard a roar of startled talk. It subsided into whispers, but the fire stayed kindled. He turned his face away from the light.

The war could be an opportunity, he told himself. His trees lived, as far as he knew, and if he were only growing timber, their longevity would not matter so long as their wood was sound. The war could give him time. His gift was not four weeks old, and still largely a mystery. With study and work, he would learn where he had blundered and fix it before he turned to the serious work of preservation.

He ground his forehead against his blankets. Once again he had been rash. No destiny was granted without trial, no great passion without sacrifice. How naive, to think he should not have to earn his gift, to assume he was already worthy of what he claimed to love.

Above him he heard a rustle. "You awake?" asked Gabriel. Rand peeled back the blankets. "You know where Merrill is? Any idea how long it'll take to hike there tomorrow?"

"Merrill? That's the train. You're going too?" Rand sat up angrily. "What the hell? I'll go tell Gray—"

"Don't bother. Weber tried, and got a speech about doing our bit." Gabriel's voice was tired. "At least there are worse places to serve than the Engineers. We'll be well behind the front. Less danger of battle . . . and Paris."

Guilt swept Rand, so fierce it was nearly panic. For his carelessness, his team was going to war. Worse, he could not stifle the small, traitorous gratitude that at least for now, he would remain with Gabriel. His selfishness made his gorge rise. He had to stop his mouth with his hand before stammering, "I'm so sorry."

If Gabriel noticed his reaction, he did not show it. "From what Gray said, this regiment's going to be enormous. I bet you're just an excuse to secure a whole crew of competent loggers." Ducking beneath the tarp, he knelt, laying his violin beside him. The ground squelched. "And I think I'm going to prefer France to this swamp, however many blueberries you stick in it."

Rand remembered that he had not yet told Gabriel about the trillium. His nausea sharpened. He was opening his mouth to speak when

Gabriel continued in a stiff voice, "I don't know how to ask you this. Guess I'll just spit it out."

His face had changed. His eyes were as stern as Rand had ever seen them, but something furtive and hopeful softened his mouth. Rand bit his lip and listened.

"You remember I said our range is overgrazed? It's worse." Gabriel's voice lowered. "My family is well off, but our land is stripped. The forage is gone, half the soil is washed out. If things keep on like this, in another five years we'll have to sell. We'll have no recourse, since—" He cut himself off with a hard breath. "I don't know if you have plans for after the war. But if my family could regrow our range, I could teach our sheepmen to manage it properly. I could even convince my father to let my sisters run the ranch." Rand saw his eyes flick down, toward his violin.

Gabriel saw that he saw. With a brutal smile he jerked back. "You're damn right: I'm shirking. Forget I asked."

Startled, Rand did not react at once. Gabriel's face seemed raw, his voice almost vicious. Rand tried to let his eyes show his concern. If he said nothing, he could avoid promises. Around him he felt the July night breathe. Somewhere within it, in places his hands had touched, patches of brown lay dying in the darkness.

Gabriel peered at him, then looked away. "Didn't you hear? I said to forget it. I don't need sympathy." His tone was bleak now. With sudden shame Rand recalled the night he'd gotten lost, Gabriel's cautious whistle and steady arm; and, later, the longing in his eyes as he tuned the dawn chorus. He seemed a man used to rescuing, who never looked for rescue. In Rand's head the red light burned. He could not be a coward about everything.

Swallowing, he reached out to touch Gabriel's wrist. When he looked up, Rand made himself smile. "Sure, I'll help."

Gabriel did not move. "You mean it?"

"I swear."

The relief on his face made Rand's throat ache. "I can't—well. Thanks."

Rand nodded numbly. In the morning, when he was rested, he would draft a strict schedule for himself of tests to run, questions to research.

Surely they would train in Washington before shipping out, where he would have the country's best libraries to consult. If he was misusing his gift, he would learn better. He would work to be worthy of it, as he had not been worthy of Clearwater, or Jonna.

For a moment he wished he were back east with her, asking advice over the ledge of her drawing table. Then he quashed the desire. The gift was his. If he could not control it himself, it had been poorly given.

"Hey. You there?" Gabriel waved a hand before his face.

"Just tired," said Rand.

The next morning they left before dawn for Merrill.

Chapter 4

CAMP JOURNAL: JULY 21, 1917

Carolina wren in the mock trenches. Good to hear them
again . . .

Rand sat alone in a small room overlooking Camp American University, watching the infantry drill.

Outside, canvas tents poked like napkins along lines of packed dirt. When the country had entered the war, the unfinished university had donated its land to the Army Corps of Engineers. Now its two completed buildings, stone pink and neoclassical, loomed above a brown surf of hastily built barracks. At the other end of campus, where the land fell away toward the Potomac, barbed wire fences guarded fields scored with trenches.

Not five minutes after piling out of the truck that had met his team at Union Station, Rand had been pulled away by a lieutenant in faded puttees. The eyes of his teammates had burned after him. They must have guessed he was responsible for their recruitment. He let their anger rake him. On the train he had apologized to Gabriel until he'd told him to can it.

On the train he had also reviewed everything he remembered from school—botany, silvics, soil science. It offered little guidance. Had his flowers died because they had been grown in the wrong place? (No: trillium was native to the northwoods). Given too little water or nutrients? (Perhaps: he would need to run tests). His best lead was the knowledge that trilliums were spring blooms, dependent on an open canopy, and he had grown them in June, in the shade. But they had withered so quickly. At school he'd learned that forestry was a branch of ecology, the youngest and most universal science, whose purpose was nothing less than explaining how nature worked as an organic whole. Yet no ecological concept he knew could account for the warm flood of energy he felt bleeding from his hands into the soil. He did not know what he should do first: consult a library or design experiments.

Watching the infantry jog in clustered formations, he wondered when he would find time or privacy to do either.

The door to the room opened. Gray stepped through, followed by a slim man carrying a black bag, whose arm bore the insignia of the army medic. His face and body were austere, composed of right angles.

Gray seemed sweaty and hurried and kept checking his watch as he said, "Mr. Brandt, this is Major Albert Manning. He's a doctor with the Engineers but has had forestry training. He'll be working with you to learn as much as we can about your power before we ship out in September."

Gray turned to Manning. "I'll expect weekly updates." He nodded to Rand. "Good luck, Private. I hope you will not disappoint." Turning, he left.

In his wake, Manning stared after him, his long, pale face pinched with what could have been disappointment. Then he turned to Rand with a curdled expression. "Randolf Brandt," he said. "You're short, for German stock. Did your family intermarry?"

Rand glanced at his reflection in the window, where he saw only his familiar wide forehead, close-set eyes, and sunburnt pallor: not handsome, but not frail either. "Sir?"

"No matter. We work with what we've got, and better it where we can." Reaching down, Manning opened the bag and withdrew a stethoscope and syringe. "Sleeves up. Any history of imbecility in your family?"

"Sir, Chief Gray mentioned updates. What did he mean?"

Manning frowned, holding the syringe. "I'm assuming the answer to my question is no. To be frank with you, I don't know why the chief believes your ludicrous story. I know he's overworked. I've told him to rest." Manning's frown deepened. "But I follow orders. The chief wants you to practice this power of yours until it's reliable. I'll study you doing it until we understand what exactly you are. Now: sleeves *up*."

Rand unbuttoned his cuffs and shoved them past his elbows. Taking his wrist, Manning laid it to the room's small table, then cinched a cotton sash about his bicep.

Rand barely felt the needle draw. "Study me? How often?"

"Don't worry. You'll still receive your basic training. Not that you'll need it, as far behind the front as you'll be." Manning removed the needle, the syringe dark with Rand's blood. "Now. Why are you in the Forest Service, Private Brandt?"

Startled by the question, Rand searched for the trick behind it. If Manning did not believe him, it could be his effort to ferret out a lie. Or maybe it was the opposite: he had sensed Rand's idealism and wanted to hear him explain it. "To preserve the wilderness," he said at last, warily.

"And that's what you want to use this power for? Preserving the wilderness?"

"Not just preserving." Despite himself, he felt his face warming. "Restoring it to what it was. Skipping succession, to bring climax forest back from cutover."

"So you're one of those." Manning sighed, as if in confirmation. He decanted Rand's blood into a glass tube, then met his eyes. "I don't expect to convince you—you Muir types think you're priests—but as long as you are part of the war effort, you will practice forestry as our great first chief defined it. There is no wilderness. There are only forests, and we must cultivate them as wisely as we cultivate our populations." He rubbed a thumb against his forehead. "If, god forbid, your power *is* real, you'll grow a lot of timber in France. And when we cut it, there'll be no whining about preservation. Do you understand?"

Rand frowned, but said, "Sir."

"Good." Straightening, Manning moved to the corner of the room and lifted a small pot Rand had not noticed before. It was filled with soil.

Manning placed it before him and pointed. "Grow a daffodil, please. The bulb is already in the pot."

Rand's jaw tightened. Though he could not know the flower would wilt immediately, he felt a terrible cold certainty as he looked at the pot, so sterile and enclosed, so designed, already, to kill what it held.

"I can't, here," he stammered. "It has to be outside, in real soil."

"Of course you can't." Manning's voice was archly satisfied. "Are there any other *accommodations* your power requires?"

He thought quickly. He knew nothing of Washington geography, only that the deeper the woods, the more easily he might hide whatever experiments he'd need to conduct. "Forest is best," he said. "Because I'll be growing timber in France, I should practice in conditions that are as close as possible to the real thing. And I should grow you trees. The troops have no use for flowers. Is there a forest nearby?"

Manning's eyes narrowed. "That's surprisingly sensible. At least you're a consistent liar. Yes, we have some woods that might suit. It's a forty-minute walk, but I can borrow a car. Come along." He rose and made for the door, then paused to smirk. "This is a city park, to be clear—not 'wild.' Adjust your expectations accordingly."

"Sir."

As the car sputtered toward Rock Creek, Rand watched the capital rattle by and thought about wilderness.

William Paquet, the service's first, conservationist chief, had carved out space for forestry in the Department of Agriculture by insisting that wood was a crop like any other. Forest was just a word to describe unlogged timber, the material reserves of a growing country. Wilderness came second, and mostly designated places that might serve for recreation—Yellowstone, the redwoods of California.

Rand understood this logic. Most of his schoolmates had been Paquet men. He could not grudge them their practicality, their sense that to be a forester was to assist the cause of progress. He was for progress himself, though it felt different in ways he could not articulate, and which added up to more, despite what Jonna said, than that he was from Wisconsin. But he was a poor advocate for his views, an awkward writer, and worse speaker. And while he could quote the language of Marsh and Emerson, it had never fit the landscape he loved. Marshes were not sublime.

Even Gabriel's offhand recollections of the Sonoran desert made a better case for preservation than Rand's misty memories of Clearwater.

"You're really interested in this?" Gabriel had said as they perched atop a boxcar chugging across the hills of southwestern Pennsylvania. "I wish I'd paid more attention."

The journey to Washington had taken a week, local trains that soaked up draftees and reservists as they went. Overcrowded, the men shimmied up to the roof for air. As the cars had filled with passengers from Michigan and Ohio, Rand had noticed that Gabriel spent more time up top. He'd followed, suppressing his fear that he'd irk Gabriel by hanging around, a reminder of why he was going to war.

"The saguaros are alive when the woodpeckers nest in them?" Rand continued. He had never seen a cactus. "Not snags?"

"Seems so. Hares nibble them for water. People too, sometimes." Gabriel slapped his crossed knees. "Ha! Glad I never had to."

Rand watched his hands resettle on his thighs. Crossing his own legs, he tried to picture Gabriel knifing water from a cactus. It was almost comically incongruous. Though Gabriel was at ease outdoors, his decorous gestures often seemed to belong onstage. Perhaps in his mind he was, too. Rand wondered if it helped.

"What were you doing in the Sonora?" he asked.

"I visited the provinces when I was returning north from my last year in the capital, at the conservatory. My last year of being indulged." He stressed the word in a gruff paternal accent. Then he winked. "Thanks to you, now I'll have to keep up my practice. I hope the men like Sarasate. He's my mother's favorite. She's from Galicia, as she never stops reminding us."

Alarm heaved below Rand's ribs. "I still don't understand what this is. I'm not sure it's wise to count on me."

To his surprise, Gabriel laughed. It was joyless. "Please. I'm not a fool. We're going to France, and then I'm going home to run the estate for the rest of my life. What do I have to lose? Why not believe in a magic boy who grows plants?" He looked down. "I've believed in stupider things."

His voice sounded bruised. Rand tried to catch his eyes. "What things?"

"Say, do you think your power works on people?"

"What?"

Gabriel thumbed his bare chin, avoiding Rand's gaze. The gaiety in his voice sounded practiced. "The army's going to make us shave off everything interesting anyway. Do you think you could grow me a proper beard first? I could even send a picture home to father. He'd hate it."

"Hell no. I might hurt you."

"Or I'd grow a few inches." Gabriel grinned again. "You're usually so scientific. Aren't you curious?"

"You're not afraid?" Rand decided it was unwise to pursue his earlier question.

"Not of that. It's a new experience, and I find those interesting." Gabriel shrugged. "Why, are you afraid of the unknowns?"

Rand flexed his hands, the dangerous warmth tingling in his fingers. He felt awe, mixed with a little horror. In his experience, men who relished being experiments were either too young to know better or too resigned to care. "I guess I am afraid. Though aren't most of the things we fear unknowns?" He glanced at the woods beyond the train, the ragged gaps chestnuts had once filled, before the blight no forester could contain. "It's frightening to think how little we know sometimes."

Still smiling, Gabriel lifted his hand to tap the bridge of Rand's nose. "You sure your name's Randolf and not Ernest? When I look that gloomy, Inés shoves me outside to ride the horse." His hand lingered. "Unknowns are comforting. They mean things can still change."

Rand met his eyes through his fingers. "Did your family really give you no choice?"

Gabriel lowered his hand and looked away.

"I'm sorry," Rand amended. Perhaps he was wrong, and Gabriel had hope he was just too timid to see. "It's not my business."

Gabriel did not quite smile. "Ernest."

They did not speak again. Beyond them the green foothills of the Appalachians rumbled past, old and not wild, unknown.

When the car bumped to a halt, Rand rose to his knees on the seat and looked out over Rock Creek valley.

It was not as bad as Manning had made it sound. The woods were in the sturdy latter half of their first century. Mostly oak and hickory, they mingled in the uplands with laurel and in the wet dingles with red maple. Rand noticed a few bridle paths, but not so many that he could not find an isolated clearing for experiments.

He slowed his breathing so that it was not so audible. When Manning wasn't watching, he rubbed a fist against the knot in his stomach.

From the road they crossed several pastures and farmers' woodlots, then turned into thicker trees. For a half mile they followed a tributary creek downward, until the meadow light was no longer visible between the trunks. Stopping, Manning nodded toward a bottomland grove of sycamore and hoof-leaved tulip trees. His voice was bored.

"Does this suit?"

Rand nodded, relieved. The leaf litter was thick and black, with a sparse understory. Whatever he grew, he would probably not kill something else immediately.

"Good. Then here, grow a white elm for our coopers." Manning reached into his pocket and produced the papery seed.

Taking it, Rand knelt. Manning leaned against a trunk and sighed audibly. Rand ignored him, too nervous to feel insulted. Despite the speed of his heart, he let the energy trickle steadily from his fingers through the soil. He could not afford to pass out, lest Manning examine him or the tree unobserved. Rigidly he clung to consciousness.

As he felt his warmth drain into the humus, he almost laughed in despair. The service could not expect much of him if it took such effort to raise one elm. He wondered how he would survive Manning's tests and his own, and whatever lumber he'd be asked to grow. Perhaps he wouldn't. The thought was grim, yet edged with a strange thrill.

He pushed it away and concentrated. Slowly the gray sapling climbed. It swelled like a molting cicada, splitting its bark into ropes. Behind him he heard Manning gasp, then crunch across the drying duff to loom over him. He tried to focus on the elm, breathing through the dawning realization that in the army he would always be watched.

Twenty minutes later he sat back, panting. His elm rose tall above the languorous sycamores, its leaves cutting their teeth on the July heat. It looks so healthy, he thought, and shivered.

Above him Manning's face was slack with wonder. "My apologies, Private," he said in a stunned voice. "This really does change everything. Our national vitality is broader than even Mr. Fisher predicted. A new world, indeed." His feet shuffled the dry leaf litter. He was kneeling down to study the elm's bole when Rand gasped, "You should cut it down!"

"What?"

He spoke quickly, praying Manning would not scrutinize the ground cover. "Whatever I grow, we should fell it at once. What if I grow heart-rot, or burls, or what if I can make good hardwoods but not softwoods? Learning how my gift works is important, but only because I need to grow sound wood. Yes?"

This time Manning's face took longer to ease. "You surprise me again. Yes, that is sensible. Tomorrow we'll bring some axes and a crosscut." Rand prayed the elm would live that long. "In the meantime," Manning continued, "refresh your memory of your dendrology courses. You are too secret to bring in additional foresters, so I'll be asking you to put that degree to use."

Rand saw an opening. "Shouldn't I do additional research, too? There are university libraries here, and the service archives. I'll go during lunch. All I need is permission."

"You're very eager to take on more work."

For once he did not have to lie. "I want to understand my gift. And there won't be time for study in France."

After a pause, Manning nodded. "Very well. I will contact George-town's library to procure you a card. It is an hour's walk from camp. On days when you plan to visit the library, you will report directly to our rendezvous at fourteen hundred."

"Yes, sir."

"Good. Now." Manning snapped open the medical kit he had brought with him. He pointed to a nearby boulder. "Sleeves up, and right arm across that rock. I want to see if exercising your power has altered your blood."

As he rolled back his cuffs, Rand craned his neck to follow the creek's slip into the valley. It was a useful landmark. To find a hidden place to experiment, he would only need to walk downstream. If he returned to the rendezvous by two, Manning would never discover that he had not visited the library. And some days he would visit it, of course. He made another mental note to compile a list of research questions.

"I wonder," Manning murmured, "if we could breed you."

The needle drew.

They returned to camp just before supper, after which Rand was belatedly registered, outfitted, and assigned his quarters. Arms grappling his mattress sack, he counted down the rows of eight-man tents until he found the one assigned to him. He ducked beneath its flap to see Gabriel, Weber, and Haines the axeman perched on their two-man bunks, reading. Beside Gabriel sat a bundle of envelopes. The handwriting on the top made his heart leap.

"Mail came," said Gabriel. A tall stack of letters sat in his lap. He nodded to the bare board beside him. "Chuck your mattress here. Straw's out back."

"Evening, Gabriel, thanks. Hello Hans, Bill. I didn't realize we were bunked together."

"Not our decision. They do it with all men from the same state," said Haines curtly. "You have a fun time with Gray? Get to keep your mop too?"

Rand realized that Haines's beard was gone, and that all the men's hair was shaven. He ran his fingers through his messy curls. "I guess I'll have to cut it tomorrow. And I barely saw Gray."

Haines waved his hand. "Don't want the details anyway." Beside him, Weber gave an apathetic shrug.

Stepping past them, Rand dropped his kit on the bed and swept up the packet of letters. He stood still for a moment. The July heat lay heavy in the tent, weighted by Haines and Weber's silence, the rustle of

Gabriel opening a new letter. "I'll just read outside," Rand mumbled. "Light's still good."

Outside, he settled on the ground a few yards away from the tent's shadow. Jonna's letter he tucked beneath the others, saving it for last. Then he opened the thick envelope in his mother's handwriting.

Greta's letter was the first and longest. To his surprise, it was in English.

> I am told we should not write German. I don't want to get you in trouble. Or me, I guess. Do you know they have had marches here on campus, to prove our patriotism to the legislature? Mein Gott! (sorry). Perhaps I'll write you in Greek next, so you'll have to learn it this time.

Rand smiled. Greta was now a coed at the university in Madison, taking a degree in classics. Two years his junior, she resented his parents' refusal to send her to one of the eastern women's colleges. Now she made up for it by outdoing Rand scholastically. Always the better reader, as a girl she'd repaid him for leading her on adventures by coaxing him to the few books he still loved. He missed her. Though he was proud of how he had weaned himself of her advice after high school, he always suspected Greta knew more about him than she let on, and had opinions about it. He wished he could ask her for them sometimes.

> Please know that Papa and Mama are proud of you, no matter what they say. Mama is happy that you're in the Engineers at least, and may not see fighting . . .

Rand flipped to his parents' letters. Much shorter than Greta's, they were stiff, formal, and also in English. *There is no shame in being drafted,* his father wrote. *You won't have to shoot a gun, will you?* asked his mother.

His hands crinkled the paper. He could not explain to them that he had not been drafted, exactly, just as he had never explained whom he'd befriended at university, or whom he'd loved. He could never tell if they guessed the extent of his deceptions. His parents were lapsed

German Lutherans. They believed in hard work, duty, and honesty. His father, son of a log rider, had through sweat and patience expanded his small cabinetry shop to a business. Bored by carpentry and forever outside, Rand had never had a hope of taking it over. He'd sensed how earnestly his father tried to hide his disappointment, just as his mother tried to hide how she indulged him as compensation. They did their best to accept his unnatural love of nature. Rand lacked the nerve to test them on any other tolerances.

Laying the letter aside, he paused to flex his fingers. Perhaps if he harnessed his gift, he could become the sort of son they deserved.

Jonna's letter was short. It began, *My dear Rand*, then continued with a line of cramped Finnish. *Haha! Too bad the joke doesn't translate.* At school Rand had picked up enough Finnish from Jonna to stumble through simple conversations. He got the gist of it: *You should assume they're reading your mail.*

His flesh prickled. Jonna was fond of decrying the government, but she was probably right. He could expect nothing substantive in her letter. Even so, he settled into it with a sharp joy.

New York is all summer haze and racket—in other words no Paris!
I am still looking for that correspondence job. Perhaps you can speak
to the army for me. If you want some samples to show them, flip over.

Jonna always sent him sketches with her letters, her return for Rand's descriptions of the northwoods. These were more detailed than usual: a New York street scene done in shadows and silhouettes; a still life of a piano covered in books; a portrait of an elegant woman, eyes just lifted. Once, at school, Jonna had confessed to Rand that she lacked the passion of the true artist, so she might as well hitch her pen to politics and draw cartoons. She'd sounded frustrated. When he'd asked why, she'd evaded the question and spent fifteen minutes vigorously detailing an upcoming eight-hour-day march. He wondered what her art meant to her now, and whether she felt ashamed of its frivolity, like some of her comrades.

And talk up my robustness. Even my paper only gives me the safe jobs, or asks me to write editorials for the Women's Dep't. Sometimes I think I should just go home and apply to ours, you know?

He noted she did not name the papers—the New York *Call*, the Milwaukee *Leader*. The socialists, of course, did not approve of the war.

Anyway, now you are out east and not getting blackflied to bones in the northwoods, I am going to try and visit. In your next letter tell me when you're shipping out, and what days visitors are allowed? I'll take the Pennsy down. Until then, maybe learn more Finnish, eh? You'll get my jokes better.

Jonna

At the last paragraph Rand pushed to his feet, turned a circle like an anxious dog, and sat down again. He had not seen Jonna in months. He imagined her pointed nose wrinkling at the drills, the clandestine ways she'd find to mock it all. He grinned, hoping they would find time to say all the things they couldn't in writing.

"Good letters?"

He had not noticed Gabriel approach, violin tucked under one arm. "Yes. You? That was some pile."

Gabriel shrugged. "Inés let it slip that I'd enlisted."

"Are your sisters angry?"

"Not at me." Untucking his violin, Gabriel sat down cross-legged, so close their knees touched. Rand held himself still. He knew whom Gabriel's sisters should be angry at. "Carmelita says she's going to ride up here and liberate me. I'm not sure she's joking."

Rand bit back another apology. "Greta says my parents aren't happy either."

"Lucky. My father is delighted. 'About time you became a man.' Hypocrite. As if last year he wasn't rooting for Villa to trounce Pershing for daring to think he could outride the guerillas." Gabriel's face clouded. Then, leaning across Rand's chest, he looked at the sketches in his lap and said deliberately, "Your sisters draw?"

Rand complied with subject-changing cheer. "No, these are from Jonna. Did I never mention it? She's a brilliant artist, does amusing caricatures. We used to stay up nights, talking, while she'd sketch." He reddened despite himself.

"So she *is* your sweetheart," said Gabriel genially. "I'd been wondering."

"No." Rand forced a laugh. "I did ask her to be, once. It was stupid."

"Stupid?"

"If you ask a girl to marry you without checking if she's interested first, you're stupid for feeling sad when she says no."

"Ha! If that's the stupidest thing you've done for love, count yourself lucky." Gabriel's voice was careful, not quite an invitation.

Rand looked at him questioningly. But Gabriel leaned back, settling his chin on the violin. He said nothing.

Earnest, Rand thought, and smiled. He had nothing to prove his trust-worthiness, but a story could be an offering. He said, "It isn't the stupidest thing."

"Oh?"

"Shall I give you the highlights?" He tried to sound playful. "As a fresh-man I broke my wrist trying to learn cycling for one of Jonna's suffrag-ette friends. The next year I got drunk and gave my father's pocket watch to an Oxford rower on exchange. And once I lived a week in a big hem-lock to impress the dean's daughter. It didn't work." He felt his face warm again; he was no raconteur. "Though falling out did impress his son."

Gabriel's brows had leapt to his hairline.

"You don't need to look so shocked." Rand thought of his reflection in Manning's window. "I know I'm not anyone's ideal."

A smile creased Gabriel's surprise. "That isn't it. You talk as if it's never bothered you, as if it were natural."

Rand shrugged through his blush. "I study nature." At university he'd decided that the only truly unnatural things were what people did to wilderness. "You learn pretty fast that every possible arrangement exists."

"Or that's what you learned," said Gabriel. His voice was low and thoughtful. It sounded like the beginning to a story, but Gabriel did not continue, only plucked a string.

In the ensuing quiet, little camp noises piled like snow, murmurs from other tents, the clang of dinner's pots being washed. Rand watched Gabriel's face as he began tuning. His silence seemed deliberate, like a turned lock. Rand knew better than to test if his offering had been accepted.

After a time Gabriel uncrossed his legs. "I should go practice. I'll sit outside the mess so I don't wake anyone. Come sing if you like. And—later?"

Rand nodded eagerly. Gabriel stood. The secondhand uniform tugged on his hips; Rand watched his hands smooth out the creases. He knew where he would begin that night. "I got a good look at the camp layout," he said. "No one guards the mock trenches after dark."

"Strategist," said Gabriel. His face was still pensive.

Rand thought of his eyes as he'd described his father's letter, his resigned courage at the war waiting across the water. How selfish his own desires were. He looked up, ashamed. "Only if you want," he said. "Only if I'm no trouble to you."

Gabriel glanced down and smiled faintly. "Not yet," he said.

Much later that night, lying on the mattress he'd stuffed with straw, Rand stared up at the tent's long peak of darkness, his body flushed and heavy. Beside him, Gabriel's breathing was calm.

He did not sleep for a long time.

Chapter 5

CAMP JOURNAL: JULY 30, 1917

First bloom: beechdrops (test: can I grow parasitic sp.?). Full bloom: coral bells, crane-fly orchid . . .

The next morning they awoke to begin basic training.

Their schedule was not as strict as Rand would have guessed, perhaps because Camp AU was barely half-finished. Piles of lumber lay beside pine skeletons of new bunkhouses and heaps of shingling cedar. As their first practice for the front, the men of the Tenth Engineers Forestry were tasked with building their own accommodations. They did not even begin drilling until Rand's third day. Their officers, professional foresters rapidly promoted from the Washington office, saw little point to rifle practice, and the recruits mostly did not need physical toughening. Lumbermen from across the country, they had arrived from harder jobs.

As his days settled into a rhythm, he began to see their gaps: the lag between lunch and afternoon drill, the half-day Saturdays, free Sundays. His first successful visit to Georgetown library was on one of these Sundays. Pocketing some bread at breakfast, he spent the day among the stacks. When he trudged back into camp, weak and covered in road dust, men gave him even stranger looks than those he encountered on returning from Rock Creek, his shirt dun with sawdust.

At least Manning had not noticed anything yet. In the little glen that had become their research station, he arrived each afternoon with axes, saws, calipers, and a set of tubes into which he shaved chips for chemical analysis. When Rand asked what the tests found, Manning stared at him a moment, as if deliberating. Then he said, "I'll worry about that. You worry about growing more and faster."

When Rand finally embarked on his own experiments, the logistics nearly defeated him, though he thought he'd planned everything carefully. To isolate how he was misusing his gift, he eliminated as many variables as possible. He would grow only species native to the valley, which preferred the test spot he'd chosen, a wet slope of mixed tulip tree and red oak. Unlike his trilliums, he would grow species that fit the season. He would take scrupulous notes, on the specimens and on himself.

But by the time he had trudged the two hot miles to the site, he was damp with sweat. The food he swiped from breakfast was never enough to sustain him through his experiments as well as Manning's. And obtaining seeds proved difficult. It was three days before he'd collected enough to kneel down on his plot between four blazed beeches and grow his first test: a patch of hog peanut, a hardy native late-summer bloomer found in mixed woods. Its hairy vine twined up his forearms and coiled in an itchy snarl about his knees. He had to slide his penknife beneath the stems and lop them from his wrists before taking readings. The motion bruised the upper pea flowers, whose soiled petals smelled faintly sweet. When he rubbed his fingers along its stolons, he found none of the vine's nubby secondary flowers. No pods had grown either. He did not know why.

Recording his baseline observations took thirty minutes. He did not finish before he had to dash to the rendezvous point with Manning. The vine died in three days.

The logistics of camp life proved still harder. Though Rand strove to be inconspicuous, his unit could not miss that he was excused from each afternoon's work of roof raising and trench digging. Dark looks followed him as he slipped into the supper line. When he began skipping lunch, the looks became gaps on the mess benches, dropped voices in the YMCA tent.

In the first weeks he tried to compensate, joining the men for card games or arm wrestling. But weighing the relief of feeling liked against the gravity of his task, he could not justify social extravagances. The Tenth shipped out in September. Every minute spent on his comfort was a minute stolen from his promises.

Gradually he resigned his efforts at camaraderie. After supper he retired to his tent to read and take notes.

The only indulgences he allowed himself were his nights with Gabriel. Often as a prelude, Rand joined him for practice, laying aside his books to sing. They never spoke of their old rules, or whether they still held. Yet he felt the shift in their attitude toward each other, like spring's green darkening to summer. With an odd new defiance Gabriel would pause to correct his posture, lifting his chin or touching his back, he said, just to straighten it.

It worried Rand that no other men came to listen. His singing was bad, but he did not do it often enough to spoil an excellent and entirely free concert. As he watched Gabriel at supper, he began to notice gaps around him too. Men nodded at Gabriel, respected his marksmanship, but he was never asked to play cards or wrestle. Rand wondered how much of their avoidance was his fault. One evening as they sat together, a passing cookee kicked a sheaf of dust at their knees. Gabriel kicked back, and the man spat and ran.

Instead of continuing to play, he cased his violin and tugged Rand up toward the mock trenches, though light remained at the horizon. His look was hard and inward. He did not say what he was remembering.

Rand kissed him once before kneeling. Then, chin lifted, he hesitantly folded his arms around Gabriel's hips. "Are you all right?"

"You learn to ignore it. It can't hurt you."

"No?"

Gabriel's fingers tensed on his scalp. "Not if you don't let it."

Not knowing what to say, Rand leaned up and kissed the dip of his navel through his shirt. They did not return to the tent until long after dark.

Around them, July faded.

In Rand's plots the specimens grew and died. Slowly, patterns emerged in his notebooks. His trees lived longer than his flowers. The more flowers he grew, the faster they died. The biggest patches of growth spread their destruction beyond themselves. Rand frowned as he waded through the brown crackle of the half acre ringing his hog peanut, like the stiffened line seaweed leaves at low tide.

But his wood was sound. When he and Manning felled his trees, their rings were so even Manning fingered them like grooves on a record. "Flawless," he said. As their work progressed he had been making fitful overtures toward Rand, as if in apology for initially doubting his power. "You have perfected the tree," he said. "It is the first time in history man has produced an ideal in nature. Do you see what an extraordinary first step this is? I've been thinking backward. How foolish of me. Of course perfection must start with the lower organisms. First plants, then animals, then the human race." He smiled, real warmth brightening his cheeks.

Rand's skin prickled. He thought of Gabriel's arch request for a beard. The unease congealed to revulsion.

"Do you understand me, Mr. Brandt?" Manning asked sociably. "Shall I explain?"

Rand held his head down. Manning waited for another minute, asked the question again, less pleasantly; then fell silent. He returned brusquely to shaving wood chips.

Later, if Rand tried to engage Manning in speculation on the meaning or purpose of his gift, the doctor gave a hostile little shrug. Rand found ever more inventive ways to keep him from examining the withered groundcover.

On the question of his gift's purpose Jonna was more philosophical, but her conjectures were so censored by caution they read too much like poetry for Rand's sake.

> Why have you received it? No reason. Maybe in answer to the
> unreason of War. No War will end wars, only the great overturning—
> yours, botanical.

Though his replies were feeble, still Jonna wrote every week, inquiring after him, requesting her usual reminiscences of Wisconsin, giving abstract, melancholy updates on her quest for Paris. He tried not to ask too often when she would visit.

In his letters home, he described the camp for his parents, who returned punctual pleasantries. He tried to answer as many of Greta's questions as he could without lying. But he wrote mostly to his notebooks.

It was mid-August before he had his first credible hypothesis. He'd found his gift depleted him in proportion to the size and number of his specimens, and that in all places he grew, the earth changed color, texture. Whatever energy he supplied was not enough to prevent soil exhaustion. Without instruments, he could not know to what extent his gift replaced water and minerals. But as he raised asters from his testing plot, he could feel himself holding back.

He was not giving his all. Perhaps his gift knew it.

Slowly, methodically, he tried to increase the energy flowing from his fingers. The resulting blackouts threatened to make him miss his work with Manning. To stay awake he held images of wilderness before him, of the burnt Clearwater peat fields or the Bitterroot mountainsides he would restore once he had learned how.

Yet after his own tests he still had Manning's trees to grow, morning drills to run. Exhaustion fogged his days. He caught himself reciting Schimper's rules of vegetative distribution—Gebietsformation, edaphischen—to the rhythm of rifle practice.

"What does that doctor have you doing?" asked Gabriel one night when he fell asleep halfway through unbuttoning his shirt. "They're just trees."

Around him in the mess hall the whispers mounted. His old team no longer spoke to him, even snidely. Falling into his cot at night, he reminded himself that the loneliness was worth it; as a trial, it was even appropriate. He would make it up to Gabriel when he drew fleets of bunchgrass from the ranch's cracked dirt, and to his team when the pineries logged before their birth burst skyward above their wondering heads. He tried not to imagine their faces, should he fail. He pushed harder, worked longer, slept less. And still his plants died.

Over the camp, September's ship-out loomed like a thunderhead.

One Sunday in late August, Rand staggered back from the library to collapse against the mess hall wall. From his pocket he drew an apple and began chewing listlessly. He must have slept then, because when he looked up again Gabriel was beside him in the red light, tuning.

"How—how much hours—time?" he asked.

"Six. You look wretched. Why don't you go to bed?"

"Rather sing." Rand sat up, fishing the library's little German-Spanish dictionary from his pocket. "I've got that one down now, the—campanillas?"

"Suit yourself. But if you fall asleep again, I'm going to let you stay that way." Gabriel lifted his bow.

As Rand began the song—something about bells and a balcony—he was surprised to see a man round the mess hall and pause close, listening. A second followed. Then two more; then five. They arranged themselves in a half moon about the music, faces blurred and intent in the sunset.

Rand's voice skated on silence. Gabriel had lowered the violin and snapped it into its case. Rand saw him stand and nudge it beneath the bench.

"Concert over, Señor Fiddle?" asked the front man. "We'd like a word."

"Would you?" Gabriel asked. His voice was quiet, but Rand saw his hand tighten on his leg. He pushed himself to his feet.

The man turned to him. "Lazy little spy, aren't you? The Kaiser's not paying you to nap."

"Spy?" Rand said. "That's absurd."

The man swayed. "What's absurd is how long they've let you operate in broad daylight. Ditching work at all hours, muttering in German!" Another man yelled from the back: "And courting the Mexican! What did he promise you, greaser? Arizona?"

Gabriel crossed his arms. It did not quite hide their tremor. "Go back to your tents. Drunk on a Sunday—you're embarrassing."

The circle of men narrowed. "You see how stupid this is, don't you?" Rand tried to keep his voice calm. "Do you think the army would miss a spy in its training camp?"

"The sarge is testing us!" the man in the back slurred. "Wants to keep us on our toes!" Another shouted: "It's our job to keep out the foreigners!" A clod of mud accompanied the shout, spattering against the mess hall wall.

The man in front spat. "Go back home. The trenches are dirty enough already." Rand realized the circle was closing, and that the man was not looking at him anymore.

"Go to hell," snarled Gabriel, a second before the front man swung.

They tried to run at first. Gabriel ducked the man's fist; Rand grabbed his elbow and lurched along the mess hall toward the small gap beside the wall. A man filled it. They skidded back, then spun to face the crowd.

Rand had never scrapped. He did not know what to do with his body and was so tired the attackers' forms smeared into a wave of fists, knees, shoulders. He tried to block a punch with his elbow and the blow deflected to his collarbone with a crunch. Beside him, Gabriel had shoved his hands into his armpits and was trying to kick his way through. The fear on his face froze Rand's stomach.

A second punch hooked Rand in the neck above the too-low shield of his arms. The pain flung him out and away, so that for a moment as he fell, he saw the whole scene as if from a great height: himself curled on the dust; a moment later Gabriel beside him, knees to his chest; and flocking over them in the red light, the pale faces, pale fists, feet fluttering like sharp wings. Then he was back on the ground again, and rolling to throw his arms about Gabriel's head and torso because he suddenly realized why he wasn't punching.

A gunshot split the pain; then another. Above Rand the shadows veered. The kicks retreated, leaving only the throbbing in his throat and shoulder and Gabriel pushing him away with a gasp. "Did they—" Rand croaked. "Your hands?"

"Fine! I'm fine."

"Get up, Brandt," said Manning, above them.

Rand looked up. The circle of men had broken. Its angry shards were watching Manning, who held a revolver above his head.

"I am disappointed," said Manning. "You are engineers, not common doughboys, and I expected more of your mental capacities. Could not

53

one of you imagine a better reason why a German-speaking Yale graduate like Private Brandt might be receiving special training than that he was a spy for the *other* side?"

The men shuffled. They peered at Rand with new interest.

Manning glanced back at Rand and Gabriel. "I trust you two can find your way to the medic. Private Brandt, I'll expect you at our normal hour tomorrow." His voice lowered. "In the meantime, I'd encourage you to consider the company you keep."

On their walk to the medical tent, Gabriel limped two steps in front of Rand. He did not speak. His head hung down, and he clutched his violin to his chest.

Rand's collarbone was probably cracked, the nurse said as she arranged the sling. He should delay heavy activity for at least a month. On a separate cot, Gabriel sat in silence as another nurse bound his ribs. Purple welts stamped down his side and back. His uninjured hands lay on his knees, flexing.

Rand watched him as from across a wide gulf. When the nurses left, he reseated himself beside Gabriel, then put his free hand to his shoulder. "Are you all right?"

Gabriel jerked away. "Damn you! I said I'm fine." His open hands shook. "Damn it. I'm a Cedillo. We do not let these things bother us." It was the first time Rand had heard him claim his father's name.

Rand edged down the cot to give him space. Below, the floor was bottomless.

Gabriel did not look at him again. Rand opened his mouth, then closed it. For all his supposed observations, he had never tried to see the camp as Gabriel saw it, or considered how it saw him. Helplessly he said, "I'm sorry," then lapsed into silence.

Outside the canvas, night fell. Dusty moths bumped against the tent's mosquito netting. Spasms of belated panic rose into Rand's throat. He pushed them back down. From the corner of his eye he watched Gabriel, whose shoulders were rigid with a shame Rand had thought he could not feel. Gabriel seemed surprised too. His eyes bored angrily into himself.

Rand had brought this shame; his presence made Gabriel a target. He felt the air thicken in his lungs. He should have fought harder. If he could not deserve what Gabriel had given him, perhaps he should not have it at all.

Several hours passed in the darkening silence. After checking in once to light the kerosene lamps, the nurses let them be. At one point a journalist from town nosed by, asking if it was true there'd been a brawl. Rand snapped at him to get out.

It was well past taps by the time Gabriel finally stood. "I suppose I don't want to sleep here," he said.

Rand nodded. "I can stay, if you'd like our cot to yourself."

"It's all right."

"It's all right if it's not."

"Come on." Gabriel leaned down and took Rand's uninjured hand, tugging it carefully, encouraging him to stand. Pain ripped across Rand's shoulder. He grit his teeth and said nothing.

Gabriel did not let go at once. He gripped Rand's fingers until he could feel tiny shivers pass down his arm. Only when Rand squeezed back did his grip ease. Then, more gently, he led Rand toward the exit.

"Looks like you have a cover story now," Gabriel said as they walked back through the blue night. "Rand Brandt, spy. Ha."

"I guess?"

"Tomorrow we pick up with the Rodríguez again, yes?" His voice strained toward cheer. "You'll want to have at least one song memorized for when you come to the ranch. With how slow you grow things, you'll have to stay awhile."

"Yes," Rand said faintly. Far off in Rock Creek, his plot lay barren beneath the dark. "Of course."

Chapter 6

SHIP JOURNAL: SEPTEMBER 10, 1917

Great shearwaters over the North Atlantic—late,
nonbreeding?; guillemots west, off of Nova Scotia . . .

That Monday the *Post* carried a story headlined "RIOT AT CAMP A-U!
FORESTERS ASK: ARE WE GROWING SPIES?" above an editorial about
the loyalties of hyphenated Americans. Manning made sure Rand saw it.
With a pique that seemed deliberately theatrical, he lit a page to smoke
Rand back to consciousness when he fainted halfway through a clutch
of pulp poplars. Rand was exhausted, having spent lunch pouring himself into a cherry tree. Gabriel appreciated the fruit, though it did not
lift the dull silence into which he fell at night, sitting cross-legged in the
tent, plucking the strings of the violin he was too bruised to play.

By the following Monday the cherry's leaves had browned. No amount
of care would revive the tree. Rand was not sure if he should revise his
hypothesis about his own energy, or whether he simply had not given
enough. He wondered how he would know when he had.

Freed from drill by his injury, he spent the next week's mornings
in the library, transcribing everything he could into his notebooks. At
night, for all his delicacy, Gabriel still flinched beneath his hands. When
Rand jerked away, Gabriel pulled him back in. "If it doesn't hurt you."

It did, but the new fear in Gabriel's voice hurt more. Rand kissed his
chin, then knelt. They both pretended Gabriel's gasp as he came was
only pleasure.

The following Sunday he received a wire—*Look for me. J.*—and the rest of his equipment: wool gloves, denim pants, puttees, and a rifle from the 1880s.

The next day they shipped out.

By foot in full battle gear to the station at Rosslyn, then by train toward the ferry across the Hudson, the Tenth Engineers traveled, cramped and chatty and clutching their secondhand rifles. Other men carried Rand and Gabriel's packs. Their injuries did not exempt them. The service could not spare men of their education.

Arriving at New York's Cunard Line Pier, Rand stared up at the massive RMS *Carpathia*, its hawsers thicker than his arm. The dock boiled with people: sailors hoisting cargo by the ship's four mast cranes; marines saluting in rows; flocks of civilians bearing flags and flowers. Already casual about discipline, the Tenth slackened into a puddle of loose lines in the chaos.

As he stood waiting to board, Rand noticed a short figure in a wrinkled corduroy skirt stomping up and down the pier. Her gray-brown hair had been cropped about her fox's face, which twitched left and right, searching. A flat artist's tote bumped at her back.

Ducking out of line, he hollered, "Jonna!"

She heard and lifted her skirts to run toward him. As he reached her, forgetting himself, he clapped his good arm on her shoulder. The motion tugged his sling, and he yelped. She stepped back in surprise.

"Rand! What have they been doing to you?" She poked his sling, then caught his uninjured wrist. "You're all bones."

"How are you here? I didn't even know we were shipping out till Wednesday."

The old, wry smile opened her face. "Heard you had a publicity problem. Something about German spies and riots?"

"Something like that."

"Your chief decided the service needed a war publicist. Someone he could trust to tell the truth to the folks back home—strong men cutting strong trees, et cetera." She fluttered her eyelids. Rand was relieved she did not press on his threadbare answer. "Someone cheaper and more docile than a man and, oh, just dying to make amends for writing for

57

those awful socialist rags. How deluded she was! How desperate to help our boys!"

"Gray actually believed that?" Rand knew Gray was concerned with publicity. He'd been promoted in the wake of a violent spat between the service's first chief and President Taft, which had so scarred the service's reputation that Gray had spent the last five years rebuilding it. Yet he wasn't stupid, however good an actress Jonna might be.

"He didn't have much choice. A five-day turnaround for an artist-writer who knows enough about forestry not to muck it up? Thanks for that, by the way. Knowing you has come in handy."

Rand smiled. "So you're coming with us?"

"Yes. Then on to Paris." She grinned back, brilliant, and Rand flushed. Acute as ever, Jonna patted him on the shoulder. "I missed you too. Come on, let's get you back before they break your other arm."

"Collarbone. And speaking of Paris, I need to introduce you . . ."

As he led Jonna back toward the shuffling formation, he saw Gabriel shimmy his way to its edge. "Gabriel! This is Jonna. She's shipping out with us as a reporter."

Jonna stuck out her hand. "Jonna Larson. Rand says you're a proper violinist, so you have my thanks. If I have to hear 'Over There' one more time I'm going to scream."

"Miss Larson, my great pleasure," Gabriel replied, lifting her hand with an easy gallantry. It did not seem forced, but was not quite natural either. "Forgive me, but they are letting someone like you report on the Engineers?"

She scowled. "You mean, are they letting a woman send back patriotic pablum while she smuggles herself to Paris? Yes, they seem to be. And it's Jonna, if you ever want to bum a smoke." Digging beneath her coat, she withdrew a case and popped it open. "Rand?"

"Thanks." He slipped the cigarette in his pocket, unsettled by Jonna's frown, Gabriel's affectation. "You know, you both—"

But Gabriel's expression had sharpened. "Paris! I hope to go too, for the music. What is there for you?"

"Art, culture, lifestyle." Jonna lifted her eyebrows. "You know?"

"Yes," Gabriel replied slowly.

"You ever hear about a place and know you belong there? More than wherever here is, anyway?"

"Yes."

Rand watched them stare at each other for a moment, some exchange he could not follow passing swiftly below their surfaces. Then Jonna grinned.

"I thought so," she said. "Cigarette?"

Gabriel took one. "Jonna. Thanks."

Rand could tell she noticed his sigh of relief, because her grin widened. This time she patted both of them, carefully, on the shoulder. "I'm berthing with the nurses, so I have to go. See you two on board."

As he waved at her departing back, the flurry of joy began to resettle in Rand's chest. Below it lay the knowledge that they had two weeks of voyage to converse. Jonna would ask about his gift and know at once he was lying. The only questions were how quickly she would unearth the truth and who she would share it with. He glanced at Gabriel, who was watching Jonna's departure with a thoughtful expression.

"You asked her to marry you?" he said.

"I said I was stupid."

Gabriel gave him an odd look. "Not stupid. Just optimistic."

From the end of the formation a whistle shrilled, and Rand heard Gray's tired voice calling them to line up for boarding.

Like everyone, Rand knew the *Carpathia* from when it had been the first ship to collect *Titanic* survivors. Now converted to troop transport, its steerage had been lined with narrow bunks, its first-class cabins refitted as officers' and women's quarters. Rand's division was berthed near the bow. The ship's kitchens had been expanded but were still not prepared to feed four thousand people. By their third day out, Rand learned to rise before reveille if he hoped to have breakfast by seven. Wrapping his rations in a handkerchief, he spent the hours before inspection convincing Gabriel to eat as he lay in his bunk, too ill even to pluck.

Onboard sickness was universal. Buckets lined the steerage berths, but the sea was rough; they spilled often, and no amount of scrubbing could scour the reek. Between submarine drills the men were allowed free time on deck for an hour, twice a day. As shifts were poorly enforced, many simply stayed up, preferring the raw cold to the hold's rancid darkness.

Rand was grateful for one aspect of the crowding: among men of so many divisions he was anonymous again. The shared misery had even tempered his unit's rancor toward Gabriel, though it did not cure the harried loneliness into which he still slipped, for which Rand could offer nothing but his hands, and silence.

Though he had no way to practice his gift on board, Rand was still required to meet Manning every afternoon. Under the pretense of checking his injury, Manning drew blood and grilled him on the reading he'd done at camp. Rand answered warily, sidestepping whatever details might imply his gift was not progressing as scheduled. It was difficult. During those last weeks he had read indiscriminately: Tansley on plant geography, Clements on succession. He had even skimmed the German agricultural journals for news of a new ammonia fertilizer developed at Karlsruhe.

What Manning made of his answers he could not tell. After each meeting he dismissed Rand with a set of vague warnings: *Remember why you're here*, or *Mind who you trust*. If Rand's failure to share his zeal for perfecting humanity had ruffled Manning, the brawl had made him flatly antagonistic. Rand could not bring himself to care about mending the bridge. "Sir," he'd reply, and leave.

The only upside to Manning's appointments was the chance it gave Rand to visit Jonna. Once excused, he was free until the end of his hour up top, so he always took the long way back, past the nurses' quarters. As the women's deck time was not restricted, Jonna met him and together they slipped aft to sit atop a lifeboat, smoking.

Once his stomach settled, he could almost pretend they were back at school. Before he'd made the mistake of trying to love her, at Yale they'd shared the pleasure of students whose passions were equally fervent but differed in focus. Jonna had liked that Rand did not grandstand about anything but nature. He appreciated her tutoring on topics he understood poorly, like politics and psychology. Now their conversation fell into familiar rhythms. Rand excitedly listed the European birds he hoped to see when they landed; Jonna sketched portraits of the shivering soldiers while relaying, sotto voce, the latest news from Petrograd. Their easiness with one another comforted him, even if Jonna's conversation remained disconcertingly direct.

"I like this one, even if he is another of your rich boys." Her voice was fond and slightly pained. "It's good to see you smitten again."

He blushed. "We can talk about something else."

"Can't we? You're determined not to tell me what's gone wrong with your magic plant power."

She waited, cocking her head at him in a challenge he recognized from endless late-night debates. His temptation to confide embarrassed him. Over the span of their friendship she'd borne too many of his confessions. But she had called his bluff, and the only shield he'd ever had against Jonna was the truth.

"I am determined, yes." He looked down. "I won't allow you to be caught up in it. It could be dangerous."

To his surprise, she gave a low, solemn laugh. "How chivalrous. Fine, I won't press you. But you should know that there's nothing you can do to me that's worse than what I've done to myself."

"What do you mean?"

"I've signed up for a war I hate to get to a city I hope I'll love." The restlessness in her voice was familiar from university, but it had focused, as if she'd labeled it and held it up to the light. She added with a defensive flourish, "I'm waiting for the other shoe to drop. I almost want it to, if I'm being honest."

"You mean, you want to be disappointed? Why?"

He watched her roll her shoulders. "Oh hell, Rand. I don't know. I should have known you'd ask me to elaborate." She laughed again, faintly bitter, and he saw that he had called her bluff too. "So let's return to your seasick violinist. Or home, even better. I've missed five springs there now. I'm worried I'll forget them. Would you mind—"

"Hello, deck party," called Gabriel. Rand peered over the lifeboat to see him advancing along the cabin wall. His face was sweaty with sickness. "Up for my hour of staring at the horizon."

Rand slid off to help him ease down into the wedge of space between the railing and the lifeboat's stern. Grousing, he pretended to swat Rand's hands away even as he leaned into them. Jonna followed, clearly relieved to have escaped Rand's probing. Her cynicism troubled him. He reminded himself to question her again later.

As he helped Gabriel sit, she produced two cigarettes that she tucked into Rand's breast pocket.

"Where do you get all these?" asked Gabriel.

"Gambling with the nurses. And I believe it's time for my refill. Enjoy the sea air, you two." She saluted them, then sauntered off.

Irritated, Rand wanted to call after her to be more circumspect. But then he imagined how they must look, huddled together behind a lifeboat. He glanced over his shoulder, then back down. Gabriel's jaw was clenched, his eyes latched to the horizon.

He would take his chances. "You keep lunch down?" he asked.

"Why would I? Sour beans, pork gristle, ugh." Gabriel wrung his spasm to a chuckle. "My stomach's AWOL already. You have a light?"

Rand lit him a cigarette and dug a smashed roll from his coat.

"Just the smoke, thanks." Gabriel sagged against the lifeboat's planks and drew carefully. The vomiting had slowed the healing of his bruised ribs. As a result he slept poorly, and flinched when he spoke too much or too quickly. During their daily hours up top, Rand had taken to telling him stories, dredging his memory for what remained of his childhood reading. The well was shamefully shallow: a little Fennimore Cooper, some Goethe, Andersen's *Fairy Tales* in a German translation. Once older, he'd eschewed fiction and poetry for Thoreau and Audubon. Naturalists did not spin good yarns.

Now Gabriel's face greened as he listed with the ship. Rand asked, "Want to hear something?"

"Thanks. Take my mind off—" He flicked ash at the gray waves. The deck pitched. "Damn it. I swear I don't usually want babying."

"It's just a story. I don't have to."

"No, please." Rand saw his cheeks darken. "Only—when we get to France, get captured so I can ride in there and save you, call this even."

"Just play me something when you're well," Rand said, though he tucked away the image of Gabriel on a horse. "Do you mind fairy tales?"

"Anything's better than the ocean."

Rand blinked, struck. "I know a story that agrees with you."

When Rand was young, each night before bed he had read to Greta and Anna from their battered Andersen. The ritual had outlasted Rand's own truncated reading and Greta's disappointment in it. Perhaps because of this, he still knew Andersen's tales by heart. His favorite was about a mermaid who gave up her voice and body, suffering great pain for love of a prince. Her sacrifice had always seemed braver to him than the exploits of Cooper's pioneers. Courage was measured not by the danger one faced but by what one was willing to renounce for love. Growing up, Rand had been terrified that he would never be capable of such devotion.

Now even as he began the story for Gabriel, his throat hitched. As he continued—the shipwreck, the sea witch—Gabriel's eyes closed, and his head sagged to the side. Rand kept going anyway.

When he had finished he stayed still, watching wind rake the whitecaps. With his uninjured arm he pulled Gabriel's cuffs over his fingers. He felt as if they floated in a small, warm bubble, calm above the Atlantic's cold waste.

It was shameful, this peace. Rand realized that aboard the *Carpathia* he had worried less about his gift. His daily trips to Manning were pebbles tossed into the sea: a brief hard splash, then nothing. It was as if the knowledge that he was between places, that he could do nothing but talk with Jonna and tend Gabriel, somehow shielded him. Even the bad food, crowding, and sickness could not puncture this silver sphere of rest. He dreaded landfall—not for the war's danger or his revelation as a fraud, but because on land he must act rather than care.

The irony was so acute he ground his knuckles into his leg. "Afraid of losing your tail," he whispered. "No wonder your trees die."

"Having a pleasant chat, Private?"

Manning stood over him, eyes narrowed.

Rand held himself still. Against his side Gabriel breathed softly. Manning could prove nothing: the ship was so crowded that men were frequently smashed together.

"Did you need me for something, sir?" he asked in a low voice. "We already had our appointment."

"On your feet. I can't hear you."

Rand did not move. "Sir," he said. "If you give me ten minutes—"

Manning leaned down and wrenched him by the neck of his coat. "I said, on your feet."

Pain arced across Rand's shoulders. His shock let him be dragged upright. Below him on the deck, Gabriel jolted forward and shuddered into dry heaving. Rand dove to help, but his throat choked on his collar.

Between spasms Gabriel was gasping, "Damn," but stopped when he glanced up. His face closed and he looked away.

Manning shook his head. "Filthy." Releasing Rand's collar, he hooked two fingers around his sling. "Come now, Private."

"What's wrong with you? You're a doctor!"

Manning tugged down hard, and Rand's vision went white. Nausea swept down his legs. Faltering, he stumbled in the direction of the least pain. If he tried to look back, Manning's fingers jerked his sling like reins. He followed.

When he felt a wash of warmth on his neck, he knew they were inside. The hit of close air tipped his stomach, and he fell to his knees to retch into a bucket he felt tucked beneath his chin. Hollowed, he glared up at Manning. "What did you need me for? Sir." He wished his voice were more menacing.

"It's not what I need." Manning wiped Rand's spittle from his fingers. "The Forest Service stands for progress. It must not be sullied by degeneracy and—perversion. You should have learned this in school. It's a founding principle of Chief Paquet. I am disappointed to have to remind you."

Rand stared down at his knees, flecked with vomit. He'd misread Manning: it had not been the brawl or Rand's mild defiance that had made him an enemy. How naïve he'd been, as Jonna surely could have told him. As she'd explained once, there are men whose entire character is disgust.

He said nothing.

"Do you not understand discipline? Your answer is 'yes, sir,' and a promise not to speak to Private Losada unless you want to be dishonorably discharged."

From the empty burn of his stomach rose an anger Rand was too tired to control. "The army can kick me out anytime it wants."

"That's enough. You are on latrine duties for the remainder of the voyage, and you will spend no more time on deck." Rand could hear Manning's breathing slow as he reclaimed his composure.

Rand refused to look at him. "Is that all?"

"You are to report to your new duties in an hour, once I've explained them to your officers. Until then, you're to return to your bunk." Reaching down, Manning hauled Rand by the collar to his feet, not in rage this time, but coolly as a man heeling a dog. "You will not stop by the medic on your way. As you say, I am a doctor, and I say you'll be fine until our appointment tomorrow. Dismissed."

"Sir," Rand growled. He backed out, bracing himself against the waves of pain.

The nurses' quarters lay astern, one deck down. The entrance to their hallways was guarded by a bored-looking lieutenant who, when he saw Rand approach, said, "Nice try, but you think you're the only man who's put on a sling to try and get in here?"

"Don't need to get in," Rand said through grit teeth. "Could you just send someone out? Name Jonna Larson. Tell her Rand Brandt's outside."

"Sorry, son, but it wouldn't be fair to let you kiss your girl just because she's a nurse."

"You can watch us the whole time," Rand gasped. "Won't even touch. Please."

The lieutenant shrugged, then opening the door, ducked in. Rand leaned against the wall. Five minutes later Jonna appeared, followed not by the lieutenant but a tall, plump nurse with serious eyes. These widened when she saw Rand. She snapped through the door behind her, "Lieutenant Brewer, you tried to send away a man with a broken arm? For shame. We should take him to the medic."

"Can't," Rand said. "Doctor's orders."

The nurse's eyes narrowed, and Rand saw Jonna touch her on the shoulder. They exchanged looks. The nurse said, "Fine, we'll treat him here. Mr. Brandt, please come with me. I'll reset that clavicle for you."

She disappeared through the door again, waving Rand to follow. As he reeled through, Jonna gave him one arm to steady himself and used the other to tip Brewer a very rude salute.

Lying on a cot that had been wheeled into a hallway lined with cabins, Rand swayed in and out of consciousness. The nurse's fingers tested his neck and shoulder, then retied his sling. Above him she conversed with Jonna, what sounded like the resumption of a debate. Their words washed hazily over him.

"Not a full break, but it's cracked. It had been healing. This is going to set him back a month." She paused. "But really, you think she flubbed the ending?"

"Ellador wouldn't have left with them. It wasn't in her character," replied Jonna. She leaned over him. "Rand, you hear that? The son of a bitch didn't break it, at least."

"You know who did this?" said the nurse. "He should report it. About Ellador—I see your point. But if she hadn't left, there would be no sequel."

He heard Jonna snort. "The sequel that killed the magazine?"

"Fair enough." The nurse straightened. "The sling is fixed. I'm going to go get some whiskey. He's even more peaked than the others."

When she had gone, Jonna asked quietly, "What happened?"

Realizing he was being addressed, he concentrated, focusing his eyes on Jonna's face to try and digest her question. "What he called us, what he called Gabriel—the bastard."

Jonna frowned. "So he's one of those. What will you do?"

"I don't know. He's my doctor, and an officer."

"How did you handle them in school? Isn't the service full of those eugenics types?"

"I didn't. I never had to." Rand swallowed. Beneath the pain drumming through his chest echoed the sting of his own flimsy principles. "I never bothered."

Jonna made a rueful sound. "Well, you can't avoid him now. Can you fight him somehow?"

"I don't know." Watching Jonna's gaze drift toward the hallway, he recalled the job she'd left behind. Guilt filled him, but he had already broken his resolution not to involve her. "Could you help me? Half your articles for the *Call* were about fighting the boss."

She laughed acerbically. He could not tell if the target was him or herself. "So I'm a professional? Sure, then. I'll help. But could I ask for something in return?"

"Of course, whatever you need."

"Careful! I didn't even ask yet. And you're not going to like this." Rand lifted his head at her sudden shift in tone. She was looking away, her eyes fixed on nothing, as if trying to escape herself. "You'd told me your unit will probably be working in the southwest?"

"That's where the biggest forests were on the topo maps. West of the front anyway."

"In other words, nowhere near Paris. But why would I need to report on you in person? I'm not allowed to say anything specific about your location. Just manly logging camp stories with a nice varnish of Our Brave Boys. I could do that from a hundred miles away, if I had the right details."

As she'd spoken, Rand felt a sinking in his chest. "Gray hired you to report. He'd notice if you just left."

"I said you wouldn't like it. But say I did find a way to make it work. Would you write me those details?"

"Yes, I suppose."

"Then it's a deal." Jonna lifted the hand of his good arm and shook. Her tone was gaily acid. "I'll help you fulfill your obligations, and you'll help me avoid mine."

"Jonna?"

"Don't. I'll tell you if I feel the prick of conscience, all right?"

"I—all right." The defensive hunch of her shoulders hurt him to watch. Jonna rarely doubted herself, at least where he could see it. But if he renewed questioning her now, she would not answer. The pain was muddying his head. He cast about for a neutral topic. "Who was that nurse? She's excellent."

"Doctor, actually. Marie's from Madison. Can you believe it? I sail across the ocean and I still can't get away from the middle west." Her tone softened, and he watched her eyes stray down the hallway again.

67

He was about to form another question when he saw her face lift. From down the hall, Marie reappeared, bearing a flask.

"Not too much," she said, tipping it to his mouth. "It's from my private stash. Jonna?"

Jonna took a swig. "Not bad. You want to play a hand for it later?"

As they grinned at each other, Rand felt suddenly obtrusive. Jonna's voice had regained its usual confidence, and he sensed that she did not want the nurse to guess she'd just lost it. He would not betray her. Sliding off the cot, he nodded to Marie. "Thank you for your help." To Jonna he said, "Where should I meet you tomorrow? I lost deck privileges."

Her brows furrowed. "Outside the stern mess, at three. Try not to annoy him again before then."

He gave her a careful hug. "I'll try." Then he turned and began the slow, subterranean journey back to his berth.

As he walked, the weight of what had happened settled in his chest. He did not know where Gabriel was, or how hurt; he had followed Manning, favoring his own pain, and had not fought back. Jonna excused his hypocrisy too easily. How many promises had he made he was not sure he could keep? They spread before him like an alder thicket, impenetrable: to Jonna, to Gabriel, to wilderness, that mute ideal which would never tell him when he'd failed it. He tried to peer over the dense branches of his fear toward the specters of disaster he might use to lash himself to duty.

"Coward," he whispered as he descended from second class to steerage. He should have known better than to expect courage of himself. But what nature did not provide, discipline could. From now on he would not let his selfishness hobble his gift or endanger his friends. He would give more, ask less.

When they made landfall, he would cut himself legs.

Climbing to his damp middle bunk, he took out his notebook. Halfway through his list of resolutions, Gabriel rolled painfully into the bed below. His face remained closed. Rand asked, "Are you all right? I'm so sorry."

"I'll live," Gabriel said. "And you? Some doctor you've got."

"He won't hurt you again."

"Sure, Ernest."

His tone was flat. Rand thought about saying more, then bit it back. He had not earned more trust.

A long time later he heard Gabriel turn over. "That story you were telling, about the fish lady. How's it end?"

Rand stared at the bunk above him. "Happily," he said.

Two days later they put into Le Havre.

Chapter 7

After a half day's rest in a British camp near Le Havre's port, Rand's unit boarded a long train of French boxcars that trundled them south, over three days, to the hub town of Nevers. Before embarking they had to wait for the train's prior cargo to clear. The regiment lounged on the pier, watching the cars back in, enjoying the sunshine and adjusting their legs to the still earth.

As the train slowed, the cars' sliding doors opened. Planks descended, and a waiting line of British medics stalked two-by-two up into the darkness.

They emerged carrying stretchers.

Around him Rand felt the engineers go still. The medics laid the stretchers in lines on the pier, where a second detail retrieved them to carry up gangplanks onto a British steamer. When they were unloaded, the walking wounded descended. Some men supported themselves by crutches; others, faces bandaged, followed a nurse in a line linked by hands on shoulders.

Silent, the Americans watched. There were many boxcars, and it took a long time.

In Nevers, it rained. Rand did not see much of the town as the train huffed past, save the arched box of some cathedral, pale on the wet sky. The Engineers' camp lay outside the city limits on a plain that had once been farmland and was now mostly thin, gray mud. As Rand slid down from the boxcar and fixed his hat against the downpour, he strained to hear the guns to the northeast. But there was only the drumming of the rain.

Behind him Gabriel said, "Want to find the YMCA tent after supper?"

Rand peered ahead, to where Manning stood with the other officers. Water dripped coldly down his neck. "Maybe tomorrow."

Nevers was a staging point, his sergeant had explained on the train. Encampments swarmed around its rail artery: aviation and labor battalions, railway operators, and two great base hospitals, long peaked buildings stamped in rows on the mud. The Tenth would wait here for a week to unpack and distribute the *Carpathia*'s cargo—narrow-gauge track, sawmill parts, engines of various sizes.

The men were bunked in tents again. Rand found he had been reassigned to an area closer to the officers' quarters. When he peeled away from his old survey crew, he caught Gabriel's questioning look and shook his head. If Manning wanted to separate them, they could not fight it without exposure. Gabriel was safer apart from him anyway. The last few nights on board Rand had woken in a sweat, raked by nightmares whose horror was their quiet credibility: Gabriel cradling the plaster of his broken wrist, or pressing a hand to his head, blood trickling from deaf ears.

At supper that night his stomach was too heavy to eat. He left early and spent the evening in his tent, studying.

There was a lot to read. That afternoon during their checkup, Manning had handed him a stack of French forestry manuals. "I've underlined the species you'll be growing, plus the dimensions we'll need," he said. "You'll start with pilings, Scotch pine, five thousand of one hundred feet or more."

Rand felt dizzy: *five thousand.* "Sir."

"Now find something to do with yourself that will let that shoulder rest. You'll need your strength."

During their conversations aboard the *Carpathia*, Jonna had advised him to keep a low profile, saving confrontation for when it mattered. Resisting now would achieve nothing. So Rand nominally obeyed Manning's command. Too injured to drill or unload machinery, he spent the week gardening for the tented Engineers' kitchen that served this end of the Nevers complex. He saw Gabriel only rarely, in glimpses near the stables, inspecting feed or scrubbing tack. His face was calmly absorbed. Rand was surprised; Gabriel had not seemed the sort of man who took solace in menial work. Rand wanted to ask him about it, but held back. He would honor his shipboard resolutions and not let desire subsume duty.

If only he knew what that duty was. The garden's repetitive tasks gave him too much time to think. As he sat pulling tubers in the plot behind the cook tent, visions wrapped his eyes like white bandages. In France he would wrench row after row of Scotch pines from the soil. When Manning discovered they were dead he would wire Gray, who would pull Rand from the Engineers and send him to the front. Or Manning would never notice the dead pines. Rand's lies in France would set the stage for greater failures. Suppose he hoodwinked his way through the war, ensuring his timber was cut before it died; suppose he were sent home, feted, and given what Gray had promised, any job in the service. He would stand amid the fireweed and larch saplings of the Bitterroot, trying to talk his way out, until at last he capitulated and knelt. From the green carpet would rise a squadron of corpses, gray naked limbs rooted in black mud, a ruin more final than the burnt hollows of no-man's-land.

He caught himself. No, that was a stupid vision, and melodramatic. If he truly proved a failure he would simply turn himself in, and let the service do with him what it must.

He buried the bleak thought. With his good arm he jiggled the trowel into the runny soil, loosened it, then pulled up a carrot. They were small and late, some overwatered to forking. But they lived.

Straightening, he craned his neck toward the squash patch he'd tucked clandestinely at the far end of the potato field. He was no closer to fixing his gift than he had been at Camp AU. There were few experiments he could conduct in secret, without equipment. The best he could do was test his ideas about soil exhaustion on squash. If an increase in his own energy could not preserve his plants, perhaps conventional fertilizers could.

His uncertainty was an indictment. Clearly something in him was not rising to the promise of his gift. What it was he could not tell. The last day on the *Carpathia*, Jonna had asked him if he was eager to see French forests. He hadn't known how to reply. France was spoiled; it had not been wild for centuries. "You mean pure?" Jonna had asked. He supposed he did. If so, perhaps his gift had to be pure to re-create wilderness where there was none. Some reticence in him was sullying it.

He sighed, then scraped mud from the carrots. Blunt, split, far from perfect, they still had been carefully tended over many months. He caught himself wishing that all of his growth were like this, slow and gracious, undestined.

Reddening, he thought suddenly of the Inselberg librarian. When he was twelve his mother had told him the story. Back in the '80s when the town's library caught fire, this mousy and retiring man had run into the building over and over to save as many books as he could. His clothes had smoldered and his hair flamed. At last the fire company had wrestled him down. But they'd been too late: he died of smoke inhalation the next day. "He knew what knowledge was worth," his mother concluded reverently. Rand sensed that it was a standard from which she deliberately excused him. Long ago, he reasoned, he must have failed to do something that would have earned his parents' regard. As a result, his mother expected little. Perhaps he should too.

To dislodge the ache in his ribs, he examined the cook tent, whose canvas the men had pinned with posters for decoration. The newest had been ripped from a magazine. It was the kind of maudlin propaganda Jonna hated, a dying Tommy gazing up at a ghostly Christ above script that read "The Great Sacrifice."

Rand once would have found it insipid. Like Jonna, he resented such posters for the lies they told about war. But looking at it now, he wondered. Andersen's mermaid could not come to land without renouncing her tail; the Inselberg librarian valued his books more than his life. No man with Rand's gift, who claimed to love wilderness, should yearn to shelter in a garden, growing vegetables. His longings were a foxhole. Inside them he hid, while outside the war raged on.

That night he was settling into his bunk with his French-German dictionary and *La réforme forestière et la propriété privée* when he heard a rustle. Gabriel poked his head in at the flap. His hat was off, his shirt slightly open. Rand sat up so quickly his tentmates raised their eyes. They had not touched since making landfall.

"There you are," Gabriel said. "I found a railway switchman from Texas who's got a vihuela, claims he can play it. There's a piano in the YMCA hall, too. I think my ribs can handle a song or two." He met Rand's eyes. "Come on, you can quit studying for one night."

Rand looked at him, the sunset framing his neck in panes of gold. His face seemed easy for the first time since the brawl. It was a peace worth preserving. "I'm sorry. Too busy."

"You sure?"

Rand nodded.

"What about later? We can smoke and—talk?"

"I'm sorry."

Rand saw confusion ripple over Gabriel's face. "All right," he said. He lingered in the door for another moment, rich light spilling down his arms. Its warmth touched Rand's cheek like a palm. Then he shook his head and withdrew. Rand's new tentmates eyed him curiously. A few shrugged, then rose to follow Gabriel.

Rand sank back on his cot. He fixed his eyes on the species lists and tried not to feel.

The next morning he woke twisted in his blanket, heartsick at the mocking vividness of his dreams. To shake them off, he added another letter to the pile he'd written onboard the *Carpathia*. No post had yet arrived from America. He was not sure how heavily censored his own correspondence would be, so he avoided dates and names, offering as anodyne an account of Nevers as he could. Greta would not be fooled, but he hoped she would understand. He prayed his parents had not seen the DC papers' account of the *riot*.

In the garden that morning, his squash still lived. Only a touch of chlorosis on their lower leaves suggested potassium deficiency. While Rand recorded their survival in his notebook, he could not honestly call it progress. He could not fertilize a whole forest. Nevertheless, he turned some potash into the soil. He'd bought it off a private in one of the Tenth's colored units, all of whom, regardless of experience, had been assigned to chopping cordwood. *Degeneracy*, Manning had spat; the service was full of men like him. Rand shivered, and wondered where Gabriel had gone last night.

Just after lunch, Jonna reappeared. Rand had barely seen her since the train. Her face was gray with exhaustion, but her eyes held a satisfied gleam. She carried several envelopes stuffed with paper.

"Jonna!" he called too loudly, as she plopped down beside him in the dirt. "Where have you been? What are those?"

"My first articles, for *Lumber* and *American Forestry*. Your Chief Gray, he's a sly one."

"What do you mean?" Though Jonna was Gray's direct hire, Rand was still surprised he handled her assignments personally.

"I was trying to sound out my options, and mentioned that I'm friends with you. He nodded—I swear, as if he already knew. Then he encouraged me to go with you to Gien. So I was 'safe from the front lines' and you could 'watch out for me.'" She snorted.

"He's just being courteous." Rand paused. "Gien? We're going to the Loire valley?"

"*You* are." She shifted as she said it; he felt she'd wanted the words to sound cockier. "But I told Gray I would too. See, if Gray thinks you're in charge of me, you'll be the one he asks for updates. So when he asks, you could tell him that I've taken rooms in Gien or Nevoy, and only visit the camp to write and sketch. And then you send whatever details I need . . ."

"To Paris?" he finished.

"Yes." She looked down. "I'm sorry. I know it's a lot to ask of you. Doing extra work, lying to keep up a cover story."

Rand thought of his peaked squash, the dead patches hidden in Rock Creek; then he thought, five thousand. He laughed, suddenly and with bitterness. Jonna raised her eyes. "Rand?"

"It's nothing. So you're in Paris but supposed to be in Gien. What will you live on? I don't think I could mail you your salary without someone getting suspicious. How will I even address letters to you?"

A pink flush crept up Jonna's cheeks. She said, "You'll address them to Marie Schulz."

"You mean that nurse from the boat?"

"Doctor. She'll be stationed at the American Hospital there. She's got private quarters in the nursing dormitory and says I'm welcome to stay as long as I need to . . ."

Rand could never remember Jonna being at a loss for words. But as he watched her blush deeper, he remembered Gabriel's pause on the pier; before that, the carefulness of Jonna's letters; and still further back, the pain in her eyes as she'd pressed his hand and said no.

"Jonna," he began, then stopped. All his memories of their friendship lurched sideways. Recalling her letters from New York, he saw that her dislike of charity was not the only reason she never described where she slept. And all her soft pencil portraits of women—it was not a complex puzzle to assemble. He reddened. He should have guessed, or been a proper scientist and extrapolated. But as always, he'd let his desires think for him.

"Jonna," he said again. "I'll help however I can."

The wry smile reappeared in her blush. "Thanks. To be clear: I'm going to Paris for Paris. Don't make me into one of your fairy tales." Her voice was taut. He wondered what she needed to prove so badly that she defended herself against romance; then he wondered about the romance.

"So what is she like?"

"Sensible!" Jonna said at once. "Solid. Like a rock in a stream." She looked surprised at herself.

He was surprised too. He nearly said so before realizing he had never met any of Jonna's lovers. He should not assume they were all Emma Goldmans. "Oh. That's swell."

She caught his tone, misread it, and looked mortified. "I'm sorry. You don't want to hear about her."

"No, no, go on. I'm only sorry it took me so long to understand."

"It took me a while too." She pursed her lips, acknowledging his invitation, but still determined to change tack. He felt embarrassed. She must think him very fragile. "I thought I was like you, and could make myself take the easy way out. But then, you're doing it the hard way anyway." She frowned. "Actually, I haven't seen him around lately. Are you avoiding each other?"

"I've been busy. So about Marie?" He tried to say it casually, but he saw her brow furrow.

"You know, whatever's happening with your plant magic, you're going to have to talk to someone about it. I'm sorry it can't be me. But you might think about letting it be him."

He frowned back. "I'll be fine. Really, Jonna, we can talk about—"

"Just think about it."

They stared at one another. A pane of hard glass had slid between them. Rand did not quite know how it had happened. For a moment longer they bumped on it, like confused birds at a window.

"You'll write?" he asked, finally. "I want to hear everything about you two in Paris. It will be postmarked from Marie, I guess?"

"Rand." Concern filled her face, then subsided. "Of course I'll write. When you get your leave, come visit us."

"Sure, we'll—" He stopped himself. "Sure I will."

Jonna rose, shifting her envelopes to the other hip. Uncertainly she said, "I have to go type these up. See you later?"

"Sure." He forced a smile. She did not return it as she nodded, then disappeared behind the canvas cook tent.

He let his eyes fall to the trowel wedged between his knees. In his mind's eye he redrew the plump doctor, placed Jonna beside her. In four days, perhaps, they'd stroll together down the Champs-Élysées. New love in Paris; Jonna could not blame him for romanticizing it. But her prickly defense of her motives troubled him. It seemed like shame, only he could not tell what she was ashamed of. At least it was not Marie.

He sighed. He'd miss Jonna, but he was comforted by what he would help her achieve. He hoped she could romanticize herself a little too. It was not so bad, wanting a fairy tale.

His fingers cramped around the trowel, and he splayed them in a bow-hand stretch Gabriel had shown him. A tighter cramp seized his chest. He craned his neck due north, toward Gien, and thought again with a tremor, *five thousand.*

Then he remembered the stretchers at Le Havre and cringed.

On the other side of the cook tent, the maudlin poster flapped. He traced its outline through the canvas. Above him on the tentpoles, small unknown birds gathered, chattering. Not until that night, after he had dismissed Gabriel for the third time, did he realize he had not once thought to look them up.

Chapter 8

Rand's detachment entrained for Gien two days later. Gray had seen him and Jonna off at the platform. "I've assigned Miss Larson to your care," he said. "Be sure the men treat her courteously. The service has a reputation to uphold." He turned to Jonna. "Miss Larson, remember our agreement. One article per week. No locations, production details, or grousing. And keep this one out of trouble." He thumped Rand's back.

Beside Rand, Jonna curtseyed. Her skirt hid a pair of shrunken trousers she'd bought at the quartermaster's. Among the stacked machinery in the last cargo car she'd wedged a bicycle, on which she would depart immediately from Gien. The ride would take three days.

"Please be careful," he could not help telling her as they alighted the next morning. She squeezed his hand, jutting her chin at him with more confidence than she probably felt. Then she walked her bicycle up the cobbled street and was gone.

Gien was a quiet town whose enormous chateau, like a great red barn, overlooked a river flanked by pollarded beeches. Rand did not see much of it. On their second day, as his fellows began putting siding up for the mill whose saws had not yet arrived, he and Manning rode five miles north to the forest in which he'd be working. Like most French woods it was privately owned, the estate of an iron magnate named Pinot, whose gray manor and stables were tucked amid the trees. These were almost entirely Scotch pine. Their plantation rows were clean-limbed, orderly, and so thick they choked out all brush save some scattered fists of bell heather. Few stood over eighty feet high.

"Here's where you'll start," Manning said, gesturing to the margin nearest the estate's wide lawn. "For the next five days while the men are building the mill, you'll be growing in the areas they'll log first. Then you'll move backward, day by day, so you'll always be just out of range."

"Won't they notice that my trees don't fit? This plantation is all one age."

Manning frowned. "Their job is to get the wood out, not ask questions. First frost is usually mid-November. We can expect the ground to freeze by December. You'll need to fill that order before then, so that we can keep logging through the winter. You'll grow from breakfast through supper."

"All day?" Rand said, trying to imagine when he might have time to test, study.

"I've arranged to have a pail lunch made for you. Now. There are five hours left today before supper. I want to see how many hundred-footers you can grow in that time, as a baseline." From their horse's pannier he drew a bag of pine cones and handed them to Rand. "Get started."

Rand took the bag and walked to the edge of the woods. Before him, strips of sun lined the trees' corridors like wainscoting. Linear crests marked the old planting rows. The forest grew as tamely as a mule in a mill rut, so far from wild it could barely be called a forest. He felt a small, sick relief. However badly he damaged these woods, at least he could not break them. They had been broken long ago.

Five hours later he sagged across Manning's saddle, steadying himself with his good arm. Behind them the falling sun lanced shadows from the wood. Above its uniform palisade a hundred new turrets rose, green and alive, for now.

Manning dropped Rand at the French barracks where the enlisted men were billeted until they constructed their tent camp. Then he rode back toward the estate where the detachment's two officers and medics slept. Too tired for supper, Rand found his bunk and collapsed.

He awoke hours later to a hunk of bread balanced on his forehead.

"I was going to complain about the mill," Gabriel said, "but it seems you've had worse." Rand curled himself upright. While he'd slept the dormitory had filled, and the room hummed with conversation. He glanced anxiously about. Gabriel caught it, said, "I can leave."

Rand wavered, then gave in. "No, please." He fumbled to make room, and Gabriel climbed up to perch beside him. He had just washed; beneath his damp undershirt the lines of his chest were visible. Rand looked away. "They made you work with your ribs like that?"

"They're healing. Anyway, it's the lightest work they can offer me. I'm to be head teamster, since none of you easterners can handle a horse. Not that the nags they gave us are proper horses."

"The estate has some. Doc Bastard put me on one earlier." Rand laughed weakly. "I'm terrible at it."

"I can give you some pointers. Starting with posture—you can't sit so rigid, in a saddle." He drew a finger down the bow of Rand's ribs, easing him into a slight slouch. The touch sent a thread of heat down his stomach.

He tried to ignore it. "I'm going to be growing trees by myself every day. Sunup to sundown. I won't have much time."

Gabriel's voice was a soft challenge. "And? That's how this works." Rand did not know how to respond. "You have time now."

Rand looked up. Gabriel's breathing was soft but fast, each breath slightly lifting his shoulders. He'd leaned so close Rand could have swayed forward to—the men's voices buzzed below. He clenched his jaw, horrified at his recklessness. "I just want to talk."

"Then let's talk." Gabriel leaned back, crossed his arms. His face was serious, with a faint crease of some rawer emotion. "So. What should we talk about?"

Later, Rand could not recall much of the conversation. He remembered only the edge in Gabriel's voice and the knot in his own stomach. Below, the men milled, their army discipline already loosening to the gruff hierarchy of the logging camp. Not even Manning might be able to stop them if they attacked again.

Rand waited, watching them, and praying he'd have enough strength when the time came.

He waited, as over the next week the unit erected a tent camp on a wide lawn behind the manor house; as they found a wainwright to make a set of ten-foot wheels for horse-hauling; as they began cutting poles from the thin margin of the woods where, four miles back, Rand crouched growing pine.

He waited. Though he saw none of the camp's regular work, he overheard details in the supper line. To his relief, Gabriel's name began to appear in these conversations—openly and with praise, not the whispers Rand had feared. His horsemanship had made an impression. As the days passed, the men's admiration spilled over into an interest in his playing. They would have been stupid to spurn a gifted violinist in a camp that did not even have a piano.

Rand also sensed how deliberate Gabriel was about being liked. The watchfulness he'd furled about him after the brawl still hung on his movements. Rand saw it on those nights when the crowd about his practice grew thick enough that he felt safe slipping in to listen. While the men sang and clapped, Gabriel played jigs and campfire songs rather than the dreamy, difficult solos he preferred. Rand wondered what it cost him. Then he remembered the survey team and "Ragtime Cowboy Joe," and Schubert. Thoughtless, he had considered himself safe. He recalled Gabriel's bravado aboard the train, asking Rand to grow him a beard. All Gabriel's daring only seemed rash; it was in fact a disciplined gamble, almost but not quite trust. Rand doubted he'd been worth the risk. Then he felt repulsed by his own self-pity.

He punched himself in the leg, and left for his tent.

By contrast, a ring of silence still surrounded Rand himself. It must have been clear to the men by now that he was no spy. Yet he still disappeared each day, returning only to eat. He would not have minded their mistrust, had the ring not moved with him. Those nights he was noticed at Gabriel's concerts, the crowd thinned. When he risked sitting near him at meals, gaps formed on the bench. At breakfast, Manning caught his eye and led it to Gabriel in a way that froze his blood.

He had no choice. Gradually he stopped attending Gabriel's performances. At supper he arrived later, when Gabriel had already chosen a seat. After, if Gabriel came to his tent with the question in his eyes,

Rand shook his head, then spent the night frigging himself, his sleeve balled in his mouth. He was pathetic, but Gabriel's safety was worth more than his pride.

He could not stop talking, not entirely. He told himself he was refusing to be cruel, though he knew it was a failure of self-control. He swore to ignore Gabriel's overtures, and the oath held him just as long as it took for Gabriel to poke his head inside the tent and say, with a look of confused frustration, "Where were you tonight?"

He swore to do better, and swore, and swore.

In the woods, his trees grew and died.

Two weeks after their arrival at Gien, he was getting faster. He could now grow thirty pines per hour, a maximum rate of over two hundred per day. It was progress: gazing at his trees crowning the anemic plantation, he again allowed himself to imagine a restored Clearwater.

Whether his speed improved his gift he could not tell. By the end of each day he was so spent he could barely conduct what limited tests he had devised, chipping the trees whose seeds he'd turned with manure and bonemeal to see if their sap still ran. He had hauled in the fertilizers one Sunday, purchased by hand signals from a local farmwife, and dragged them as far back in the plantation as his shoulder allowed. The injury was not healing. He ignored it, and pushed on.

Though neither the mill's saw nor engine had arrived, by the second week in Gien, Company E began logging in earnest. Two men, armed with axes and a crosscut, could down a small tree in ten minutes. One of Rand's hundred-footers took twenty. A high deck of logs mounted beside the millsite.

As he had feared, the men at once recognized his trees' deviance. His giants sprouted haphazardly between the neat plantation rows, as if they had grown later—though that was clearly impossible. When they were cut, some had already died, though of what no one could say, as they were free of burr, bug, or fungus. Their grain was straight and fine. Their rings caused a sensation: the dark latewood was as thick as the earlywood, and the rings themselves perfectly even. One man, the unit's only other trained forester, was so baffled he took to measuring them with a ruler.

Rand had seen all this already, with Manning at Rock Creek. It had not struck him as eerie then. But now as he watched his fellows recoil, he was troubled. Perfect, Manning had called his logs. He ran his fingers across their faces, unblemished as if raised from Eden. No hard winters had contracted their girth, no fire, no years. They were trees without history.

Rand held up his good hand, and felt his gift pulse through it like the blown ember of a forest fire.

What is France like? asked Greta when her letter finally arrived, the first week in October.

How are you doing? wrote "Marie" two days later.

Swell, he replied to both. *Just swell.*

As he filled the woods closest to camp with piling pines, each day he had to walk farther. The men cut faster than he could grow. By the end of his first week, he was losing more than three hours a day in transit. By the end of his second, Manning lent him a horse from the estate.

Jolting in the saddle, he lay his hand on his stomach and thought about posture.

At the beginning of the third week, he sat with his lunch pail in his lap, gazing emptily into the hundred pines he'd grown that morning. Behind him on a long lead, his horse nibbled the bell heather. He should be using this break to study, test, experiment. Try as he might, he could not whip his body to action.

It was a childish melancholy. His shoulder ached; the men from the camp continued to snub his company. Gabriel, finally taking the hint, had not spoken to him for three days. He knew he should consider these pains worthy burdens, proofs of his devotion. But devotion required effort, and for the past week he had done nothing to solve the problem of his gift—only stare at his piles of fertilizer and half-filled notebooks. The terror of exposure was a red coal in his stomach. Not even the sear of a cigarette against his wrist could rouse him to duty.

At least Jonna was safe in Paris, Gabriel unhurt. Nor, for all Rand's poor acting, had the men connected him with the plantation's mysteriously perfect trees.

He examined them now. Where the plantation's pines sprouted in obedient rows, his muscled wildly skyward. Any preservationists who saw them would call them older, by which they would mean purer, more natural.

"Act natural," Jonna had advised him the day she'd left, when he had asked her how he and Gabriel might avoid suspicion. He was not sure what she'd meant. Certainly not what he longed to do: gallop back, pluck Gabriel up, and spend an afternoon elaborately demonstrating his contrition. However natural it felt to him, the men would not see it that way. At the same time, he refused Manning's label of perversion. Years ago he had concluded that nature accommodated his existence. He had needed it to. If nature was pure, he could be too, despite what the newspapers claimed.

Yet his gift's trail of dead things was as far from natural as Gien's tame plantation pines.

He studied them again, longer this time. Down the plantation's green sleeves wound stitches of sun, like an aged shirt darned many times. At the trees' feet, hands had removed brush for kindling, spaced the saplings so they would grow straight and tall. Other hands, at the forest's edge where the pines shaded into Gien's common woodlot, had coppiced birches for faggots and oaks for cordwood. They had probably done so for centuries. The woods were not natural, not pure. But they were loved.

As he sat watching, wind opened the branches, curtaining the aisles with gold.

Through that wash of light he noticed a shadow bobbing. Vaguely he followed it, wondering what animal was approaching. Then suddenly he stood and ran, his heart cracking like river ice.

"It's an hour's walk!" he gasped once Gabriel was in earshot. "You won't make it back in time."

"I was hoping I could get a ride," Gabriel said. He nodded toward Rand's horse.

"Oh. Yes." Rand stared at him. Sweat had cooled in his hair, frizzing its short curls. His shirt stuck to his back. He'd clearly walked fast. The wrinkles in his khaki pants were damp, hugging his broad thighs.

Gabriel let him stare for a moment longer. "That answers that question." There was no amusement in his voice. "You know, I was always impressed with how open you were. And now I have to hunt you down to ask if you want to stop." He stepped forward. "We can, if you don't want this anymore."

Rand's throat ached. "That isn't the problem."

"I'd guessed."

"I'm dangerous for you."

"Which you decided without asking me."

"I—you might have disagreed."

"Yes, I understand that to be the point of talking." A thread of anger laced Gabriel's voice. "I had thought you wanted something where we talked. If you didn't, why did you spend all of boot camp trying to confess me?"

"That was before—" Rand stopped, not wanting to remind him. Around them his pines were closing like a cage. "I'm sorry. I wanted to protect you."

To his shock, Gabriel shuddered into low laughter. Rand edged back, too startled to feel insulted. When Gabriel finished, he rubbed his eyes. "Protect me?" His voice was hoarse but gentler. "Christ save us from our saviors. Back at camp you asked me the stupidest thing I've ever done for love? Well. It was trust the last man who told me that."

Rand held himself still, waiting. But the laugh had thawed the space between them. "What happened?"

"Oh, the usual melodrama." Gabriel sounded as if he were determined to find himself amusing. "He was a professor at the Conservatory, offered me a spot in the city's orchestra. And when I got boring and he reneged, he told me he was trying to protect me from the scandal of having fucked my way to a position."

Rand hid his flinch. Unsure whether sympathy would embarrass Gabriel, he said carefully, "That's awful."

"Thanks."

"Is that when your family—your father . . . ?"

"One of the times. Some protector, eh?"

Rand frowned. "But that's not what I meant at all."

"Then maybe you could have said so."

Rand looked at him across the ripples of gold light. Gabriel had crossed his arms, but his face was open—if not trust, then the courage to entertain it; like the courage, which Rand also lacked, to stamp through the woods after a man who'd avoided him for three weeks.

Why he bothered, Rand could not understand. Face burning, he repeated, "I'm sorry. I guess I didn't say anything, because I do want something where we talk. And that's riskier for you."

"I know."

"But you want it anyway?"

Gabriel's smile was faintly ironic. "Among other things we haven't done recently."

He stepped closer, and Rand could no longer keep his eyes on his face. Through the flare of his anger at himself he mumbled, "But if Manning?" even as he was hooking Gabriel's belt loop, tugging him closer.

"We know how to do this," Gabriel said against his cheek. "We'll figure it out."

Then his hands were on Rand's jaw and his thumb against Rand's lips, in his mouth, warm and rough. Gabriel laughed, saying, "You know we can swap sometimes," until Rand kissed the words from his tongue and proceeded down, unbuttoning as he went, trying to taste as much of him as he could and wishing they had more time.

It did not feel long, but when Rand checked his watch the lunch hour had nearly ended. His knees shook as he stood. Cinching his belt, he hurried to untie the horse. "You in front," he said to Gabriel, who nodded and shimmied capably up, despite his healing ribs. Rand clambered astride behind him. Gabriel on a horse: he kissed his neck and arched futilely against his back.

"You're the one who hid for a month," Gabriel scolded, then clucked the mare to walk.

As the horse moved through the green aisles and Rand became able to think again, he remembered Gabriel's story, how his body had stiffened with shame, telling it. A slow anger pooled in his calm.

"Your professor," he said. "He lied to you about a position in the orchestra? How old were you?"

Gabriel's tone was warmly surprised. "Oh, you know. Old enough to know better. Still young enough to believe love could save me from my fate." He paused, and his voice went light and hard. "By the way! That promise you made me, about restoring our range. Forget it. It was just a lark." As he spoke he stared straight ahead, rigid as a pole in the saddle.

Through Rand's chest an opening wind swept. It was an escape—bought, yes, with Gabriel's cynicism, his stoic acceptance that his life was not his own. But it meant what they had could be without debts, beyond their mutual fears for safety. A surge of hope filled him. It would be so easy to say yes: abandon his promise, hide his failure, take, again, what he did not deserve.

"Rand?"

"No!" He felt Gabriel start. "I still want to try. I can grow two hundred trees a day now."

"You sure?"

The pines were crowding him again. He heard himself say, "Absolutely."

"Well. I—thanks." Gabriel craned back, half turning. Their cheeks touched. "Guess you really are serious."

Rand curled his good arm about him, then let his head sink so his chin rode on Gabriel's shoulder. His stomach was a wire snarl. It was not a lie yet; he still had time. He stared ahead into the sunlit pines.

Above them his trees gouged the sky like smokestacks, lifeless, pure.

Though he dropped Gabriel off well before the camp came into view, Rand was unsurprised when that evening Manning caught his eye over the supper table. He even broke the loggers' convention of mess hall silence to say, "My tent in ten," as he passed Rand on his way out.

"I'm not stupid, Private," he said when Rand appeared. "I know what you're up to."

Act natural, he thought. They knew how to do this. "The pines, sir? I know I've slowed down some. My apologies."

"Don't be cute. You'll make your situation even graver."

"My situation, sir?"

Instead of rising to the bait, Manning's face went coy. "I'm glad you feel innocent, Private. I'm not sure Losada will feel the same when he's arraigned for assault. The law is quite clear on these matters."

Rand's heart skidded. He tried to keep his voice level. "I don't know what you're talking about, sir."

Manning smiled, and he knew he had failed. "See that you continue not to know. Because if I ever find proof that you do . . ." Manning looked him up and down. His eyes narrowed, but his tone grew almost wistful. "What a waste. You should be grateful for how useful you are to the service. Dismissed."

As Rand turned to leave, he kept his back straight, pace measured.

He made it all the way to his tent, tucking himself unobtrusively beneath his blankets, before the panic took him. He was not Jonna, bold enough to fling cheek in the face of power. He should never have believed he could follow her lead.

Against his closed eyes the familiar demons of his panic rose: Gabriel's broken hands; the mocking bones of a dead forest; the downcast eyes of everyone to whom he'd given his word. If he fixed his gift, he could still preserve the northwoods, the range, the marsh. But he did not know how to preserve Gabriel, now that they had chosen to walk open-eyed into danger.

To slow his breathing he imagined his mind as ruled paper. *We'll figure it out*, he wrote, first in English and then German. *We'll figure it out.* He wrote it over and over until his heart calmed, and his stomach subsided to its usual upset.

To distract himself he rehearsed that day's observations, which he had forgotten to record in the field. Sitting up and opening a notebook, he jotted down what he remembered: which of his trees still lived, their needlefall, color, sap. Unlike his Nevers garden, here the fertilizers did not seem to make much difference. Likely he had not used enough, or something else was wrong.

He did not know. He was so tired.

He closed the notebook and crushed his face to the blankets. They would figure it out. Though he was a coward, and a failure, and a rifle sight on Gabriel's chest, he would figure it out.

Chapter 9

DECEMBER 4, 1917

My dear R,

I had your description of the new sawmill last week. It was perfect.
If you could send more of those awful songs too—Gray thinks they
show "spirit," & was talking about putting them into some sort of
enlisted men's paper HQ is cooking up. A paper the men own, not the
bosses? "Flying pigs." Though the AEF sounds like it could use
cheering. M's casualties say their lines are a shambles. No rations,
stragglers everywhere. You could walk right up to the front lines & no
one would bat an eye!

Paris remains cold & drear. The "City of Light" & yet we have no
coal . . . I hide in the hospital when I'm not working the metro. The
wounded—I don't know how M survives them. Was that part of your
training? Fake cheer even when you're rotting inside, legless, faceless?
My complaints are so minor by comparison. E.g.: I can't afford the
Ballets Russes. Boohoo. But the set designers live in Montparnasse,
so I see all the important parts anyway.

M's French improves every day—she's almost as fluent as me now.
You know she plays piano, & sings too? (see reverse) When you visit
we shall have a concert, brighten things up. When is your leave again?

My L. Superior friends are still celebrating October. I help where I
can, though I ought to be doing more, much more. How bourgeois
I've become, staring out windows for no reason.

I know it's a waste of paper, but could you write me just a little paragraph about home? The black lakes, the larches, the trout lilies in spring. You know.

And you: how are you, really?

Love,

Marie

Rand flipped the letter over. It was two weeks old. Damp had faded the pencil sketch, but he recognized the round doctor from the boat, shoulders sloped as if at a piano, mouth crooked in a smile. Jonna had always been good at expressions, and this one, as always, said more than her carefully offhand words. Solid, he thought, like a rock in a stream.

His bunkmate, a sawyer from Boston, leaned over. "That your girl? She's cute." The men were talking to him more now that the ground had frozen and Manning reassigned him to log scaling. "Though I'd look out for the guy she posed for. Whew, that smile!"

"She's just a friend," Rand said.

"Too bad," he replied, and returned to his own letters.

Rand wished Jonna had sketched Paris, or herself, so he could know more about either. He recalled her similar moods at school, when for days she could not draw or write but stared listlessly at nothing. These often preluded some revelation and a new burst of activity. But now she simply sounded stuck. He wondered about the mood in the capital. He had lived in France for three months now, and the front still seemed like something happening a world away. Only on wet chill days, when the mill was silent, could he sometimes hear the distant rumble of guns. Otherwise he knew the war only by its absences: horses, white bread, men over fifteen.

But rumors told of mutiny and food riots. Jonna's Lake Superior friends—the socialists, so coded for the community of working-class Finns from which she hailed—were, he gathered, trying to import Petrograd's revolution to Paris. Jonna made it sound possible.

Perhaps the unrest was sufficient reason for her dejection. He hoped so. He would find a cautious way to ask her in his reply.

Unfolding a sheet of paper, he propped himself on his elbows, pencil to his lips. His left arm trembled. After he had stopped growing trees in mid-November, his collarbone had finally begun to heal. Never had he been so excited for convalescence, or so shamefully grateful for the frozen ground that prevented his experiments. Tomorrow was Sunday, when the officers dined for a reliable five hours in the estate house and the enlisted men trooped into town or squabbled over the few bicycles that might take them to Orléans. The plantation's back stretches lay empty save for birds and sunlight. Even Manning could not keep track of which men went where, or with whom.

Though Rand had elaborately scheduled a few of those Sundays—Gabriel demanded a level of cleanliness for some things that was hard to achieve outdoors—they spent nearly as much time talking. In all acts they were tentative, vulnerable. The bridge between them was the same, but it now bore more weight. Rand ventured across gingerly, listening for creaks.

One sunny noon in February, when he still sprawled in the horse blankets they'd spread on a patch of cleared ground, Gabriel sat up to smoke. Abruptly he began describing the summer he'd returned from the Conservatory, only to find the rumors had followed. His voice was hesitant. Rand nodded him on, hiding his surprise at the suddenness of the confidence. As Gabriel spoke he looked away, as if refusing to admit the story was his helped him to tell it.

By that autumn, he continued, the whispers had spread, and the eligible daughters of neighboring ranchers had withdrawn their bids. To prevent loss of face from becoming loss of business, Gabriel's father had taken a liaison position between the New Mexico Wool Growers Association and the Department of Agriculture. It made the Cedillo family indispensable to the government. "That's when my father decided I should go away for a while, join the service and learn range management," Gabriel said. "If I couldn't marry into more land, I could restore what we already had."

"But there's not much range in the northwoods," Rand said. He had wondered about this for some time. "Why did you go there? What did you expect to learn?"

"Exactly," said Gabriel, in a tone of tart satisfaction.

Rand nodded. "So now your father works with the DOA. Doesn't he despise Washington?"

"If you can't rely on your neighbors for security, you make deals with whatever devils will offer it." Gabriel blew smoke. He did not sound disapproving, and Rand wondered if both he and his father prized loyalty to people over ideals. For some reason it made him feel immature. He tried several times to put the feeling into a question, then gave up.

Instead he said, "But you're so careful." With me now, he added, picturing a younger Gabriel who wasn't. "And your professor wouldn't have advertised it. How did anyone find out?"

"Family gossip, how else? I still have nephews in the city who address their letters to 'Uncle Forty-One.'" When Rand gave him a strange look, he waved his hand. "An old city scandal. There was a dance, some men got caught. It's not important. Don't your cousins whisper about you?"

Rand shook his head. Though he'd talked Gabriel's ears off about wilderness and Clearwater and the Forest School, beyond his college amours, he had shared few home stories. He'd always considered his family life dull, what Gabriel might have called provincial, and Jonna bourgeois. His parents were too formal to pry into his affairs, romantic or otherwise, and Greta, whatever she suspected, kept her mouth shut. Anyway, he had no real griefs to conceal. His lovers had only left, never betrayed him. It would have been insulting to meet Gabriel's story with one of his own, as if they were equivalent.

He sensed that sometimes Gabriel found these one-sided conversations frustrating. One day he'd been reminiscing to Rand about the orange poppies that sometimes filled the meadows east of Santa Fe after rain. *Eschscholzia californica*, Rand had guessed, shorter and more drought-tolerant than their red relatives. Once he fixed his gift, he could weave them into the grama and bluestem on Gabriel's range. He'd breathed down the specters of wilted prairie, rolling dust. When he had looked up from the vision, he realized Gabriel had stopped talking. "Are you taking notes in there?" Gabriel had asked.

"Sorry," Rand had replied. "I was just planning."

"Planning what? You look so earnest, Ernest."

Rand had given him a weak smile. "Nothing interesting," he'd said. "Just plants."

For cover's sake, they always spent their Sundays far back in the woods, returning to camp through the plantation. Snow crusted the ridges between the pines. In the unlogged areas it lay clean and blue in the shadows. Only sometimes, closer to camp, great rusty stains of needles ringed the largest boles. When Rand saw them he tried to walk faster.

But that day Gabriel stopped and pointed. "Don't know if you knew this, working the deck like you do, but some of those big pines you grew—their wood's good, but they'd died before we hauled them in." He must have seen the blood leave Rand's face, because he added, "So you didn't know. Want to go look?"

Color and sound leached from the world. Rand let himself be led to one of his trees. Kneeling down, Gabriel took a handful of needles. "The men say they've never found bugs or rot. Not my area of expertise. What do you think?"

Rand steadied himself on the trunk. "I'd have to run tests. It's probably something in the soil."

"Just for your trees, though? Seems strange." Gabriel glanced at Rand over his shoulder. "It's not a problem with you, is it? Maybe Doc Bastard drove you too hard this fall. What was it you said, three hundred a day? No surprise some got botched."

"Sure," Rand said. His knuckles were white on the bark. "I'll have to pace myself, come spring. Nothing to worry about."

Gabriel did not reply, but a crease appeared between his brows. Forcing a smile, Rand leaned down to kiss it. Though Gabriel must know he was lying, at least he might think it was about overworking himself.

They walked on.

The pencil was still to Rand's lips. He refolded Jonna's letter and put it away.

Outside the tent, the camp was settling into its night noises, fires being stoked or doused, horses stamping, the distant thump of the day's last big tree being limbed. Nerves burned in his stomach like a live wire.

He knew he would not be able to sleep again. He might as well do something useful.

Shrugging on his coat and gloves, he unhooked a lantern from the tentpole. "Off to town for the fiddling?" asked Boston. On weekends Gabriel sometimes played in a little tavern by the river. The tips were good, he'd said.

"Going to look at the deck," said Rand.

"On Saturday night! And here we all thought you were a loafer."

Rand smiled wanly and left.

Since the ground had frozen, he'd spent most days near the mill, pinching logs with calipers and converting the measurements in a tally book from board feet to cubic meters. At first he'd held the job because his injury allowed no other. Now he continued because he was quick with math, and, though technically trained, had never worked in a logging camp.

He was grateful for the assignment. Under the guise of scaling he was assembling a mass of data, counting rings, sampling resin, measuring the relative thickness of heartwood, sapwood, bark.

So far his study had yielded little. Nutrient deficiencies had surely caused some of the needlefall Gabriel had seen. How responsible they were for the trees' death Rand could not tell. He had long since abandoned his old energy hypothesis. Whatever his gift contained, he clearly had enough of it to grow thousands of trees. Yet fast or slow, they all died. There must be some question he'd failed to ask, some detail he'd overlooked.

His fist clenched on the lantern as he raised it before the deck. Maintaining his deceptions felt increasingly perilous, their edifice less stable than the tangled heap of cordwood behind the mill. One slip and the pile would topple. He was exhausted. As winter had fallen he'd acquired the bad habit of sleeping through the nights. He would need to break it before spring.

He must also decide what to do about Manning. Rand did not know what he was waiting for. With each new dead tree that came down, he tensed for the call: *Private Brandt, to my tent.* But Manning said nothing. That silence frightened Rand almost more than his broken gift itself.

Above him, the dim light polished the logs' faces like the raised rounds of a typewriter. Here and there huge keys loomed from the shadows. Rand's trees looked as out of place here as his white pine had in the alder thicket of the northwoods.

Out of place, he thought slowly. A cold sickness bloomed in his stomach. Despite everything, he had still been thinking of his work in Gray's terms, as timber gardening. Gardens were controlled, their growth dictated by their tender's whims. Their purpose was to be out of place.

Wilderness was different. He remembered a chapter from Clements's *Plant Succession* he'd hastily reviewed at Camp AU. *The unit of vegetation, the climax formation, is an organic entity, a unified mechanism in which the whole is greater than the sum of its parts. As an organism, the formation arises, grows, matures, and dies.* Forests were mutually dependent on the interaction of hundreds of species. Had Rand's trees sprouted naturally, they would have grown in time with this organism. Their age would fit their surroundings.

Instead, everything he'd ever grown had been out of place. At Rock Creek he'd drawn a flurry of climax trees from second-growth woods. Here, he raised pines a hundred years too old for their soil. He was like a doctor grafting a man's heart into a child's chest.

Anger washed down his body. What a fool he'd been; how long it had taken him to see it. The problem with his gift lay not in himself, but in how he'd been trying to use it—in his ignorance, not his effort, though his ego was responsible for both.

He recalled his fantasy of striding Clearwater's scorched peat, bulrushes lifting behind him like flags. It was a thoughtless, arrogant dream. Wilderness could not be cultivated like a squash patch. If he were ever to be more than a bad gardener, he would have to regrow the entire organism: raise the whole man from childhood, heart and chest and limbs together.

His anger hardened into resolution. Against the ragged edge of a log he slammed the soft belly of his forearm. Pain arced up, and behind it, clarity.

If he spent winter acquiring knowledge and materials, when spring came he could find a way to test his new theory. Thanks to Manning's pilings, he was strong enough now to grow a complete succession sequence. If he raised a whole forest at once, from dominants to groundcover, his trees might finally survive.

He would need a testing site. It would need to be deforested recently, so that some seeds might still linger in the soil. It should be land no one cared for, where a new wood would be ignored, since it could certainly not be missed.

The logs' faces winked at him. His lantern swung in his hand. A chthonic rumble rolled from the northeast. Far away the night's shelling had begun over no-man's-land, that gun-tilled expanse of empty mud. No one would blink if a man rose and disappeared there, or a forest.

He lowered the lantern.

In his head he heard Jonna's voice warning him how stupid the idea was. But still it drew him, with a cool, heavy certainty, as if he were swimming down through dark water toward the seafloor.

When spring came, everything would be over. Gabriel would find out he'd lied; Manning would call his bluff. The front would be dangerous, but if he could salvage his gift for the only purpose that had ever really mattered—if he could still restore marshes, forests, look Gabriel truthfully in the eye—it would be worth it. Perhaps the risk was even necessary. He had never made a real sacrifice before.

In the swinging light, shadows flapped like a dark poster on canvas.

That Sunday Rand was quiet. He'd stayed up all night planning. He would have to leave at first thaw, which meant going AWOL; at least Manning could not blame Gabriel for that. He'd need terrain maps. He'd need floras for the region. He'd need—

"Not interested today?" Gabriel's hand fell from his cheek. "We can just walk."

"Sure," Rand said. They stood huddled against a woodlot oak, shielded by a bowl Rand had dug from the snow, like a rabbit's scrape. Gabriel was pretending not to mind the cold. Rand had cowled their coats around their bare chests.

Gabriel's fingers lingered on his collarbone as he pulled away. "Was there something bad in the mail?"

"I'm just tired."

"You've been a lot of that lately. Or 'thinking.'" Gabriel frowned, then corrected to a half smile. "So what is it? 'Just tired' is what an old wife says before she turns over."

"It's nothing to do with you," Rand snapped, surprised at how much his fear sounded like anger.

"All right." Gabriel's hand was gone.

Rand shook out a smile, said desperately, "You said you'd heard from Inés?"

Gabriel gazed at him for a long moment before answering. He shrugged his coat back on, his cold fingers fumbling the buttons. "I don't know where she finds all this gossip," he said. "We barely get the Paris papers, and we're in the damn country. But she says Peeters has agreed to perform a series of concerts. He does more conducting than performing these days. If I had the chance to hear him! You think we'll get a leave anytime soon?"

"Not before summer."

"What's the point of a European war if you don't even get to see Europe?" Gabriel sighed. "I'm going to return home and be just the same."

Rand watched the thought move down his face. "You want Paris to change you?"

He saw Gabriel follow his eyes, then catch himself. "Nothing so naïve. It's more like what Jonna said in New York. There are some places that just fit you. I don't want to belong to Paris, or anywhere in Europe. But I do want to bring back something to remind me of—me, I guess. A souvenir, to put on the shelf when I'm a rancher and too busy for fiddling." He smirked, and this time did not try to make it seem natural. "Listen to me whine. Hammy as an opera!"

The false brightness in his voice made Rand wince. He touched Gabriel's arm. "You're not—" Gabriel stiffened, and Rand amended quickly, "I know what you mean, though. The place I fit is that marsh I told you about. It's my place, somehow. Though . . ." How strange:

beyond saving it, he had not thought about Clearwater in a long time. "Anyway, whatever you bring back from this war, I hope it's more than a souvenir."

Gabriel laughed. "Like you?"

"Of course not. I meant—"

"I know what you meant." The laugh returned, harsher. All at once Gabriel seized Rand's arms and swung him up and around. Rand's old wound pulsed; his snow shelter burst in a hail of glittering shrapnel. "Shall we make our own souvenir, then? Desert to Paris with me! We'll live like thieves in Montmartre! I'll storm the Conservatory! You can sell violets on corners. Ha, ha!" Gabriel let him down but kept laughing. It had a bruised sound. "Don't worry," he said at last. "I'm just joking."

Rand started to reply, but Gabriel had already turned and begun to walk away. When Rand caught up to him, he stared straight ahead, as if in a drill line. They did not resume the conversation. Behind them, late December heaped its gray drifts against the farmers' fences. The snow clung icily to Rand's perfect trees.

December 22, 1917

Dear Greta,

    I am sorry I haven't written for so long. I have been so busy! I miss you and Anna a great deal. Please give Mama and Papa my apologies for not writing to them as well . . .

December 24, 1917

Dear Marie,

    "Hyvää joulua"! Is that right?

    I shall send another letter later with the information you requested, but I thought this would make a good present. I snipped it from my Muir (no, don't protest). It's the chapter "Life on a Wisconsin Farm," including his description of spring—pasqueflowers, lady's slippers, etc. I know he was too far south for you, but I hope something resonates anyhow. It always makes me happy to read it.

It's funny: Muir's farm was not wild at all. It was as unnatural as the plantation here at Gien. I guess you don't mind, when it's home.

I promise to write more soon. In *your* next, tell me about Paris, & you.

As for me: don't fret. All's well. I hope to visit soon.

R

Chapter 10

In mid-April, snow still lay on the ground. It had been a long winter and the coldest in recent memory. In his notebooks Rand had documented it: sap running, February 27; common cranes migrating, March 10; snowdrops, April 4. Nearly all of his pines were cut and shipped west.

He watched the ground for signs of softening and waited.

At night the roll of the guns was louder. In late March the Germans had launched an offensive. They were aiming for Paris, Jonna had written, and had nearly gotten close enough for bombardment. People were fleeing again. Stubbornly her new companions remained, debating the impact of the Russians' separate peace, the Germans' rejection of the Fourteen Points, everyone's anxiety about how much power the Americans would have, the longer they stayed. *They only tolerate me because I'm L-Superior, & M because she's gorgeous*, she wrote. *Artists tolerate anyone gorgeous.*

As the snow had mounted between January and March, beneath Rand's cot mounted drifts of État-Major maps, field guides, and books from the town's one ancient bookseller, with whom Rand had haggled a borrowing arrangement in halting French. Into his notebooks, purchased from the same shop, he had laboriously translated incomplete floras for the areas near the front, plus their common associations, dominant and secondary trees, subdominant societies, and successional stages. He longed to ask Gabriel for help—his French was fluent—but feared he'd ask more questions. He had already asked too many Rand could not answer.

Manning continued to hold his silence. It felt like a waiting quiet. Once Rand had tried to probe him, remarking in what he hoped was a casual tone about the health of the estate's trees. Manning had narrowed his eyes and asked him if he'd found anything deficient in the wood. "No," he'd said, too quickly.

"Good," Manning had replied. "Dismissed, Private."

To calm his fears, Rand spent his scaling hours confronting probable futures. If Manning guessed, and passed his guess to Gray, Rand might be pulled from the service, his family humiliated. Gabriel would depart in disgust; Jonna's cover would be blown. This was the best outcome. If Gray found his lies a form of disobedience—Rand did not know military law, but he knew how men like him fared in military prisons. He swore to bear it, if it came.

April passed. Snowbanks dissolved into brown mouths of water. Beneath, the soil was nearly soft enough. Rand lengthened his evening researches, reading by the light of the mill's night shift. The men laughed at his dedication. Gabriel said, "You're not sleeping again." Rand smiled, apologized, and kept working.

Beyond the question of determining which dominant he'd choose (black alder, because it was a pioneer species and nitrogen-fixing), which landscape (riparian, for the alder), and which successional stage (hydrarch, less than fifty years old), he had to determine which shrub and ground cover species he could realistically count on having seeds present in the soil, to what extent he should leaf out the trees (it was only April), and a thousand other considerations, of which he seemed to remember more every day.

Then he had to cross-reference his coarse terrain maps against what he knew of the current front, identifying areas likely to have the requisite qualities: abandoned battlefields where forests had once stood, no longer under fire but freshly wounded enough to have little regrowth.

At times, crouched bleary-eyed and shivering at midnight in the yard, he wanted to hurl his notes into the millpond. There were so many factors he could not control, so many unknowns. Perhaps it wasn't worth the risk. Then he cringed at the cowardice of the temptation.

One Monday in early May, after a night he'd spent trying to determine which spring ephemerals appeared first in the Meuse valley, he was dozing in the weak sunlight against the mill's siding. The boards buzzed with the whine of the saw within.

"Good nap, Private?" Manning shouted. "Come on out where you can hear me." Rand snapped straight, then walked to the skid road where Manning stood. "I've got an assignment for you."

Rand glanced around him. "I'm to begin growing again?" he asked in a low voice. He watched Manning's reaction: maybe this was finally it, the confrontation.

Manning's face betrayed nothing. "Not yet. And not here. You've noticed that we've nearly cleaned this plantation out. We'll have to move camp in June. Until then, you're going to put that degree to use. For the next few weeks you're reassigned to timber acquisition. The Pinots have generously offered to lend you the horse you rode in fall. You'll survey available woodlands further up the Loire. Here are your orders." He handed over a sheet of paper. Rand glanced at it. Following a standard set of timber cruising instructions—determine the stand's character, age, size—he saw a list of towns. According to his maps, all lay at least a day's ride north.

He was suddenly very awake. "These aren't day trips."

Manning raised an eyebrow. "You know your geography. No, they're not. You're authorized to lodge elsewhere during your surveys, up to a limit of five days. We don't have much time before the growing season, so you'll return to camp only to deliver your reports, then depart again immediately."

Rand tried to conceal his bleak excitement. Unlike Gabriel, he did not believe in fate. But surely this was a sign: nearly a week where he would not be missed. He felt the front call him in its voice of deep water. "Is five days a hard limit, sir?"

"Five or six, I won't count." Manning looked satisfied. Rand realized he was probably pleased at separating him from Gabriel, stamping out their Sundays.

He kept his voice sour. "When do I leave?"

"Tomorrow morning. Come up to the estate after lunch today, and we'll outfit you." Manning met Rand's eyes. "Until then, you've got work to do."

"Sir."

Rand made motions toward the deck, untucking his pencil from behind his ear and reopening his tally book. He watched Manning from the corner of his eye.

When he had disappeared up the skid road, Rand jogged toward the deck's far end, where the jammer crew and their battered donkey engine were hefting logs into place. Gabriel would be along presently. While the unit had finally received a truck in February, it was useless in the spring mud, and until the ground dried they'd returned to skidding with high-wheeled carts.

"Hey, Brandt!" From atop the jammer, Boston waved his cant hook. "You graduate to real work today?" Rand waved back coldly.

Five minutes later Gabriel appeared, seated atop the lefthand nag of a three-horse team. Behind him, two of Rand's giants strained against their chains in the high-wheeler.

Casually Rand called, "Hey Losada, mind joining me for a minute?"

"What's wrong? You didn't even think of a good cover question," Gabriel said as they walked quickly back toward the mill.

"Doc Bastard assigned me to timber cruising. I'll be in and out for three weeks. I leave tomorrow morning."

"Damn. Only three, though. That's not so bad."

"No," Rand said, but a hollow had opened in his ribs. Glancing over his shoulder, he tucked himself into the shadowy angle between two protruding logs. Pitch still lined their perfect rings.

Gabriel followed, eyeing the pitch. "Romantic."

In the little pocket of shadow Rand looked at him. "Three weeks isn't bad. But I wanted to say goodbye." The danger of his plan, so nebulous before, abruptly sharpened. "Ah, damn." Quickly he caught Gabriel's chin in his hands and kissed him.

Gabriel frowned. "You should get back," Rand said, watching his eyes. "I'll come hear you play tonight."

"Sure." Gabriel backed away into the sunlight. "Hey. Don't do anything stupid?"

From his chest the hollow was spreading like a plume of smoke. "I won't fall into your lap during a number, promise."

"I'd prefer that," said Gabriel, and left.

That night he did not fall into Gabriel's lap, though it was hard not to want to, hovering at the edge of the stove-warmed recreation tent watching him catch Rand's eye. He played, to the men's confusion, a haunting, naked-sounding solo Rand knew belonged to a Sibelius concerto.

For the first time Rand stayed until the end of the concert. In the straggle of departing men he walked Gabriel back to his tent, one eye over his shoulder. They did not speak, but before parting Rand drew Gabriel's hand to his face and kissed it. He tried to ignore Gabriel's frown as he walked away.

In his own tent, his tentmates were already sleeping. Rand took his notes to a lamplit blanket outside, where he spent the night recopying and consolidating them until they fit discreetly in his pack. Beneath them he tucked the fistfuls of black alder cones he'd spent the past weeks collecting in the thaw. He could only hope they were still viable.

As he worked, he hummed a tune nervously under his breath. On realizing it was "Gute Nacht," he laughed quietly at his own drama, then continued in silence.

At dawn he was outside the stables. Manning met him there, where he handed over the bay mare's reins. Rand squirmed himself astride, his caulked boots catching on the saddlebags.

Then with a kick he was trotting up the estate's carriageway to the long road north.

He waited three hours, until he'd passed Montargis, to turn east. According to his maps, the ride to the Meuse should take two days. He would have no time for timber cruising. He'd think of excuses for Manning in transit.

Riding was slow. The winter's melt had scored runnels of mud in the macadam, and Rand let the mare, wiser than he, nose her way. As he rode he replayed his possible futures in his head, priming his courage by making each version a bit worse than the last. At last his nerves were so ragged he could no longer think, and he had to look up and around.

On the train to Nevers he had seen little of the French countryside. Now he found the landscape black and wet with a strangely familiar spring. Save the little towns, huddled around stone chapels like children in tile caps, he could have been riding at home. The sloping fields, sodden ditches, gnarled orchards clutching ice in their shadows—all reminded him so strongly of Inselberg that he kept expecting an ancient sea stack to rise rustily above the horizon.

A pang of queasy nostalgia swept him. How luckily he had been stationed in this war. How deliberately he was squandering that luck.

He rode. Around him day brightened and faded. Tired women appeared and disappeared in the fields. Once a convoy of French relief troops passed, bound for the Ardennes, once a bumping line of Red Cross trucks. No one asked Rand to identify himself, though some of the farmers, recognizing his uniform, climbed to the edge of the raised road to stare. Otherwise the only sign of the front was the occasional clap of the guns, like ice breaking on a far-off river. He spent his first night in an auberge south of Sommesous.

The next day the war drew closer. When he approached the latitude of Paris, the roads began to fill with supply trains: munitions, rations, mule-drawn field kitchens, and even, once, a great square box filled with pigeons. From the east rolled hospital convoys and truckbeds of weary infantry on leave.

The roads worsened. Still no one asked Rand for his pass, though some of the more alert officers eyed his horse, glossy and well-fed. He wondered why no one cared, given what Jonna had written about stragglers. Then he wondered if it was because he was riding toward the thunder.

He did not begin seeing evidence of the front until the fields had risen into hills patched with woodland. The shellfire was now regular to the northeast. At some point he began following the signs—scoops of earth from old barrages, a biplane's timber skeleton half sunk in mud, and men, on foot or pumping handcarts or queued before a field hospital, men lapping sluggishly back and forth like a gray tide.

As if he were surveying, he triangulated their flows and followed.

Even so the first line of trenches startled him. He'd expected more security. But these were reserve fortifications, the nerve clusters from which communication ditches spidered out toward the front lines. Men on their six days of relief lounged about, hats over their faces. From their uniforms Rand saw that they were French.

Since no one seemed bothered by him, he slid off his mare. Addressing a man who was eyeing her, he said in French: "Forest dead. Old battle. Where?"

"American?" The man looked closer at Rand's uniform. "Ah, Engineer. What do you want with the dead forest?"

"Dead?" Rand repeated. "No men? In forest?"

"No, no, we"—some words that included *abandoned, months*. The soldier's eyes flicked skeptically over Rand's mudless trousers. But he waved a hand vaguely northeast, said something else quickly.

Rand had reached the limit of his French, but he understood the gesture. "Thanks," he said, and handed the man a cigarette. Remounting, he rode in the direction he'd indicated. The fear was passing. He felt only discouraged, conscious that the risk he was running was somehow not the right kind.

He rode. Gradually the line of trenches edged east. Below the mare's hooves old narrow-gauge ties ribbed the black mud. If the front had been here, it had advanced long ago. As he picked his way northeast, the terrain buckled into short hills and the men thinned.

At last, cupped in a low valley, he could see no one. He edged the mare across its far crown and looked down. Inside him a great silence fell.

It had, perhaps, once been a hollow through which a creek fed the Meuse. The creek was invisible now, buried beneath a cindered snarl of trees. Above them, broken-backed trunks lay caked in mud like tallow. A few still stood, snuffed wicks. Long tumbles of muddy scree traced paths from blast holes downward. The holes held metallic-smelling water. No clear-cut he had ever seen, even the razed hills of the White Mountains, had seemed so dead.

He dismounted. Making to tie the mare to a stump, he realized he did not know how many hours his experiment would take. Cursing his stupidity, he untacked her and gave her one last pull at her sack of oats. If he blacked out for too long, at least she was free to leave. He stepped away, dropping his hands. She watched him with docile patience. Perhaps she would stay. If not, he would have to find another way home. He tried not think about it.

After a drink from his canteen, he snapped a stick from a half-buried snag and unpacked the sack of alder cones. Slowly, prodding the mud for stability, he clambered across the hillside, casting cones as evenly as he could.

As he went, he paused to press his fingers to the earth. Over the winter he had practiced extending the reach of his gift. Now if he exerted himself, it could serve as a rough dousing rod. If he sent it combing through the soil, buried roots flashed like autumn tamaracks through fog. While he did not recognize all the species, he could make some educated guesses.

The hillside was roughly three acres wide. Seeding, dousing, and recording, his mind numbed gratefully into routine. At some point dusk fell. When he glanced back up the hill, he could no longer see the mare.

Too weary for a fire, he slumped atop a fallen beech to swallow a cold portion of rations. In Gien, Gabriel would be tuning before the recreation tent, perhaps thinking of his family, or of his home, the miles of range he trusted Rand to restore.

Guilt burned in his chest. He must do this tonight, or not at all.

Wedging his flashlight between the beech's upturned roots, he spread the saddle blanket on the mud, then fanned his species lists across it. These he cross-checked against his educated guesses. He spent a minute chanting their names below his breath: *Alnus glutinosa, Prunus padus, Rhamnus frangula, Rubus idaeus, Urtica dioica, Caltha palustris, Viola palustris*—trees and shrubs, herbs and flowers. On each binomial he hung an image, like loops of ribbon on nails.

Finally he touched his fingers to the ground and sent one last dousing pulse. He plotted where clutches of each species lay, their relationship to the soil and creek and one another. Like a root he drew this knowledge up through him.

Then he planted his hands to the earth.

At first he released his gift slowly, like water testing a dam's gates. It leaked through the soil, kindling with warmth the thousands of seeds and bulbs and spores. He focused, apportioned more energy to the alders, less to the buckthorn, a rivulet to the communication systems between roots. Then he drew the sluice wider.

His gift plunged through, a controlled torrent. The mud shivered into life.

For a long while he held this posture, propping the gate, his gift thundering up to drive shoots like nails through the soil. Around him the dark writhed with swelling trunks, creaking branches. The starlight disappeared, and the sky, and time. In his own darkness hope and pain vined together about his lungs. He gave himself up to them, to the forest surging through him. He knew what it was worth.

He did not remember when the sluice finally swung free, and he became the torrent, falling.

He awoke to shadows and the taste of water on his lips.

Instinctively he drank. Feeling arms beneath him, he jerked away.

The man holding the canteen blinked in surprise. Fuzzily Rand registered his uniform—American, signalman. Beside him a second signaler was reading Rand's notebooks. "This is . . . I've never seen anything like it. Douaumont is our area. Why weren't we told?" He glanced over his shoulder. "Did you really do this?"

"I don't know what you mean," Rand said in a thick voice. He followed the second man's eyes, and his heart dropped.

It was midday. Around them, an alder wood sloped as far as he could see. Sun scratched through the new trees' leafless branches. Their trunks were sturdy, circular, like a statue's rigid arms. Below them, buds of kingcup daubed the pale soil. He dug his fingers into it and his throat closed. What had been mud was now dry and silty. Atop it were scattered thousands of pebbles—alder buds. The air had an arid smell.

He could not look longer, because hearing him the second signalman had fumbled backward. "Your accent," he said. "Where are you from?"

"What do you mean, where?" Rand began, then suddenly recalled what language his notebooks were written in, and to which he had reverted without thinking.

"He's a real American, I think," said the first signalman to the second, then glanced again at Rand's wood. "Shit. Whatever this is, it's not ours." He held out the canteen to Rand again, paused, then drew a flask from his pocket and took a sip before offering it as well. "I'm afraid we're going to have to question you. Please drink more first, though. You look spent. This one's schnapps."

Rand accepted both drinks. He knew he should be frightened, but he could not stop staring at the soil, gray as dust. "Are you taking me prisoner?"

"Yes, I'm sorry. We're a reconnaissance team, but we're authorized to make arrests if we have to. Don't fight, we'd rather not hurt you."

The second man held up Rand's notebooks. "Where's the machine? I've read through most of these but can't find operating instructions. Did you destroy it?"

"I don't know what you mean," Rand repeated, more deliberately.

"Please don't play stupid. We shelled this area to nothing two years ago. Now there's a forest here. I bet if you turn over this technology willingly, they'll put you in one of the officers' prisons. Those bastards eat better than we do."

Rand continued to stare past him at the soil. The alders' roots twisted above the pale powder, looking hungry and desperate. He was almost afraid to touch the earth again, lest he absorb their pain. Leaning down, he was caught by the second German, who waved a hand before his face. Rand blinked at it dully.

The man sighed. Standing, he refolded Rand's maps and slipped them into his backpack. The first man took Rand's wrists. "Look, maybe on our way to the safehouse we can convince you to talk."

He was pulling Rand to his feet when with a ringing crack, his helmet flipped off his head. It clanged against his boots, its steel crest grooved. Stumbling backward, he threw his hands over his head and shouted, "Sniper!" Behind him, the second man leapt forward, but then his helmet too flew off, whirling into the trees.

"Don't move!" came a shout from above. A second set of shots accompanied it, spitting at the Germans' boots. They froze. But Rand had recognized the voice, and was beginning to inch cautiously away when Gabriel hollered, "You too! If you move it changes my line of sight!"

It took longer than Rand expected for him to emerge from the trees. He walked behind his rifle. His uniform was muddy, and his face was like stone.

When he was finally level with Rand, he did not look at him but trained his muzzle at the first German and said, "Walk backward, slowly, until I can't see you anymore. Then you can turn around and run. Take everything off first." Rand translated hastily, trying to catch Gabriel's eye.

The Germans did not move. The second stared at Gabriel. "You're not going to shoot us?" Again Rand translated.

"I don't care about your stupid war," Gabriel said. "Now put the guns down. Rand, translate that, then get their gear."

As Rand prodded the Germans' boots for knives, he said in English, "They know about me."

"I'd guessed," Gabriel said. He still had not met Rand's eyes. "Do you want me to kill them?"

"No."

"Then we need to leave as quickly as possible. I have a horse tied above." He circled the muzzle at the Germans. "Tell them to start walking, hands behind their heads."

Rand complied, and the two men began backing away. "Thanks for the schnapps," he added. The second German tipped a salute. The first merely nodded with a look of bewildered resignation.

They began walking away. Rand watched Gabriel watching them. Neither spoke.

When the Germans were at last out of earshot, Gabriel's eyes flickered to Rand, though he did not lower his gun. His voice was too heavy for anger. "If I'd been five minutes later . . ." A shudder crossed his face, followed by a long curse in Spanish, too low for Rand to understand. "What the hell were you thinking?"

"I needed to test something." It sounded like an excuse even to him.

"Test what? You can grow a forest anywhere!" The Germans were matchsticks now. "And you went AWOL to *Verdun*?"

"I'm sorry." Rand dug his fingers into his thigh. A crazy part of him longed suddenly to dash after the Germans. He looked at Gabriel, who was at last lowering his rifle. "How did you know I was AWOL? What day is it? How long was I—how long have *you* been away?" Beneath his fury at himself a cold fear broke.

"It's Thursday afternoon. I left on Tuesday night, after giving Weber my whiskey ration to translate your notes and keep his mouth shut. If you don't want to be followed, you shouldn't do everything in triplicate." They could no longer see the Germans. Gabriel reslung his gun across his back, then turned to Rand. "Once I knew where you were going, I stole one of the good horses. The Pinots won't be happy about it."

His face was ashen with dust. With a cigarette, he could have been facing a firing squad. Rand wanted to drive his knife into his own leg. He said, "I'll explain. You saved my life. This is my fault. I'll fix it."

Gabriel gave a harsh laugh. "Don't insult me. I knew what I was doing, and so did you." He sighed. "Well, at least you're alive. Let's go."

He clasped Rand's hand, once, as if closing a door. Then he turned. Ribs aching, Rand sought any apology that could convey what he felt. The words dried in his throat. Up the slope he followed the sagging bow of Gabriel's shoulders. Their boots slipped in the white dust.

About them sounded muffled raindrops: the shriveled alder buds, falling. As they climbed Rand tried to observe his wood, gauge the damage. But details slipped from his mind like sand from glass. Unlike the British, the Americans rarely shot their deserters. Imprisonment or discharge were the usual penalties. Gabriel would have known this, when he left.

The horse stood well within the trees. Strapped carefully to her back was Gabriel's violin. "You brought it. Why?" Rand asked, before remembering he had no right to speak.

"I don't know," Gabriel said. He began to remove the saddle, favoring the instrument like a wound. Over his shoulder he flashed a labored smile. "We could sing, tonight. Since when we get back . . ."

Rand watched Gabriel weigh his anger against his relief, convince himself that this sacrifice, too, had been worth it. It seemed an old equation, performed many times. As their gazes held, Rand saw it conclude, and Gabriel force a smile. "Come on. I'll give you a leg up."

Something like panic seized Rand, a horrified disgust that surged up from his chest to his mouth. He could not love as Gabriel did; all his imagined futures had been too safe. Again the deep water rippled, calling him down—until a memory caught him, swinging him up over the snow.

He lifted his eyes over Gabriel's shoulder, to where through his dying alders the sun was angling west. No souvenir could repay Rand's debt. This one was not even his to give. But that did not mean Gabriel had not earned it.

He said slowly, "We don't have to go back to camp." He saw Gabriel straighten, as if tuned. "We're AWOL, we're together, I lost a horse and you stole one, and in a week the entire German high command will know about me. I've fucked us." He met Gabriel's eyes again. "Let's go to Paris."

Gabriel stared at him. His expression was depthless. "You're serious?"

"I am. But only if you want to." Selfish, he'd made the gesture without thinking. If they returned to camp, Gabriel's delivery of Rand from German capture might excuse his desertion. That chance at pardon could outweigh whatever Paris offered. He held his breath and waited.

Gabriel lay his hand on his violin. "They'll find us."

"I know."

"And still you'd risk it?"

Rand could not bear the hope in his voice. "It's more your risk than mine."

"Well. I've got nothing to lose, do I?" He sighed again, and Rand could almost see it flash, the silver underside of his fatalism. "All right. We'll go to Paris, and I'll hear Peeters and the Lamoureux, and play the 'Devil's Trill' in the streets until they catch us. I hope you like ballet."

"Never been. But I'll try." The pressure in Rand's chest eased, though its escape was sharp as a puncture. "Gabriel. I'm so sorry."

"You look it," said Gabriel, with almost a real smile. "Say, I don't suppose your triplicate plans included directions to Paris?"

Rand dug in his pack and withdrew two maps. Folding them together, he traced his finger along a route. "We can avoid major roads this way, with a night's stay in Étoges. I have Jonna's address. She'll take us in." Though as he spoke he realized their presence would endanger her, too.

"Thorough as ever," said Gabriel drily. "Come on, then." He cradled his hands, but Rand shook his head and floundered his own way up the horse. His body felt leaden.

Gabriel mounted and sat before him. Rand gripped the saddle blanket for support, avoiding his waist. At Gabriel's kick they began to weave through the trees. The horse's hooves raked up plumes of silky dust. Rand's alders rose above it, as cold and perfect as lampposts. He stared at them. His earlier panic was returning, not as a flood but a slow brimming, filling his limbs with cold weight.

Gabriel stared, too. Rand saw his shoulder lift, the motion that usually preceded crossing himself. "When Weber read me your notes, there were all these different species," he said. "Trees, shrubs, flowers. But this forest is dead. The soil reminds me of our range, after the brush went. What were you trying to do here?"

"It was just an experiment. It failed. It doesn't matter."

"All right." But Gabriel's back had gone rigid. Rand kept his hands on the blanket and did not touch him.

Together they rode up the white slope and into the sunlight. Pale as lime with the clinging dust, they drifted across the broken roadbeds and gutted lanes. To either side the front rumbled—the thunder of the first storms of the wet spring, which was riding, like them, toward Paris.

Chapter 11

In Paris, June gardens bloomed. Rand knelt in the dirt footprint of the city's old rampart at Saint-Ouen, clipping asparagus from Jonna and Marie's tiny allotment. It was one of thousands raked into existence over the past three years, as produce from the countryside grew scarce or expensive. Around him wood pigeons perched on stray islands of rubble, burbling softly. Little European robins—not thrushes but bright round balls—pecked the plots for insects.

He struggled with the impulse to lay his hand to the dirt and simply raise a head of cabbage. It wasn't safe. But he was tempted because they needed the food. When he and Gabriel, thirsty and pale with mud, had first knocked on Jonna's door at midnight two weeks ago, she'd gaped at them before muscling a smile across her face. Cutting off Rand's apology, she'd pulled them inside. "Of course you can stay," she'd said, sitting them down with glasses of wine. "But you're going to have to help out. Bread's hard to get now and will be harder with four, even if Rand never eats enough." On the bottle's neck her knuckles were white.

With four people now crushed inside Marie's two-room flat, they took turns tending the allotment in their off hours. Only Marie was exempt, working at the American Hospital from dawn until dusk. Jonna spent mornings at the Metro and afternoons weeding, notepad open beside her with her latest for the *Stars and Stripes*. Gabriel played the lunch hours at a café-concert. Rand hired himself out as a day laborer, gardening on Mondays and Wednesdays, when the shops were closed. Both men wore civilian castoffs pilfered from Marie's influenza dead.

They did not bother to obtain forged passes; there was no point. Their time was borrowed. They had not come to Paris to hide.

What they had come to do was a question Rand tried not to ask himself. He enjoyed the concerts to which he accompanied Gabriel and the revelation of the Montmartre cafés where Jonna brought them at night. He even enjoyed their cramped quarters, despite the lack of privacy and the bedroom schedule they'd had to adopt after the mild disaster of trying it all together a few times. When alone, he enjoyed evening strolls through the city—the roses at the Tuileries, the espaliered pears of the Luxembourg.

His joy was a shelter, he knew. He spent whole days inside it, hiding from the failure of his gift.

His dereliction appalled him. If he could not prevent their eventual arrest, at least he could spend these few free weeks absorbed in study, so that after their sentence, if they both survived it, he would be ready to keep his promise. Yet he could not work. No matter how he wrenched the reins, he shied from his notebooks with a reckless dread that made him wish he really could whip himself like a horse. He had not even grown a testing plot in the allotment. He only scanned the papers each day for the inevitable news of his no-man's-land disaster. When Jonna or Gabriel caught him at it, he pretended to be absorbed in the political news, about which Jonna always had an opinion. Gabriel he could distract less easily. But he never asked: only looked at Rand once, then away.

Though he had made them many times now, all Rand's apologies still seemed insufficient. What Gabriel felt he could not tell. His moods were energetic and frayed, as if he were keeping up a whirling dance. Every night at the cafés, he perched on a stool and played tarantellas, drinking in the crowd's admiration. When he left for another man's flat—sometimes with Rand, sometimes without—he always returned to Marie's the next morning laughing. Following the laughter came always the same, sad smile.

Rand too felt as if he were dancing above an abyss. He wished he were as fey and defiant as Gabriel. But his legs caught under him. Below, the guilt yawned bottomless.

Jonna, for her part, dismissed Rand's apologies with a wave. "I'm glad you came," she insisted. Her voice was glum. When Rand pressed, her shoulders hunched, and she explained that she'd been trying and failing to write something *L'Humanité* would publish. "I'm disappointed in myself," she said. "That's all."

Trying to cheer her, he asked her how things were going with Marie. Because of her work Rand rarely saw them together, and then only at night, at the cafés. "She's such a comfort," Jonna said. Her pale face brightened. "I never thought I'd cling so. No, not cling. Follow, like she's in the grass ahead of me, cutting a path." There was a waver of charmed surprise in her voice. "Like your surveyors. Ha."

"And you?" he prompted. "You're a Parisienne now. What do you like best?"

Her forehead creased. "It's fine. My mother would be proud, even if I can't vote here either. Soon I'll be a real European, and a comrade, just like I'm supposed to . . . but how are you?"

"Me? Fine," he echoed.

They stared at one another; between them, the mirror of their mutual pretense glinted. In the old days, one would have cracked. Now neither spoke. At last Rand mumbled an excuse and rose to start supper.

A few streets north, the big bells of Saint-Ouen's Notre-Dame tolled noon. He looked up from the asparagus. Down in the café-concert near the Gard du Nord, Gabriel's lunch show would be starting. It had been three days since Rand had last visited one of his concerts. Brushing the dirt from his knees, he covered the vegetables in their basket. If he jogged, he could drop them off at the flat before Gabriel's second performance began.

The Sirène was modest for a café-concert, and cheap, since it mostly served the permissionnaires who poured north up the Boulevard Barbès from the train station. Its stage was low and simple, its productions scattershot. Gabriel liked it for these reasons: between acts he'd convinced the owners to let him drag a chair to the stage and keep the tips. Playing on a stool before an appreciative crowd, he was mesmerizing, and seemed more himself than Rand had ever seen him.

He was there now as Rand entered, eyes closed, wrapping himself in something cheery and baroque. Behind him the curtain bobbed, the dancers changing their outfits. Few among the audience seemed to be paying attention, so Rand didn't either, ordering a tea and stationing himself at a side table where he might listen while seeming nonchalant. If he kept to the back and did not watch too closely, he could usually escape notice.

As he sat he saw another man listening intently. He had a table before the stage, and as Rand watched, his calloused fingers twitched.

An hour later the midday show ended. Gabriel had taken the stage two more times. On the second he had noticed Rand and smiled. Now as he climbed from the pit, shirt gray with sweat, he swept by Rand's table and nodded his head at the exit.

Rand was rising when the man seated before the stage pushed out his chair and called, "Monsieur!"

Rand saw Gabriel tense, turn. They caught each other's eyes, then looked away. But the man ignored Rand. Offering Gabriel a slight bow, he addressed him in French, slow and un-Parisian enough for Rand to understand: "Who did you study with?" Rand fixed his own gaze ahead, trying not to seem like he was listening. For a few moments they conversed. Then the man paused and asked, this time in incredulous Spanish, "The school in Mexico?"

Gabriel's mouth soured, and he replied with affronted clarity, "We have music there too, you know." The man's eyebrows jumped. Then he said something that sounded placating, too low for Rand to hear. Gabriel's shoulders eased. He asked another question in Spanish; then they were speaking so swiftly Rand could not follow. He heard Gabriel give the name of the café they frequented at night.

When the man finally bowed and left, all the bristle had bled from Gabriel's voice. He was flushed, and so dazed he slid down without pretense at Rand's table, not even bothering to glance over his shoulder. "That was Fernández Arbós, of the Madrid Symphony! He's only in Paris on his way back to London. I don't know what he was doing at this café. He said I reminded him of—" His fingers curled on the table. "That was just flattery. But he said he wants to hear me again, that I could have a solo career if I wanted. Well, if I pretended to be Spanish. That can go to hell, of course. But he knows Peeters, said he's going to

Chicago at the end of the year to be music director. Said if I wanted he could speak to him for me. The Chicago Symphony!"

His eyes were radiant. The pulse in his cheek beat so hard Rand had to catch himself from reaching up to cup it. Instead he tapped their knees together below the table and said, "Outside."

In the street Gabriel was calmer, but in his walk there was a height, like a flame reaching up. "It's fate taunting me," he said. "It's too easy."

"Easy." Rand glanced at his ill-fitting flu victim's shirt, how he scanned the avenues for MPs before crossing. "When will Peeters hear you? I can pick up extra shifts so you don't have to waste practice time at the caf'conc'."

"Don't, you're just tempting fate." The same hard laugh, sad smile.

"And sheet music. I know you have a lot memorized, but if there's anything new you'd like, to impress him?"

Gabriel slackened his pace and met Rand's eyes. "I suppose. It's Peeters, so I'd want something with feeling. But I wouldn't want to challenge him on his own ground—no Franck, no Beethoven. Bruch's first concerto?" Rand nodded him on. "But maybe not difficult enough?" His steps quickened again. "I should prepare some solos for technique. Tartini? Too expected? Sarasate of course—what mother would say if she knew he'd compared us!"

As they walked, talking, Gabriel's elation rose into a hope so uncut by bitterness Rand could barely recognize it. Hesitantly Gabriel spoke of his family, how his sisters would celebrate were he to take a symphony position, a real one this time; how with such proof of vocation they might even sway his father.

The light in his face was transfixing. Rand could not stop staring.

Turning finally down Marie's street, Gabriel said, "To think, if we hadn't come to Paris."

"To think."

And he did think, fumbling the keys to Marie's flat, Gabriel's fingers brushing his hips: Paris achieved what his promise had not.

The door opened in a gust of cold.

At the little table Jonna glanced up from *L'Humanité*. "Will Marie be back at the normal time tonight?" Rand asked into the chill silence.

"You'll want to wash. We're going to the Hyacinth to celebrate. I'll let Gabriel explain." But Gabriel was already rummaging in the closet for his thin folder of music.

Jonna smiled with half her mouth. "She'll be home," she said.

The Café Jacinthe was their usual nighttime haunt, along with what seemed half of Paris's glittering demimonde. It lay in the Rue Norvins, an hour's walk east. After ten its blackout curtains swept down, guarding its bright belly from zeppelins above and roving police below, and offering the latter a pretense for overlooking what went on there each night.

After eleven, the overlooked arrived. Often Rand would ask to go early so he could watch them enter. "Always birdwatching," Jonna teased, but sometimes she sat beside him. Together they marveled at the handsome women, graceful men, their plumed defiance of the gray wartime city.

Tonight, though, he went straight to the bar and slid two francs to the bartender, plus a pack of American cigarettes. "Your good red wine. From Loire, please. All, not cup." He described a bottle shape with his hands. "For the violinist." Gabriel played frequently. The café's owners considered him free entertainment and encouraged his loyalty.

At their table, Jonna downed her first glass quickly. "What a waste," whistled Gabriel. Beside him Marie was adjusting her hair, eyes down. On the walk over neither had spoken directly to the other.

Rand looked at Jonna, then Marie, then back. Gabriel followed the look. "Help me choose the next bottle?" Rand asked him clumsily. Sighing, Gabriel filled the women's glasses, set his violin case neatly against his chair, and plucked the bottle from the table to follow Rand.

"I doubt they're going to sort it out here if they didn't at home," Gabriel said. "Why did they have to choose tonight? Well, dammit, I'm going to celebrate anyway." He tipped the bottle to his lips.

Rand glanced back at the table. Marie had stood and was meandering toward the piano along the back wall. At the table Jonna drummed the stem of her glass.

He felt Gabriel's hand in his hair. "Go ahead, Ernest." Rand snapped his head back, but Gabriel's expression was bemused. "You're not going to be any fun until you've tried. Meanwhile I'm going to let the ladies buy me drinks. You can come save me later, all right?"

"As if I could ever save you from anything," Rand said softly. Gabriel did not hear. Lifting Rand's hand with his glass in it, he drained it, toasted Rand with its empty bowl, then moved off toward the bar.

Jonna gave him a grim smile as he resettled next to her. "Meddler."

"You looked like you wanted meddling."

"Now you sound like Marie."

"Is that what you're fighting about?"

She frowned. "Not everything's a fight, Rand. Sometimes things just don't sit right, and you can't explain why. You know?"

His eyes fell on Gabriel's violin, propped beside her. In the weeks they'd been in Paris he'd sensed something dull and tentative in her. He'd assumed it was the danger his presence had put her in, which she had simply been too considerate to mention. But it seemed she did not know either. "Are you not getting along? You did start living together very quickly."

She huffed. "It's not Marie. It's me. Well, mostly me. She just got word she's being recalled in August to Madison, for the flu. She asked me to go with her." She gulped at her wine awkwardly. Rand had rarely seen her trying so hard to get drunk. "So that's it. Back to the middle west. Finis."

"I don't understand," he said carefully. "You mean you said yes?"

"No, I asked her to let me think about it." He watched her loosen her necktie. "Am I that eager to throw in the towel?"

"On what?"

"I don't know! What good am I doing in Paris anyhow? I was so sure I'd love it here, but—" She cut herself off, looking almost ashamed. "Still, to lose it would feel like losing, well, me. Ha, I'm getting as dramatic as the French."

He looked at her rolling her shirtsleeves, smirking painfully at herself, and felt a rush of tenderness. Despite her grousing, she had a focus now that reminded him of her at her easel. "You could never lose yourself."

"Wait until I'm in Madison. You'll see."

"Jonna, I grew up near Madison. It wouldn't stand a chance against you." He tried to catch her eye. "You're the most you of any person I know."

"Always so soft," she scolded. But her shoulders relaxed. Draining the glass, she craned her neck to look for Marie. "I should apologize, I was an ass today. I can't believe she wants to take me with her . . . why do they bother with us, Rand? The ones who know where they're going."

"I always thought you were one of those," he said quietly.

This time a real laugh cracked her gloom. "Flatterer. Well, I'm off to my contrition." She rose and began weaving her way through the crowd.

Rand sat a moment longer, saw her reach the piano where Marie now stood. They exchanged a few words. Marie's golden head flashed over her shoulder. Her eyes met Rand's, and she smiled once. Then the crowd swelled between them. Turning, he half rose from the table and scanned for Gabriel at the bar.

The café was filling. Along a row of stools women in smart suits perched, some with other women on their laps. Little clumps of foreign servicemen crowded at tables, whistling at the queens who swept by in silks. The close air smelled of powder, cologne, and the wine sweat of excitement. Only the café's exterior was furtive; inside the people flocked like birds. They knew where they were going. So did he, as far as sex went. In that sense he belonged here too.

So soft, he thought, and colored. Across the darkened city his mind groped east to the front, his dead alders in their white dust. During these two weeks in Paris he had done nothing but be a tourist, attending Gabriel's concerts and courting Jonna's rants, waiting, head in the sand, for the blow to fall. The shelter made him happy, but it was a shelter.

Now watching the birds' display, he wondered what it would feel like not to care, to take joy in his sheltered self. He felt as he so often did, that he had mistaken the purpose of his life, like the knight whose confidence spoiled his grail quest. But he could not amend it now. Habit had become nature.

He shook his head violently, then drained his glass. No, nature was no excuse. His trees proved that. His gift was also his nature, or was supposed to be, in the same way that he was supposed to be a forester, and a lover, and a man who kept his promises.

At the bar Gabriel was leaning backward, flirting with some French queens. When he saw Rand looking, they all waved. Rand was embarrassed by the fuss they made of them, *the fugitive lovers*, as if they were characters in a romance. But Gabriel found it charming.

Rand felt the wine flush his neck, and with it an exhausted resentment. He was so tired of guilt, however merited. What harm if for one more night he gave in to the shelter, just let himself be?

Standing, he retrieved the violin for safekeeping and threaded to the bar. The queens kissed and parted. "Such a long face!" Gabriel said. "Are the girls still fighting? From here it looked like Jonna felt better."

"For now, anyway. What are you drinking? I'll get us two more." He waved to the barman, handed the violin over. In his bad French: "Two gin. And guard this, please?"

He tossed the cheap gin in one go. It surprised him how much he needed it. Gabriel matched him, too elated to notice. Rand bought him another glass of wine, then let himself watch him sip it, his joy rising in waves like heat. When Gabriel slid off the stool and asked with a jokey flourish if he wanted to dance, Rand laughed and let himself be led out. He felt proud and stupid and free.

Dancing became fumbling in a corner; singing at the piano; more drinks; Jonna tipping her hat at the exit, making sure he had the key. About them the café darkened, the crowd thinned. Gabriel retrieved his violin from the bar.

Then they were in coats and reeling out together into the cool night, arms linked like schoolgirls. Rand felt as if he were escorting a maestro downstage and told Gabriel so. Gabriel bowed, grinning. Rand felt as if they were still dancing, the abyss far below, harmless. He could not remember what he'd feared before.

Passing the cemetery, Gabriel pushed gently away. They'd reached the border of the safer streets. A few other revelers had appeared, servicemen of various flags making their way home. "Time's up," said Gabriel. "Look indifferent."

"Wait," Rand said. Bordering the entrance from the Rue Caulaincourt were flower boxes. Within, May's spent bulbs slept. He jogged back and pressed his fingers to the soil, willing the bulbs forward through their seasons.

He cut the daffodils free with his pocketknife. Soft—but oddly, he could not feel ashamed.

On his return to Gabriel he bumped against an American engineer who had been pacing across the avenue. "Excuse—pardon." The engineer gaped at the flowers. Rand teetered on.

"I haven't even debuted yet." Gabriel laughed but laid the daffodils carefully in his arm. "You go first, you have the key."

Rand stepped a safe distance ahead. Then, Gabriel lagging in his footsteps, he resumed the long walk west to Marie's apartment.

The sirens were quiet. Even the grumble of the bombardment seemed distant. Above him the starless city sky stretched, a great soft shelter.

Chapter 12

Dear Greta, I don't know how to say . . .

Dear Greta, You must not tell Mama and Papa, but . . .

Dear Greta . . .

This time he scrubbed so hard the eraser tore the paper. Crumpling it, he tossed it into the box of kindling beside the stove. Greta deserved more than half-truths. If he could not give her honesty, maybe it was best to hold his silence.

Across the room, Gabriel paused in his practice, and Jonna looked up from her mess of papers.

He raised a smile for them both and retreated to the bedroom. "I'm going to get some sleep before tonight." Since meeting Arbós, they had spent Thursday through Sunday nights at the Jacinthe, remaining until closing. Gabriel could not be sure when Peeters would come.

The fingertips of his left hand had grown raw. Each day Rand arrived at dusk, dusty from digging or bricklaying, to find him coiled like a spring before the clothespinned line of sheet music they'd strung across one wall. While he stretched his wrists Rand tried to calm him, reading him funny poems from Jonna's *Stars and Stripes* or retelling the same fairy tales he'd told on the *Carpathia*, a world ago. Beyond Peeters's audition, they avoided discussing the future. But Gabriel's hope seemed to burn through his skin. Watching him, Rand could dream escape was possible. Perhaps the service would never catch them. Rand could abandon his broken gift, his futile preservationist's hopes. They could take new names, start over in Chicago—maybe, someday, even write their families. These dreams never came as vividly as his nightmares of military prison, but courting them helped him sleep sometimes.

He did not tell either dreams or nightmares to Gabriel. Would he still want Rand in Chicago? He never mentioned Rand's promise now, as if he'd forgotten it. He only smiled, listening to himself play. Rand bit back his questions, reminding himself that it was better this way. He could not love well; it was not in his nature.

Later, when the stifling afternoon had cooled and Gabriel slid behind him on the cot, he turned over. "No?" Gabriel asked, reaching around to stroke him. "Why?"

"Save your energy for where it counts," Rand said.

He felt Gabriel recoil in sleepy irritation. "Not this again."

Rand wanted to explain he was doing it for his sake but could not find the right words. Gabriel yawned another question, which Rand did not answer. He was saved by Gabriel's exhaustion. His breath went soft on Rand's neck, and his cramped fingers relaxed. No more questions came.

Rand's gift prickled his palms.

Every night his tension and Gabriel's distraction amplified the silence that still gusted nightly between Jonna and Marie. It blew in waves: the women would be chatting furiously, then one or the other bent the conversation awry. They jointly tried to right it, but the rudder snapped and they both fell silent. Then, an hour later, a stray comment would start the cycle over. Presently Marie would yawn and gather the dishes, Jonna turn to some editorial, and everyone would wait separately for nightfall.

Rand found himself looking forward to the café, where his unease was veiled by smoke and darkness. While the girls danced or drank, Gabriel played languidly, one eye on the door. Rand watched him and tried to bend his feelings in the proper direction, like the topiaries he'd seen in the Tuileries. His joy in Gabriel's success should be purer. It was not Gabriel's fault he'd had to find it alone. He should probably even be angry at himself on Gabriel's behalf.

As he sat watching him, he tried to summon that anger, use it as a winch to squeeze his fear into gratitude. It required more gin than he was used to.

"Don't celebrate too much," Gabriel said when he returned to Rand's table after another night without Peeters. He eyed Rand's glass. "I don't have the audition yet."

"But you will!"

"Aw, thanks."

"You will, you will! You'll be great, I just know it! Brilliant, world-famous!"

Gabriel's nose wrinkled. "Maybe you should go home to bed. See you tomorrow, all right?" And he moved back toward the bar.

Rand let his head swing above his drink. He felt chastened, and somehow satisfied.

Two weeks and a day since Arbós had come to the caf'conc', he nursed his third gin at a back table. Across the room, Jonna and Gabriel were involved in separate arguments. One of the tuxedoed women had called Sarasate a mere imitator before Gabriel, while a second had asked Jonna why her name was so Swedish if she was a Finn.

"When is she up to?" Rand asked Marie when she slid down beside him with a fond sigh. Tonight had been a good one: the cycle had spun quickly out of its silences. Marie's gaiety had manifested in her best dress, scandalously red and frothy. It complemented the confidence she always wore, which Jonna rakishly called her surgeon's hand.

"1809," Marie said. "Another half hour at least." She glanced at Rand's gin. "You really are the Swamp Boy this week."

He was too surprised to be insulted. "Where did you hear that name?"

"I'm from Madison, remember? You were all over the papers when I was sixteen. My brother even signed your petition."

"Oh. But you didn't."

"No." She smiled, so calmly unapologetic that Rand felt it would have been absurd to expect otherwise. "It's funny. You know Jonna really believes she's cynical? While she lies awake worrying she's not at the Jaurès commemoration. I wonder if it's because you've been friends for so long."

"Because I'm such a terrific idealist?" He had not spoken much to Marie alone, and felt somewhat attacked. "It's not such a bad thing."

"I'm not insulting you." She laughed, then tipped her glass to where Gabriel was tuning. "I've surrounded myself with your type. I'm a Grantaire."

"A what?"

"Never mind. Did you really join the Forest Service because you couldn't save that swamp?"

"Marsh. And there were other things." He flushed, took a sip. "I had an uncle from Sturgeon Bay who remembered the great fire. He took me to see the new growth around Peshtigo once. I always thought how fine it would be to help bring places like that back. And be a fire marshal, I guess." He did not tell her about his mother's eyes after the Clearwater campaign had failed, when she'd slipped the service's leaflet beneath his plate and he realized for the first time that he could disappoint her. "I figured the service would teach me to love the real job."

"What, saving people from fires?"

"Yes? No. I don't know what I mean." Across the room Gabriel had launched into a spirited piece that reminded Rand of *Carmen*. A crowd was forming. "I had to make sure I was doing it for the right reasons. But you're a doctor, you wouldn't understand."

Marie smiled. "Another thing about idealists, you think everyone is like you. I'm a doctor because they said I couldn't be. And I'm a good one to spite them."

"Oh. Is it, ah, working?"

"You really are worse than Jonna." She laughed again, then looked to where Jonna was emphatically drawing a coastline in the air. "It makes me feel dirty, wishing she were more selfish for my sake. As if I'm ruining her, you know?"

From the crowd around Gabriel came a rush of applause. Rand looked at him. His eyes were closed, his body leaning into the music. "I know," Rand began, but a bustle at the door of the salon cut him off.

A tall, portly man in a fine cloak was making his way to the bar. There he retrieved a glass of wine, not removing his cloak and barely looking at the barman. His head was cocked, listening.

Rand's breath caught. He looked to Gabriel, willing him to open his eyes. But he was too absorbed. By the time he'd finished the fifth movement with a flourish and lowered his bow, the man had edged his way into the crowd of listeners. As Rand rose and jogged across the room, he saw the blood rush Gabriel's cheeks. He was just in time to hear his first startled question.

Behind Peeters a ring of whispering onlookers swelled Gabriel's original audience. Peeters frowned at them. Brow furrowing, he helped Gabriel from the stool and gestured toward a corner table. Rand could hear his grumbling Wallonian-accented French and Gabriel's clipped answers as they passed.

Some nosier members of the crowd made to follow. "Away them!" Rand snapped, too agitated for better French. For the next few minutes he herded people back, until they gave up and he returned to sit numbly beside Marie. A minute later Jonna joined them.

"You don't need to try and talk," she said, pressing his shoulder. "I'm watching too."

At the corner table, Peeters's back faced Rand. He strained to lip-read, following the moods flickering across Gabriel's face. These were unmistakable: his cheeks darkened, eyes brightened. Rand felt his own stomach contracting. Gabriel certainly did not need him. Ashamed, he downed the last of his gin.

Peeters and Gabriel spoke for less than twenty minutes. Though Gabriel's violin lay before him on the table, he did not play again. As Peeters rolled to his feet, Gabriel finally glanced across the café. His smile was dazed. Rand smiled back, trying to nod his question. When Gabriel nodded back, he rose, heart in his throat.

From the front of the café came a heavy crash. Rand ducked instinctively, hands flying to his head; he had missed the air-raid sirens. Behind him he heard Jonna yelp as she pulled Marie to the floor. Glass thudded against the blackout curtains, and the oily smell of city summer rushed the air. Further back he saw Gabriel scoop his violin from the table.

He flinched, waiting for the next blast, but a second later bodies were surging by him. The barman was calling, as if it were a command, "The police!"

He felt Jonna catch his sleeve. "It's a raid—back entrance!" she cried. "Get Gabriel, they never arrest that many." Then her voice died and she released him. He turned to follow her eyes, past the table where Gabriel was scrambling to case his violin, the bar where Peeters had stopped, his body rigid.

At the front of the café a knot of men was shoving through the crowd. They had shattered the window and forced the doorway, whose yellow light now swung into the street. But they were not police. Their uniforms were not the gendarmerie's dark cobalt but a familiar olive on whose lapel flashed the bronze Engineers' castle-in-a-circle. Between them two men stood in dusty greatcoats. Manning's lip curled as he surveyed the café. Gray looked only very tired.

Rand straightened. Turning, he pushed the air at Gabriel and Jonna—go—then walked slowly toward Gray. He must be Gray's main target; if he came willingly, the distraction might buy time. A burning dragged at his chest, as if he'd breathed chlorine. The crowd's surge split around him.

He risked a glance back. Neither Jonna nor Gabriel was running. Jonna was trying to shoo Marie off. Gabriel had reslung his violin and was inching toward Peeters, who still stood at the bar, looking offended. Rand tried to catch his attention, but he did not look up.

When Rand turned again Gray was frowning at him. "This is some hideout, Mr. Brandt." The flesh had thinned on his face. Unlike Manning, he did not seem disgusted, merely sapped by anger. "I would have expected more discretion from you."

"You didn't have to break the window."

"We had to do something to signal our official distaste," Manning said. "Since the French won't give us the authority to—"

"Major," Gray growled, and Manning set his jaw. Gray resumed, "I'm sure I don't need to tell you that you and Private Losada are under arrest." He looked over Rand's shoulder and his mouth bent in surprise. "Miss Larson? My god. Did you flee here with them?"

"I've been here. You should really check your postmarks," Jonna said. "No, Rand, stop it. I'm not leaving."

Gray and Manning exchanged a strange look. In Gray's exhaustion a red spark flared. "I can't say how disappointed I am, miss. You are fired, effective immediately. And you are most certainly leaving." When Jonna did not budge, he waved at one of the engineers, who began roughly escorting her away.

Rand's heart dropped. He lunged for the man, but at another flick from Gray a second engineer pinned his arms. In his shoulder the old wound throbbed. "Jonna," he called. She squirmed, spat; she did not seem afraid, though her eyes when they met Rand's were anxious. In twisting back toward her he saw that Gabriel had reached Peeters, but also that two more engineers had spotted him and were approaching with cuffs.

The burning in his chest seared to panic. Again he lunged forward, trying to wrench away from his captor and interpose himself—but an elbow clipped his head and he stumbled.

Gray pulled him back up. "Spare us your Greek heroism," he said wearily. "You've embarrassed the service enough as it is." A moment later Gabriel passed him, cuffed between the two men. He did not struggle, and his half-closed eyes were fixed on the floor. Rand looked back at the bar. Peeters was gone.

"Gabriel," he began, but Gray repeated over him, "I said spare us. Or at least save it for your trial." Rand jerked out of his hands, about to protest, but Gabriel raised his chin and shook his head at him, just slightly.

Rand dropped his shoulders. The panic was receding, and in its place opened a cold gulf of horror. How stupid his dreams of escape had been. They had both expected this, had chosen it together, but it was no less Rand's fault. He imagined his ribs bursting, knives or bullets flaying his sides. Nothing seemed painful enough. His eyes burned, and he drove his palm's heel into them at his failure to summon some braver emotion.

As they were led out of the café, jostled together through the door, he glanced at Gabriel's violin, still slung across his back. It had not been damaged. But Gabriel caught the look. "Tempting fate," he said under his breath, then chuckled. Before he hung his head again Rand saw the edge of the old, sad smile.

Chapter 13

The court-martial came six days later. Rand was impressed they'd assembled the paperwork so quickly. On his second day of confinement in the American barracks he'd been served his charges. They were joint, which meant he would see Gabriel at the trial, and that what he'd hoped would be simple AWOL was desertion and conspiracy.

The young lieutenant who served him had handed him the papers, then flattened himself warily against the back wall. Below the first charge was a second, also joint, for assault with intention of sodomy.

When the lieutenant left, Rand let his head fall against the window and stared out across the summer city. He hoped Jonna was safe, and that the loss of her income would not hurt her and Marie too badly. He could not say what he hoped for Gabriel or himself. He would do what he could to mitigate Gabriel's sentence, but that would not restore Peeters's regard. His betrayal was now total. Whatever punishment they dealt him would be too lenient.

Below in the barracks courtyard, a row of lindens tossed their light-green heads. Watching their leaves lift, he could not tell anymore whether they seemed natural.

The trial took place in a small office on the north side of the same barracks, with the same lindens waving outside. He had never bothered to learn much military protocol, so he could not tell if the court—Gray as judge, Manning as judge advocate, no defense counsel, and a small jury of five—was usual. He'd been placed in a chair near the center of the room, with Gray and Manning at a table in front.

A minute later Gabriel was brought in and seated beside him. It was the first time Rand had seen him since the arrest. His hands lay unharmed in his lap, but a blue shadow ringed his left eye.

"Your face," Rand whispered. "What did they do?" Gabriel shook his head, then flashed the same smile he'd worn in Rand's alder wood— the calculus smile, that had weighed and accepted the cost. Again the gulf opened in Rand's chest, and he felt himself slipping toward it like water.

He was saved from the plunge by Gray standing and shuffling his papers. His voice sounded worn. He read the names of those present and the order appointing the court, swore in himself and Manning, then continued, "Let's get right to it. Privates, you're here to be arraigned for the following charges and specifications: in that Randolf A. Brandt, Company E, 10th Engineers, and Gabriel C. Losada, Company E, 10th Engineers, acting jointly, and in pursuance of a common intent, did willfully, knowingly, and unlawfully violate Numbers Fifty-Eight and Ninety-Three of the Articles of War."

He listened as Gray relayed the charges and Manning presented the evidence: of his absence from timber speculating, Gabriel's flight, their meetings in the camp and on the ship and at the estate—had they really been so obvious?—their escape to Paris, their intentions not to return. He was asked questions, answered them flatly; heard Gabriel echo his replies in a hard, dead voice. Manning spoke again, longer this time.

At some point the words blurred. Rand's chin sank to his chest. He counted Gabriel's breaths beside him, recalled his shoulder's trusting weight on the *Carpathia*. Outside the lindens washed the sky, unwild, alive.

At length the little clump of men beside Gray left to stand in the hall. Five minutes later they returned.

Gray rose again to announce their findings: guilty, all charges.

Rand roused himself to listen. Punishments for desertion ranged from death to hard labor; for sodomy, discharge to imprisonment. In his place,

Jonna would have been lit with fury. He felt only sick and cold. He snuck a glance at Gabriel. If the world had worked like Andersen or Goethe, Rand could have bargained for him, offered his soul or pound of flesh in exchange for his safety. A vision flared extravagantly before him: kicking back his chair to deliver a fiery speech, Gray stirred, Gabriel uncuffed, and, later, Rand blindfolded against a wall.

His fingers curled into his thigh. How silly and craven. Of course he would dream of ideal sacrifices, now he had failed to make a real one.

He was roused again by Gray's voice. "Losada, you'll be sentenced first," he said. "You had entered a plea of not guilty. Would you like to amend that? It might be wiser."

"No," Gabriel said. Rand watched him. His eyes were lifted, voice steady. He straightened his own shoulders. "I just don't feel guilty, sir."

"I didn't ask for commentary," Gray said. He sighed. "Though I admire your spirit. You would have made a good ranger, if not for your unfortunate connection with Private Brandt. As I've explained, the usual sentence for this combination of charges is dishonorable discharge with five years' hard labor. As judge and your commanding officer, I could, however, choose to be lenient. Off the record, it is a pity that these matters are not negotiable—that there is no clemency you could purchase with your promised cooperation."

Gray's voice had slowed after his slight stress on *your*. Rand saw that he was not looking at Gabriel but himself. His heart jumped. It was no sacrifice, but it was something. Meeting Gray's eyes, he nodded firmly. Gray did not nod back, but his tone shifted.

"However," Gray said, "it would be a pity to lose that spirit in a labor camp. Private Losada, I therefore sentence you to be dishonorably discharged with no pay. You are dismissed from this court. You may file your paperwork outside. Sergeant?"

He nodded to one of the door guards, who rose to escort Gabriel away.

In the few seconds before the guard took his arm, Rand turned to him. He could not speak. His face felt frozen, his lungs full of cold water. Gabriel said nothing. They had known this would come; only Peeters had fooled them into believing in a future. Now it was truly over. He held Gabriel's eyes, not insulting him with a plea or even an apology, only looking as long as he could before the guard raised Gabriel and led him out; then, as Gabriel's back slipped behind the door, reminding himself that no pain was enough, that he deserved nothing else.

He was still watching the door when Gray said, "Private Brandt." He turned back, numb. At the table Manning was regarding Gray with a small smirk. "Yes, yes, you were right," Gray muttered, rearranging his papers. To the remaining court he said, "Brandt's sentence contains confidential information. Please wait outside."

Rand watched them file out. He felt suspended from his body, as if he were watching himself in the cinema, his voice mute, his limbs gray as a ghost's.

When the men were gone, Gray gave another sigh, longer and more worn. Rand noticed how pale he seemed, and how narrow his wrists were beneath his uniform. Vaguely he recalled the gossip he'd heard at school: that Gray resented this job, having taken it only from a sense of duty. That had been in '10, four years before the war. Rand wondered if Gray handled him so leniently because he hated playing soldier too.

"You've caused a lot of trouble, Private," Gray began, breaking Rand's thoughts. "It's partially my fault, underestimating the lengths you'd go to try to correct your power. We should have known you wouldn't be satisfied with hidden garden plots, that you'd need to be an ecologist about it." He rubbed his forehead. "By the way, your story for that wood is that it's dead because of poisons in the soil, from shelling. I hope that's what you've been telling people?"

The question finally slid a knife into Rand's paralysis. Fear needled his ribs, but the chill in his heart was still too thick for surprise. He said dully, "You've known it's broken. For how long?"

Manning's smirk fell. "Since boot camp, obviously. You hid it about as well as your perversion."

"*Doctor*," Gray said wearily. "He's already agreed to cooperate." Turning to Rand, he said, "Let's be level with each other. Dr. Manning realized your power's limitations during your training at Rock Creek. He offered you as much help as he could, giving you library access, turning a blind eye to your experiments. But on my orders he refrained from revealing what we knew. You are a bad liar, and irritatingly prone to apology. I thought your fear of discovery would be the best means of ensuring your discretion. Manning thought your wish to hide your connection with Private Losada would help keep you quiet. We were both wrong."

Manning sniffed. "We were right for a good eight months."

"And during that time we did not change our tactics once," Gray said. "That's bad policy. The service is full of it; it's why we're in this situation."

The suspended feeling was fading. He stared at Gray's pinched, tired face, Manning's faint sneer. Self-disgust replaced enervation. They knew, and he should have guessed months ago. "So what do you want from me now? It's broken."

"First, stop using that word. We can't afford to be defeatist."

"But it *is* broken." Anger prickled his throat. "Why did you keep me growing pilings if you knew? The damage I was doing!"

"Because your job is not growing pilings." Gray's air was slightly long-suffering, as if reprimanding a pupil. "You're young. You don't know how important reputation is to the functioning of a large organization. Taft dismissed Chief Paquet a decade ago. Are you aware the service is *still* living down that scandal? And the Department of the Interior wants to wrest us back from Agriculture, where we have freedom and a budget. And we're conducting a war on a shoestring, with donkey engines and handsaws, which the public barely registers because our boys aren't out dying with the AEF."

His thin hand passed across his eyes. He sat silent for a moment, then seemed to compose himself. "My point is: it never really mattered what you grew during the war. When peace came, we were going to unveil you as a figurehead, a Good American Boy with a magic power who'd done extraordinary things for the war effort. A Forest Service hero."

The word shivered down Rand's neck. For an instant the old dream flickered before him, striding the cutover as climax oaks sprang up behind him. His stomach pitched. "And now I can't be one."

"Obviously, we can no longer reveal you *after* the war. Your bungle made sure of that." Gray's tone grew irritated. "Now every branch of the government knows all about you. We'll have to share you for a while."

"Share me? For what?"

"Don't act stupid just because you dislike the idea. First you'll be deployed tactically, and later—god willing—act as a goodwill ambassador for America during the peace negotiations. Growing olive trees, that sort of thing. I'm still awaiting Wilson's specific orders. If you do well, the service gets you back."

"You want me to lie." The nausea became a kind of smoldering. He glared at Gray. "Just pretend that my gift works, that I'm a miracle? You should be going to the press to tell them I killed that forest."

Manning, who had been stewing, broke in. "Remember you're being court-martialed, Brandt."

Gray frowned. "I understand your reservations. But the situation is more complicated than truth. And as the major points out, you don't have a choice. The minimum sentence for desertion is five years' hard labor. Not to mention," Gray added as Rand began to protest, "that I have not finalized Private Losada's sentence."

From searing inward, the heat seeped out. He might be a coward, but he would not be a hostage. "That's right, you haven't," he said. "And I tell you I won't grow a damn thing unless you downgrade his discharge and ensure he's let free in Paris. No jail time, no mark on his record."

"You can't demand that," said Gray, his anger finally provoked.

"And you can't force me to use my gift. You want it, you let Losada go. If I find you've lied, I will do everything in my power to smear the service." Rand curled his fists on the desk. Gray raised his eyebrows. He saw Manning's hand go to his holster, and he met his eyes, the burning part of him urging Manning to draw, aim. "I'll do it. I don't care what you do to me."

For a moment they sat there as if in a tableaux, Manning's fingers on the grip, Rand locked in his fury, staring at Manning's gun. Gray let the silence hang. His expression calmed, then grew thoughtful. At last he waved Manning down. He said to Rand, "No. I really don't think you do." His voice was troubled. "All right. I accept those conditions. Don't scowl, Doctor. Let's be grateful. Private Losada has ensured Brandt's cooperation. Think what we would have had to resort to if he didn't have a lover."

Manning snapped, "We could have waved the carrot!"

"Carrot?" Rand's breathing was slowing, but his eyes still held Manning's.

Gray sighed, fingering his temples. "For the last time, it's not a carrot if he's getting it anyway." He turned to Rand. "We're giving you a research team. It's small, but we've assembled some of our better available foresters. We even found you a botanist from Wisconsin. They'll work with you to overcome your power's limitations. I'm only sorry I didn't do it sooner. With their help, you won't be lying to anyone. You really will be a hero."

Rand stared at him, trying to assess the wheedling in his tired voice. In his chest the embers of his hopes glimmered. Gray's plan might solve the problems that had agonized him for months, might, as Gray implied, honestly make him into what he pretended to be. He waited for the flare of relief in his heart. But he could think only of the men at Gien, uneasily tracing his logs' perfect rings. What had Gabriel said about tempting fate? His mind felt smoky, hazed by grief. "All right, sir."

"Glad to hear it," Gray said.

The satisfaction in his voice cut through the smoke. How easily Rand had folded, accepting Gray's conditions when his gift was still a chip, bargainable, and he still had debts to pay. Shamefully he thought of Jonna, limping home jobless from the Hyacinth. "One more thing."

Manning finally burst, "Sir, you're letting him treat this like a negotiation!"

"For god's sake, Al, he's going to be our public face. We can't have him wholly miserable." Gray drummed his fingers on the desk. "Make this fast, Brandt. Is it reasonable?"

He spoke with as much acid as he could summon. "You've already said I'm a bad liar. So if you want me as your show pony, you'll have to train me to jump. I want a publicist." He took a deep breath. "Specifically: Jonna Larson. I know I lose my wages by deserting. I want them transferred to her. You fired her for disobedience, but you know she was good at what she did. She writes fine patriotic dribble. And she knows me, so she'll write it in a way I can stomach to repeat. Reasonable enough for you?"

He'd been steeling himself for Gray's brush-off, so he was thrown by his surprised blink, then bloom of amusement. Even Manning grinned, as if Rand had told an obvious joke.

"Quite," said Gray, smiling. "You do realize that's why we hired Miss Larson in the first place? *American Forestry* has plenty of writers. We wanted a journalist who would keep close by you during the war and be your handler during the peace—someone who knew you well, could help you tell your story in the way we wanted."

"Also a woman," added Manning. "Not that it helped much."

Gray resumed, "When we found Miss Larson in Paris, we assumed she'd abandoned the job. But if you want her, you'll have her. Thank you for your vote of confidence in our initial plans."

The room seemed to tilt. Faintly Rand asked, "Did Jonna know?"

"Give your red friend some credit. You think she would have agreed?"

"No." He gripped his seat, feeling outmaneuvered and hopelessly filthy. "No, she'd never."

Gray raised an eyebrow. "But it sounds like she would, if you asked her now. We always did wonder how we'd get her to make the switch from fake journalist to real publicist. Now you can ask her in good faith. A real silver lining."

Rand let his chin fall to his chest. The air was thick as water, choking. Not a single step he'd taken in the past year had been his own. Yet he had barely noticed; he'd even convinced others to leap with him toward the snare. To think he had considered himself an observer, when he was more dangerous than even his own disgust had suspected. His heart felt like wet ashes.

Gray let the silence hang again. When it must have been clear Rand would offer no further resistance, he signaled the jury to reenter. Rand heard them shuffle in. Briskly Gray read his sentence: five years' hard labor, labor being defined at the Forest Service's discretion. No sympathy remained in his voice.

Rand did not lift his head, but turned it at a drum of wind against the windows. Outside, the lindens' skirts flashed silver. A summer storm was rising.

He wondered where Jonna was now, and what she would do if she said yes. Would she have to travel with him, leave Marie behind? And would Gabriel continue living with them, now that everything was over? He did not know if he hoped so or not. He could no longer trust his hopes not to do harm; he could not even trust they were his. If he were stronger he would give them up—simply empty himself, let himself be used. Perhaps he would try.

The wind threw silver leaves against the glass.

The jury left. Rand sat alone again before Gray and Manning. For a time they said nothing. He heard the sound of papers, scribbling, brief tired sighs.

Finally he raised his head. Though his life was no longer his own, at least he might learn what he'd be used for. "You said I'd be deployed tactically?"

Gray put down his pencil, looking haggard. "In April the Germans made a push to break the British line near the Somme. It's their last chance. Now that America's in the war we can replace troops faster than they can. But we'd rather not let them keep mowing down dough-boys until they surrender. A few tactical displays of our resources might encourage them to yield sooner." He looked at Rand. "And they don't know we've only got one of you."

Empty, he thought. "What do you want me to do?"

Through the lindens beyond the window, a gray rain began to fall.

One week later, two biplanes strafed the muggy dawn above Reims. They wove above no-man's-land, crossing between the facing lines of trenches. From their wings poured sheaves of brown sleet. It slopped into blastholes, bounced from debris with a shushing sound.

Along the trench wall beside Rand, British soldiers peered from beneath their steel helmets. A few upturned them, collecting. "What a waste," he heard someone grouch. "Crazy Yanks." Leaning over the muddy lip, he hoped the Germans were hungry enough to wonder the same thing.

When the buzz of the engines faded, he closed his eyes. The seed was a hard winter variety, normally sown in fall and reaped in spring. It was July now. But the plants did not need to live. Pressing his fingers to the mud, he threaded his gift through it, nosing it up past the old roots and new bones to the grain piled above.

Then, concentrating, he pushed.

As always, he did not remember when he blacked out. But an hour or two later, when he felt himself being hoisted by the armpits, the guns and voices were still. Above them, in the silence, rushed a sound he had not heard for so long he'd nearly forgotten it: the wind's long click and sigh through an endless field of wheat.

Two weeks later, Chancellor Michaelis wired President Wilson on behalf of the Reichstag to discuss the conditions of an armistice.

Chapter 14

When the last camera had finished rolling, Thom the Oxfordian—the youngest member of Rand's research team, and thus designated mailboy—picked through the pale dust to hand him a letter. "Came through the post at Belleville," he said in his slightly plummy accent. "You'll take some lunch before the afternoon's sampling? Ned shot a rabbit, and we're roasting it."

"I'll join you later. Tell Jonna not to worry? I've got biscuits." Rand waved his hand vaguely at his lunch sack, slung on one of the fallen alders. Thom shrugged and strolled off in the direction of the packing newsreel crew. They moved slowly to avoid ruffling the white silt that caked the dead trees like curing salt.

A chalky cloud rose about him as he sank against a bole. He had been allowed to write his family a week after coating no-man's-land in winter wheat. His parents would have seen the armistice in the papers before they received his letter. A return this early meant they'd replied immediately. He'd addressed the letter to Greta in the hope that she might read it first and so soften the news of his gift, AWOL, trial. He prayed she would not alert his parents to the holes in his story, which she could fill with guesses uncomfortably close to the truth. If the writing on the envelope was hers, he might have hope.

He flipped it over and his heart skipped.

The hand was fine and forceful; he knew it only from signatures, or other people's letters. He hadn't expected to see it again. Before opening it, he rubbed his thumb wonderingly across his own name.

R—

I hope you get this. I've had a hell of a time figuring out where to send it. But M gets J's letters every few days, and she always mentions you. Why haven't you written?

About what happened—we can talk, when you return to Paris. I thought you'd want to know that they changed my sentence from a DD to a GD. Your doing? J implied it, before she left. I know it can't have come cheap. What did you promise them, Ernest?

I saw a sketch in *Le Petit Parisien* of you at Ypres, growing poppies among the crosses. You looked awful. What are they doing to you out there?

I guess I mean: are you all right?

You'll want to know about me, I hope? If I'd written last week the news would be bad. But yesterday at the caf'conc'—they don't know, and I won't tell them—who would you believe appeared but Peeters! He'd got the name of the place from Arbós.

And here's the miracle: he's still interested. Turns out he's sympathetic to our *situation* (no wonder he had no trouble finding the Hyacinth . . .). He sails for New York next week, then on to Chicago. He'll ask the current music director about an audition.

I still haven't written my family. I guess I won't, if the audition goes through. There's no point, if the army has already told them about my discharge. I shouldn't feel so bad about it. That was always the trade-off, right? I'm terribly ungrateful, aren't I?

Meanwhile I busk to help M make rent. I hear "La Madelon" in my sleep. If you were around I'd risk some Schubert. German music isn't quite back in fashion, but Paris seems too happy about the armistice to care.

The city is wild with peace. Half the nation was in the streets for Bastille Day. You'll probably get a parade when you come back. People talk about you alongside Wilson, you know. "The Wheat that Won the War" is in all the papers.

I feel like I should be more stirred by it all—peace, the rebirth of Europe, the end of War, et cetera. But it all feels hollow.

The flu, by the way, is bad here. M says she's grateful for the experience before she leaves at the end of August. Will J go back with her? M hasn't said. I'll have to find a flat of my own soon. But then you would know that, from J.

Why didn't you send word through her? I'm beginning to think you don't want to talk.

G

PS: that forest you grew—the press has named it Whitesoil Wood. They say it's from the poison, because they swallow whatever Gray tells them.

What's going on with that power of yours, magic plant boy?

Rand laid the letter on his lap. He could hear his breath move through his throat. A miracle, Gabriel had called it, and it was. Rand imagined him cross-legged on Marie's threadbare rug, drawing his bow across the cake of rosin. His movements were calm and radiant, the orison of a believer for whom fate has finally come through. He had never needed anything but his faith, after all.

The vision brightened; Rand blinked it away and looked up. At the edge of the wood, the Pathé men were wiping the camera box with rags. Around them the pale dirt spread, crosshatched with debris: fallen buds like spent bullets, the withered violets' limp black spangles. The wood seemed more dead now than when he'd first grown it. Two months of balmy summer had failed to revive the hardy buckthorn or curl a single new kingcup from the bleached soil. Even Gabriel's hurried glimpse at the wood had been enough to make him uneasy. If he could see it now, he'd be as horrified as Rand's team had been when they'd first trudged over the silent hill, powder mucking their damp boots like lime.

From downslope, past the testing plot where he'd been growing alders for the past three days, Rand caught the scent of roasting rabbit. On the survey team at home, Gabriel had shot him game on the condition he be the one to cook it. He could rely on him for that, at least.

He scowled. Such miserable self-pity—he was lapsing into it too often. He socked himself in the leg a few times to blunt it. The old bruises throbbed.

144

A few blank pages remained at the end of his latest notebook. He cracked its spine and removed just one.

Dear G,

    I'm glad your letter reached me. I am sorry I haven't written yet. I'm so sorry, for everything. If you ever do write to your family, please tell them it's all my fault.

    Give M my love. J does want to go back, I think? She won't talk about it much to me.

    As for me, I'm working with a FS research team on how to improve my gift.

    After you get the position in Chicago—

He paused, then erased it.

    You know you don't have to keep writing if you don't want to. It's fine. I'd understand.

And then in a final flourish, which felt stupid even as he wrote it:

Gute Nacht,
R

He folded the paper quickly. For another minute he stared at it in his lap, soothing himself with the image of a knife scoring his ribs. Some high dim part of him wished he could describe the image for Gabriel, to prove his contrition. But the tethered part of him knew it was best to say nothing.

A slim hope existed that the research team might help. If so, he would still have something to give. Even if Gabriel no longer spoke with his family, Rand could write. From what he had told Rand, his father was a practical man. If he believed Rand, he would not spurn his offer. Rand would cherish that hope but leave the door open for Gabriel. Anything less would be unfair.

His head ached. Dully he fumbled in his sack for a biscuit. Then, chewing, he rose and walked toward the smoke.

His team sat around a shallow firepit a half mile from the testing plot. They spent mornings comparing what he grew there to Whitesoil Wood—he might as well call it that. A nearby canvas tent held their field equipment: increment borers, soil augers, mallets, thermometers, and a bulky collection of platinum plates to measure acidity.

They had been working for three weeks now, and what they'd discovered so far confirmed only what Rand already knew. His trees were straight and flawless, free of bugs and rot, and sucked the soil about them dry—the more trees, the greater the depletion. His private observations were even less encouraging. Not just one but many things seemed sickly in the organism he'd tried to grow. No insects crossed the bleached earth, no woodpeckers knocked at the snags.

Each day's round of tests felt like tossing a bucket of water on a raging fire. Ecologically, Rand had no new ideas. He'd had none since Verdun, despite his now-regular access to the best libraries in France. His current experiments merely repeated his own earlier work. He pushed forward anyway, in the hope that the same methods, done better, might finally succeed. Unease plagued him. He knew he was missing something, and all his reading and thinking could not tell him what.

However many doubts he voiced, he could not tamp his teammates' enthusiasm. Most were not a decade older than he and still saw him as a miracle. Their botanist, Gray's promised Wisconsinite, had even greeted Rand with a vigorous handshake, exclaiming, "The Swamp Boy! Ned Fawcett, from Janesville! I signed your petition, remember?" Rand did not, but he liked Ned. He was the kind of solid middle-western man he'd grown up with. His presence was comforting, even if he did seem too much like he'd played football in college.

Now as Rand shuffled into view, Ned stood and waved. "Thom said you'd eaten? I'm done too, we can check the dirt." Because of the morning's filming, they had skipped their usual tests: coring trunks and digging down to see how far Whitesoil's white soil reached. Behind Ned, Manning caught Rand's eye, then shrugged at a log atop which the augers, mallets, and borer had been set. Rand lowered his gaze and retrieved them.

At the edge of the little ring of men, Jonna sat revising her notes for a speech he would give next week at Amiens. As he shouldered the equipment she frowned, then drew her arm back and hucked. He caught the apple. "Actually eat it!" she called.

He returned a tight smile. Jonna's acceptance of his offer still surprised him. He did not know if she'd agreed from pity or her own motives. A troubled inward stare sometimes blanked her face as she sat at her letters. At these moments she seemed eerily like the Jonna he'd first known at Yale, unsure of herself and falsely confident to compensate. But whenever he tried to broach it with her, she changed the subject. She had received the news of his broken gift with weary satisfaction. She was too kind to rag him for lying. It was punishment enough, she'd explained, that between the photographs and newsreels he was desperately fixing the power for which he was being feted. "I know what you do to yourself," she'd concluded. He had not known how to respond.

She'd reacted less well to his plea that she keep the secret from Marie and Gabriel. "You mean you haven't told him yet? For god's sake, why?"

Prickling, he'd said, "I don't ask you what's wrong between you and Marie." What he had written Gabriel was true. Jonna never showed him her letters, and replied to his inquiries with single words or vague nods.

"Liar, you ask every day! It's just not worth talking about."

"So you do understand," he'd said.

For a few moments they'd stared at one another. As in Paris, Rand had the odd feeling of gazing into a mirror. Why did they hold back now, when they were more aware than ever of their resemblances? He could not answer, and they'd parted to do other things.

Ned reached him. Clapping Rand on the shoulder, he steered him back uphill, chatting as they high-stepped through the pale dust. Rand kept his eyes down and gnawed the apple.

Like most of Rand's team, Ned had not been in Europe long. "Such puny trees," he said, laughing, as they reached the messy juncture where the testing plot's heaps of combed mud faded into Whitesoil. "We're wasting our time with these French forests. There hasn't been a natural succession here in centuries, even before the Germans blew it all up. What's the point of trying to restore it? We should get you back home, away from human meddling." He unfolded a tarp for the soil samples and smoothed it neatly on the ground.

Rand thought of the alder wood outside Merrill, a continent away. "We've meddled everywhere."

"Us easterners have," Ned said as Rand handed him an auger. "Out west they've still got proper wilderness. You ever been to the Cascades? Climax forest, mostly untouched."

"Except for the miners and lumber barons."

"Sure, but that's our job." Ned looked confused. "Keeping the wilderness wild. Forest science progressing so it can guide nature's progress."

Rand bit his lip. He agreed: wilderness was Muir's first principle, and his own. Yet something about Ned's confidence bothered him. Grasping the auger's T bar, he twisted; the bucket's twin teeth slid into the loose earth. At ten centimeters he jerked it up, then shook the sample onto the tarp. It sighed out, dry and pale as sand. "You talk as if we're outside of it," he said. "Nature, I mean. Are we?"

"Of course. It's a responsibility, a charge. *Replenish the earth, and subdue it.* Our state's bald because men only heard the second bit." Rand watched him dig, yank, and deposit a sample from his own auger. "All that virgin forest, gone in fifty years! Think what the service could've done, had we gotten there first."

"That's true." Rand knelt down to pinch the soil. It dusted his fingers like flour. "I was surveying near Merrill before the war. Miles of stumpland."

"See? Another couple centuries and it will look just like this." Leaning on his auger, Ned shrugged dismissively at the alder wood, France, Europe. "But with you on the job, we could bring nature back in a few years. Revirginize it." He winked.

"I suppose," Rand said slowly. He brushed his hands clean; had the loam always been so silty here? No humus remained, as if it had been dissolved and consumed. "If we fix my gift."

"Have some faith in yourself. A little pioneer spirit! You've read Turner, right? He's one of us too—from Wisconsin, I mean." Ned looked at the samples. "Well, this is grim. Why don't we do the cores instead?"

Rand nodded, then rose. Together they walked deeper into Whitesoil. At his side swung the canvas bag with mallet and borer. Already he knew what they would find, because he had spent winter sawing through it: sound, hard wood, grain as pale and chiseled as the men's cheeks on the war posters about Paris. Übermenschen, he thought, and the word chilled him, though he did not remember where it came from.

Beside him, Ned stomped in cheery silence through the dust. His belief warmed Rand, though he did not know how he could have faith in himself when he was losing faith in science. He looked at his alders, skewing from the silt like burnt sticks. His new testing plots wanted nothing: water, potash, manure, a carefully chosen network of dominant and subdominant species. Yet these miniature climax communities—an acre of maple, a slope of oak and high beech—did not survive a week. No ecological reason he knew could explain why his blackberry and eagle fern withered in a day, his beeches in seven.

Faith in myself, he thought again. After he'd learned to grow so many pines at Gien, he'd abandoned his initial hypothesis: that his gift's failure lay in him rather than how he used it. He'd thought he was being a good scientist. But nothing about his gift had ever been solved by this sort of science.

His feet slowed in the pale dust. Perhaps he'd been wrong to turn outward all along. A forest had a character; so did he. If ecology saw nature as a whole, why shouldn't it encompass spirit, self? His gift lived in him. Its life was his. Was it so unscientific to ask how he was failing—not as a naturalist but as a man?

They topped the ridge, breaking Rand's concentration. Descending toward the dell that held the testing plot, he saw two men milling there, camera stand planted between them. The cameraman started grinding as he and Ned jogged down, waving no.

"You can't film here," Rand began, but the journalist had flipped back his pad and said, in fine Parisian-accented English, "What are you growing in these plots? Is it secret? Are you measuring the poisons still present in the soil? As a German American, what have you to say about the German pollution of French land? In your opinion, should Germany offer forest reparations as part of the peace negotiations?" He took a breath. "Would you give us another demonstration? We could always use more reel."

"No, I won't demonstrate. And yes, it's secret." Rand palmed the lens, then withdrew his hand when the cameraman looked delighted. "Please leave."

"Fine, fine." The journalist shrugged, but signaled to the cameraman and said in French, "Come on, now we've got an exciting finish." Rand watched as they hiked the camera up, then began climbing out of the dell. A plume of pale dust followed them like a train's smoke, marking their progress, all progress.

One week later, sitting beside Jonna in a dark Amiens cinema, Rand watched the plume hiss up, silent as the trace of a far-off fire. His own body bumbled in the smoke, speaking.

RANDOLF BRANDT IN THE WHITE WOOD, flashed the French title. The shot cut to a different image: his hands, dug in dark mud, which paled as between them unwound a cluster of cowslips. A NATURAL MIRACLE—AND A SECRET. He watched his hand sweep over the lens.

A series of text cards followed, interspersed with shots of himself standing awkwardly at a podium, speaking into a microphone. *The US Forest Service says Mr. Brandt's power is for peace. He is a symbol of the American commitment to advancement through science. The healthy vitality of young America, given to old Europe to help restore . . .*

Rand's palms were damp against the armrests, his French finally good enough. *For ecology, he is a savior, able to renew in a few hours what two centuries of industry has blasted . . .*

The screen was suddenly too bright, the dark too thick and hot. He pushed from his seat and stumbled along the aisle. His teammates turned to look at him, but none followed.

Outside on the rubbled street, he leaned against the cinema's wall. His skin felt filthy and tight, like muddied leather. He thought of the cowslips in the film, how the next day they had wilted in their round of cracked soil. *Savior:* a world ago, Gabriel had said, *what you could save.* Was the old lie worse because it was intimate, or this new one because it was bigger? He hugged his arms around himself.

At some point Jonna appeared beside him. "Is it that bad?" she said quietly.

"I can't do this. At least when it was just me the world didn't think I was a hero."

"Plenty of men have pretended to be more while being less." She stopped, pursing her lips. He knew she knew this would not convince either of them. "Isn't the team helping?"

"They're just doing the same tests I did. We're going in circles." He rubbed his eyes, debating whether to tell her about his latest intuition. Though an atheist, Jonna was practical about spiritual matters. She would not think him crazy for believing the problem lay in him. But she might think he was scourging himself uselessly again.

"So there's no progress," she prompted.

"No. I'm beginning to think I'll never know enough to use my gift safely."

"What do you mean?"

"I don't know." He drew a long dusty breath, craning his neck at the sky. Starlings circled there, chips of dark iridescence that were pests, in America. "I don't know what I mean. I haven't felt like myself in so long."

"I understand that," Jonna said, sympathetically. She had leaned against the wall beside him and was staring across the street, her mouth tight. He felt a swell of disgust at his whining.

"You don't have to stay in this job," he said. "I'm grateful for you being here, but I know you want to go back to Paris. I'm sorry I've kept you."

"Rand! Stop whipping yourself! Not everything is your fault." She dug in her pocket for a cigarette, lit it. A small part of him laughed to have guessed her reaction so precisely. "I'm here because I chose to be, all right?"

"Is it because of Marie?"

"*Why* do you keep asking that?" She blew smoke.

Why did he keep asking, he wondered, before the obvious answer presented itself. Though he could not call neglecting to write to Gabriel a fight. "I'm sorry."

Jonna stabbed her cigarette, then glanced down at it. Her fingers were gaunt and ink-stained, her thumb flat from pressing the barrel:

the hands of someone rehearsing the same motions and wondering why nothing changed. "It's all right," she said. "As it turns out, I am going back to Madison with her in August. Spare me your worried face. I've more or less accepted it. Though I don't like leaving you to the whims of Doc Bastard."

"I'm at his whim anyway. Maybe without you, my speeches will be so bad they'll excuse me from making them."

He'd meant it as a joke, but she was silent for a long time. Then she said, slowly, "No. I've written you plenty of bad speeches. To get out of them for good, you'd need a speech that would make you useless for propaganda. Something seditious."

A shiver touched his neck. "You're serious?"

"First tell me if you're willing. They might punish you for it."

He thought of his supposed current sentence: not hard, barely labor. If he was afraid, it was because his skin was still so thin. He had suffered very little for the risks he'd run. "Good," he said viciously. Jonna looked startled. Stumbling, he amended, "No, that's not what I meant. I'd just do anything not to have to lie anymore. I don't care what you have me say. The problem is, I made a deal with Gray . . ."

He trailed off. Gabriel was discharged, no longer subject to military law. His movements were his own. Soon he would be back home, safe in a position he'd won despite Rand's blunders. And refusing propaganda might buy Rand time to delve into himself and finally discover why his gift kept failing. His chest tightened. "All right, I'm willing. So how would I do it? Just tell the truth, that my gift's broken? Gray would consider that pretty treacherous."

"Of course not." Jonna's eyes were skeptical, but there was a new energy in her voice. "You do know most people don't care how long your plants live, right? For the purposes of propaganda, you're still magic. No, I'm thinking about a different sort of truth."

Her brows tensed. He stared at her for a minute before understanding. When he did, he whistled. "You'd definitely lose your job."

"I'm going to quit anyway. This way I gain a bit of myself back in return." She smiled with ghastly purpose. "I'm thinking your big speech next week, for Wilson's arrival. Are you all right with that? I meant it, about them punishing you."

He repressed another shiver. "I meant it too." The visions he thought he'd overcome after the trial crowded him again, the dark prison, white blindfold. To quell his fear, he fumbled for practicalities. "Could you work forest policy into it somehow? If I'm going to do this, I want to say my piece. Start with how most woodlands in France are privately owned. But they're well managed, unlike ours. Then talk up the Weeks Act. You saw what happened with Philipp in 1915. We can't count on states, or private owners. National forests are our best chance to preserve—"

"Slow down." She flipped her pad open and began scribbling. "You'll have to give me your notes." Her cheeks had pinked, despite her own fears. Brave Jonna, he thought reflexively, then paused. What could she need to prove so badly that she would endanger herself for it?

"Hey," he began, but her head snapped up, and he turned just in time to see Manning slide out of the cinema.

"There you two are. Hope I'm not breaking something up." Manning's voice attempted heartiness, but his grin fell when he saw Jonna's stubbed cigarette. "Not interested in the film?"

Rand tipped his cap. "Just taking a break." He wondered if his speech would restore Manning's itch for retribution. Then he wondered why he cared. A ghostly ache throbbed through his old wound. "Heading back in now, sir."

He held out his arm to Jonna. She rose and curtsied. Together they walked back into the darkened theater. The piano was still going, and Rand never had a chance to resume his question. Jonna wrote through the rest of the film like a fiend, her face pinched, possessed.

The following Saturday Rand stood on a platform at Versailles. He breathed slowly so his voice would not waver when he began. Fear was useless; or rather, fear was the point. Below him, a scree of hats and signs tumbled down the long aisles between the fountains. Many speeches had preceded his. Many more would follow. Gazing out over the crowd, he caught himself scanning for Gabriel's face, though he had not written to tell him he'd be speaking. Ashamed, he screwed his knuckles into his shaking thigh and tried to focus.

At his side on the podium Jonna had positioned a low flowerpot. Before flipping open his speech—tucking away the false one she had prepared for Manning—he knelt and touched his hand to its soil. The nearer crowd oohed.

He'd deserve it, he reminded himself, as he let his gift stir the seeds.

Poppies sprang up to flutter in the wind like flags. They were tall and fragile, and very, very red.

Chapter 15

In the end he was impressed they let him finish the speech. Nor did they drag him from the podium when he was done, stand him up against a wall, lash him to a pole. This alone indicated Gray would probably try to rehabilitate him in America, where he was now bound, he learned, in early September. Until then he was hidden from view, as the service waited for the press to move on to its next scandal.

AMERICA'S WHEAT-HEART CALLS FOR NATIONALIZED FOR- ESTS, read the *Times*. HAVE OUR TREE-MEN GONE WOBBLY?, asked the *Stars and Stripes*.

The French papers contained even worse puns. In his last conversa- tion with Jonna before she left the barracks, she'd brought him her favorites. *L'Humanité* had reprinted the speech in full. "They finally published something of mine," she said. Then her face fell. "Will you be all right?"

"Don't worry." He tried to smile. "It's like you said. I chose this."

"I know," she said. Her eyes were troubled.

Later, he wished he could have told her that the punishment was not as bad as she'd feared. It was not even, echoed some dim part of him, as bad as he had hoped. He was too valuable a resource to dam- age, as Manning put it. Since he could not be jailed, he faced only a grueling step-up of his research program, with no visits, no correspon- dence, and little unsupervised time.

The acceleration surprised him. He had less energy than ever to devote to his new, secret investigations, searching within him for what might be frustrating his gift. Sitting up late in his small-windowed room, furious at his shortsightedness, he smashed a lit cigarette to his arm to rouse himself. He usually fell asleep anyway.

The last letters he was allowed to receive—his family's replies—were brief and formal, with an air of censure. Greta's reassurances that his parents still loved him implied the army had relayed more of his charges than he'd hoped. Her own carefully worded disappointment implied she wished she'd heard about them from Rand himself. And by now the middle western papers must have picked up the story about his traitorous speech. He was almost relieved he was not allowed to respond.

Before she departed, Jonna had also asked him what she should say to Gabriel. "Tell him I'm fine," he'd said.

"And? He'll want more than that. Anything about your work? Plans?"

Rand paused, then shook his head. If he could not explain it to her, Gabriel would certainly not understand.

Jonna gave him a hard look, then left.

In the absence of publicity stunts, he returned to growing whole biota—three or four per week, with testing and reading in between. He devoted little attention to the work. For hours he mechanically dug trenches to measure root depth or screwed bores into trunks, while his mind bored through himself. Self-analysis was a tool he rarely used, and it felt blunt and awkward in his hands. What did his forests need? What was he not giving them? Even as he plowed his energy into a service tree or skimmed Tansley's newest in the British *Journal*, he turned inward. However deep he drilled, no answers came.

He felt sorry for his team, who must have sensed that his focus lay elsewhere. They were kind not to resent it. Seven days a week they appeared early at his cell to drive him beyond the Paris suburbs, then return him after dark. Their eyes grew as hollow as his; he caught their scowls at Manning's back when it was turned. They talked to Rand readily, their shared fatigue overcoming their new distrust of his politics.

Even Manning seemed tired, after a while. It was his schedule too. His frustration, having no outlet, calcified into blame. Sometimes he would waggle a headline in Rand's face, as if to remind them both of the severity of his betrayal: ET TU, BRANDTE? MIRACLE FORESTER INCITES REVOLUTION.

The papers gave Rand a strange satisfaction. Their disgust at his politics was misdirected, but close enough. He imagined it as a beam of light that he could turn to illumine those failures for which he should rightly be reviled.

Meanwhile his team was beginning to realize what Rand already knew: their science produced no answers. "You'd do well for flower boxes," Thom groused, examining the neat, well-fertilized plots in which Rand's smallest specimens lived for a week before wilting. His larger tests were worse.

He felt so stymied he tried out some of his more abstruse ideas on his team. "'A forest is the triumph of the organization of mutually dependent species,'" he quoted as they rested beneath a stand of brown-leaved Norway maple. He and Ned had just felled and bucked two trees. Rand rubbed the logs' faces. Their sapwood was eerily dry. "A biome is more than the sum of its parts. If I'm only making parts, what's missing?"

"Nothing. And you should stop reading that trash," Ned said. He disliked Whitehead, who was both British and not a real ecologist. On the log across, Thom sniffed; he'd gifted Rand the printed lecture during one of his periodic efforts to culture the Americans—Whitehead, Pater, Shelley. "Maybe it's not you. We should get out of this exhausted country."

"My trees died at home too." Rand's breath shortened. "Everything I touch dies."

Ned patted him on the shoulder. "Courage! You'd think you want to fail, the way you talk. There's so much less to fix at home. Europe's been destroying its wilderness for ages."

"And now I'm helping!" Rand cried. "Look at this wood. It's not just the trees. The entire organism is dead, like the life's been sucked out of it." He could hear his voice cracking but couldn't stop it. "How do you fix a forest's *spirit*, Ned?"

He saw Ned lean back, surprise lifting his comfortable linebacker's jowls. Behind him, Thom straightened on his log. Rand imagined how he must look to these easy, curious men: a wild-eyed prodigy spouting nonsense, undone by a bunch of dead leaves. His head felt heavy, and he was irritated with himself.

Ned was peering at him attentively now, a new expression on his bland face. "Rand," he said. "You know, despite what a miracle this is, you seem pretty miserable about it."

"What's your point?"

His ire bounced off Ned like a football. "It's funny. Seems the only time you look happy is when you're scribbling in those notebooks of yours. You've got a good eye, you know." He regarded Rand sympathetically. "Say. After your obligations to the service are up, if you don't want to do this anymore, maybe you could come work with me. I'm nobody at the university yet, but I'm doing some studies you'd find interesting. There's a little research station I'm thinking of, isolated and quiet. You might like to spend some time there, when this is over."

"When this is over," Rand said bitterly. Above, wind scratched through the scraggly branches.

Ned looked at him with a pity that made him want to dig a hook into his side. "Think about it. Until then, maybe don't judge your success on Europe, all right? This continent's forests are crawling with people. We've still got time to clean ours out."

His tone was deliberately bracing. When Rand did not reply, he shrugged. "Just think about it," he repeated, and walked off. Thom sat for a moment longer, then shrugged and rose too.

Rand was left alone among the dying maples.

Too tired to continue working, he slid down beside the bucked log. He put his nose to its dry sapwood. It smelled spicy, like it had cured a year in the sun. Yet Rand had grown the maple only a week ago, giving it all the food and water it needed. Something deeper was lacking. Spirit, he'd told Ned. What did he mean?

Above him the dead trunks towered, their bark stamped with a deep lace of grooves. He could sense when spirit was missing, if not exactly what it was. So too any forester who saw these maples would recognize that they were individuals, not a community; parts, not a whole. They were missing the essence that weaves trees into a forest, as time weaves a man's disparate years into a life.

A life—he sat up. He gazed along the fallen maple, its split trunk like a sleeve of spilled coins. On each face sixty-four rings circled uniformly.

A healthy Norway maple could live to eighty, as long as a man. If left alone, a second-growth forest could regain climax status in a hundred. All biota eventually replenished their spirit, regrew the bonds that transformed a clutch of trees into a wood. What his gift gave in speed it stole in this connection, this maturity—this lifetime, precisely.

If he could restore it, where would he get it from? He had always sensed he wasn't giving enough. Before, he'd dismissed the idea as unscientific. But maybe he'd only been afraid to face the truth. He spread both hands across the log's face. Its grain was warm as skin in the summer sun, ridged with lines: a palm, just like his own.

Of course—it came with sudden clarity, like a plummet dropping to his depths. Of course: that had been the answer, all along.

If a lifetime was what his woods lacked, he would give them his.

He almost laughed. How absurd he'd been, training himself to grow hundreds of trees, as if he were Mr. Ford's production line. More was asked of him; his gift was both greater and narrower than that. As Ned had said, it was a miracle. Like all miracles, it could only be worked once.

A warm, fierce pain lit his chest. He thought of the Inselberg librarian, burning, and of Andersen's mermaid drowning at sea. They gave themselves gladly. What was one Swamp Boy compared to a sea-green maple wood, the cathedral of an oak savanna, a silver marsh at dawn? He should be grateful. The true wonder of his gift was how cheaply the life of such a place might be bought with his own.

Joy sheared through him, filling his head with light. He saw himself lying down in the Argonne's poisoned mud and breathing out, and from that breath spooled a green thread knitting the great-rooted English oaks to their understory of rustling hornbeam; tying the bilberry on the seeps to the goat willow in the creek beds; weaving a shared life into all the nubby carpet plants he did not know and could not name. Above his green and empty body, the sighing canopy stretched toward the sunrise.

He would never be a hero, but this was an act of love. He could walk into death with head lifted.

Dizzily he pushed up from the maple log. At once practical difficulties assailed him. How would he prepare himself? How would he choose which landscape to save, since he could only save one? And how would he keep the service, and his family and friends, from understanding, until it was too late?

His heart rose, then sank again. Now he could keep his promise to Gabriel—if he forsook Clearwater, the Bitterroot, the northwoods. Reproach filled him, so vivid it became a kind of shining. One family's blasted range versus a murdered old-growth forest: he already knew which he'd choose. This, too, was part of the sacrifice. The light burned in his limbs, raising him, purifying.

Far below his body trembled, still tied to earth. He would refuse fear, feel only joy. To steel himself he tried to picture what wilderness his life could buy—one long slope of Douglas fir in Idaho, or a single hardwood autumn in New England. Instead he saw only carrots in gardens, blueberries in marshes, a field of California poppies, orange sparks in the far, tall grass.

The joy shook him, and shook, and shook.

Some time later he heard Ned say above him, "Hey. You all right?"

They returned early to Paris that day. On the ride home he'd thudded against the seat like deadwood. Even Manning had the grace not to ask him any questions. At the barracks his phlegmatic guard took pity on him, not shuffling him immediately to his cell but allowing him to sit awhile by the westward-facing window in the office. Grateful, Rand slipped him one of Jonna's last cigarettes.

"You know, someone telephoned for you earlier," the guard said, taking it. "Told him you're not allowed, then left the number on the desk. I'm going to go and smoke for a half hour. I'll be by the door, so don't try to escape while I'm gone."

He did not wink, only swept briskly out to leave Rand staring at the telephone.

The exchange put him through to the American Hospital. He asked for Dr. M. Schulz. There was a long pause; he counted the minutes. Then he heard the receiver lift.

"Marie said it was you," said Gabriel. "I was about to leave. The man told me you can't take calls."

"I can't," said Rand. His own voice sounded strange to him. "We have ten minutes. How many other—?"

"None, but there are doctors passing. Jonna says hello. She's back with us in the flat. She says you can't write now?"

The floor of his stomach opened. He prayed she'd kept her promise. "No."

"And yet you didn't send word through her."

"No."

"Well, dammit, why?"

"I didn't know what to say. I'm so sorry, Gabriel."

"Nothing, for weeks." His voice was cold. "You must not have been that sorry."

Rand was silent. The urge to explain crept up his throat. He swallowed it down. The same radiance that had filled him in the maple wood was buoying him, so that he seemed to peer down at his cramped body as if it were a fallen toy soldier.

Gabriel waited a minute for him to respond. When he didn't, he tried again. His voice wavered with a desperate cheeriness. "Anyhow, I read your speech—Jonna's speech, I guess. Really, was it so bad to dance a little in exchange for your freedom? Now I won't see you until you're back in the middle west."

"The middle west? That means—"

"Yes." He could almost hear his strained grin, Gabriel's pride fighting his irritation. "The music director is a German. I gather that my discharge is rather a plus. And the flu has hit Chicago so badly there are a lot of open positions. Not to mention they've had five concertmasters in as many years, which means lots of chances for advancing. I sail in a week. Until then I'm raising merry hell practicing Strauss, whom Stock apparently likes."

Rand let him go on. Chest aching, he smiled against the receiver. Gabriel's courage had been rewarded; Rand's betrayal would not hinder his freedom. He stared down at the guard's desk, proud and despairing.

When presently he noticed silence again, he asked, "Did you tell your family?"

"Of course not. Don't you remember my letter?" Gabriel sounded hurt. "The old you would have been happy for me."

"Congratulations," Rand said. Another silence followed.

"Christ, Rand! You talk like you've got a gun to your head! What's wrong?"

"Nothing. Now you don't need me to regrow your range before you can have a career." He clung to the receiver, a manic terror filling him. "It's swell, terrific, a miracle . . ."

At last, into the long silence, Gabriel said slowly, "It doesn't work, does it? Your magic plant power. That's what Jonna meant, and why you won't talk to me. There's something wrong with it."

So it had finally come. "Yes."

"Well, hell. You could have told me. Why did you keep making promises if you knew?"

"I don't know."

"Don't you trust me?" Gabriel's voice was pained. "I'm not a child."

"I know. I'm sorry."

He heard him curse. "This is just like at Gien. You don't have to protect me."

"I know I don't."

"Then why didn't you tell me? If you can't trust me, you don't see me as—as more than what we started as."

He lay back beneath the anger, submerged himself. "I know."

"Damn you, can't you say anything else?"

All at once Rand knew that he would keep up this small lie forever— that he preferred Gabriel believing he'd merely failed, rather than broken his promise, chosen some unknown forest over Gabriel's range. It was nearly true; it didn't matter.

Gabriel continued, "Is that what you were trying to tell me, in your letter? You should have just said so, and saved us both the trouble. If that's all we are, I can get it as easily in Chicago."

Rand closed his eyes and breathed in. "I know."

"So that was it, all along?" Gabriel's voice shook. "Stupid me. All right, then."

"All right."

There was a waiting pause, like a held breath. Then: "Well. Guess I won't see you."

The line clicked.

Rand did not replace the receiver in its saddle. Slowly he let his head sink to the desk, then covered it with his arms, as if he were holding it underwater. Outside, the sun fell, brimming the room with shadows. He felt at once terribly cold and as if some deep part of him had been melted down to its essence.

He did not know how long it had been when he heard the door swing. He dimly remembered that his guard was only supposed to have left for thirty minutes.

"He's still here," he heard Gray say. "Thank goodness."

"The guard will be punished, sir," said Manning. Rand felt his shoulder pulled up. "You still in a funk? Wipe your face. The chief's here."

Rand pushed himself up, swabbing his eyes with his sleeve. Gray was standing in front of the desk. Looking faintly embarrassed, he reached over to resettle the telephone's receiver. "You're not allowed to take calls, Private."

Rand shrugged. Now that he was forced to think again, he wondered what would happen that night in Marie's flat. Jonna would think him an idiot, but at least he would not have to explain it to her. Perhaps Gabriel would, before he left. If he did not understand now, he would eventually. The version of Rand he'd cared for did not exist. It was cruel to let a man love a lie.

"I said, your first American appearances will all be internal, keyed to reframing you as a useful conservation resource. The Office of Farm Management, those Parks people." Gray tilted his head. "Are you listening?"

A barb of pain stirred the drowned part of him. "You want me to lie to the government now," he said.

Gray rubbed his forehead. "Not this again. We're working on your power. You're not lying. Why can't you understand this?"

He realized he had not yet worked out a story convincing enough to forestall the service's demands. His head ached. "I can't take on big projects," he fumbled. "They've all failed. And they'll keep failing."

"You have no idea if that's true. We've only just begun to research—"

"Then I refuse." He clung to the radiance that had lit him in the maple wood. This was his purpose: he would say whatever he needed to fulfill it.

"You are not in a position to refuse."

"No." He said it quietly once, then again, louder. His heart thudded.

"Remember our agreement, Mr. Brandt."

He was as surprised as Gray when he half rose, pressing his hands to the desk. His voice shook. "You have no power over him anymore. I refuse!"

Gray held out a hand. "Private—"

"Goddamn it, I'm not your hero!"

He rocked, bracing himself on the desk. The words had swept out of him on a crest of blank rage. The room swung in and out of focus, as though through a wet lens.

Manning's fists had balled, but Gray waved him down. Rand saw his eyes flicker to the telephone. He did not speak at once. When he did, his voice was cool. "You're rather hysterical tonight, Mr. Brandt," he said. "I would have liked you a little calmer to learn about your first public conservation job."

"I already told you, no big projects." Rand swayed at the desk but did not sit.

"What a shame," said Gray drily. He met Rand's eyes. "I did think that the Swamp Boy would have been interested in Clearwater Marsh."

Rand's breath caught. He had thought he was wrung dry of feeling, but even standing a continent away, eyes red and lungs aching, he could hear the drip of fog in cattails, their dry rattle as a sora waded through. In the cold confusion of his heart, a warmth bloomed.

"Sir?" he said shakily.

Gray looked satisfied. "Don't think I'm being charitable, Mr. Brandt. Remember I'm not one of your preservationists. As far as the service is concerned, Clearwater is expendable. The only people who care about it are sportsmen and idealists like yourself. If you fail it, I won't mourn, just ask you to learn from the experience." Gray paused. "You've been agitating for a more organic approach, haven't you?"

He bowed his head, barely listening. The joy was buoying him again, so keen it was almost pain. To think he'd worried about choosing which landscape to save, as if it were not already chosen for him, as if it were not fate.

"When you take this job," Gray was continuing, "you'll have a full team of Wisconsin naturalists at your command, and half a year to prepare the marsh in whatever way you wish. I've convinced Washington to buy most of the land and flowage rights, so you'll be free to dam. But if you are serious about refusing all big projects, we'll just sell it back to the onion farmers. And we'll find something else to do with you. Grow wheat for the Department of Agriculture, perhaps." Gray shrugged, regarded Rand. "What do you say?"

He closed his eyes. Even in his most shameful fantasies he could not have imagined a more resounding proof of his purpose. It was Clearwater; it always had been. He could not return the vital spirit to France's maples, but the marsh was infused into himself. He knew it at a level beyond species lists. Its sunlit windings had shaped the paths of his own life. He would save it, if he finally gave his all.

The flash of sun in the reeds became the pewter sea seen from the deck of the *Carpathia*, its warmth a sleeping weight on his shoulder. All that was past now; he had given it over. He was still a water creature—finned, spineless, sacrificing nothing for what he claimed to hold dear. But he would cut himself legs, at the last. He would love one thing well.

"Well, Mr. Brandt?"

He opened his eyes. "I'll try, sir."

Chapter 16

On Clearwater Marsh the snow lay clean as a plaster bandage. The previous week, the first of the new year, a thaw had softened its upper layers, which had refrozen to a gleaming crust of ice. Above, the pale sky hung soft as gauze. Sounds soaked upward into its chilly silence.

Along the bank of the frozen main ditch Rand scuffed his shoes over the ice. Occasionally he lifted his binoculars to watch a troupe of snow buntings forage the buried hummocks of a meadow. As the marsh had dried—a slow process, which had begun long before the speculators had scored it with drainage ditches—the bulrushes and cattails had ceded to margins of sedge and bluejoint grass. These were in turn invaded by shrub-carr. Its spikes of red dogwood, like fire beneath the willows, were the brightest color in the landscape.

He paused to count the buntings—twelve—before wrenching himself back to his task, mapping the boundaries of the marsh's seres. His walks were growing too long, Manning had complained. "You've already decided where we're putting the dams. What else can you learn out there?" But he had been unable to stop himself, or staunch his traitorous joy as he idled on the mudflats, watching the redtails circle for field mice.

Over the past four months he had made research trips of two weeks to Clearwater, alternating them with longer visits to other parts of the country, where he performed minor feats intended to ingratiate him with various skeptical agencies. In March he would depart for northeast

New Mexico on his longest trip yet, testing dry farming for the Office of Farm Management. As Manning had said, "They cut wheat right away, so it won't matter how fast it dies."

Like a mill horse he let himself be circled through these exhibitions. Growing longleaf pine for navy bureaucrats did not excite him, but it was useful practice in burying his needs. With each new task he nudged himself further out of life. He did not know how other men prepared for death. When the fear seized him, he recalled the French soldiers he'd seen at the front, exhausted, resigned, their terror ground beneath the daily wheel until it was a gray dust behind their eyes. He comforted himself that courage was not necessary, only that he did his duty when the time came.

Otherwise he tried to focus on Clearwater. Yet on each visit to the marsh, he found it harder to plunge into his dreams of what it had been, and would be again if he succeeded. His feelings were not right. Try as he might, he could not see beyond the moment next summer when he would wade into the reflooded flats, surrendering himself to the quiet water. His failure to picture his triumph troubled him even more than his fear of death.

Perhaps it was because he was learning how incomplete his dreams really were. For all his sense of Clearwater's spirit, he had known it only since the turn of the century. Earlier descriptions, which he'd spent November ferreting out of farmers' diaries and voyageurs' journals, evoked a richer, wilder place than the one he loved—where stands of wild rice whispered, and the thunder of settling pigeons bowed the ridges of oak to the west. It felt ungrateful to do what he was doing today and delight in the marsh as it was, counting its small stirrings like the breaths of a convalescent.

He pushed on anyway, lashing his imagination to flesh out what memory could not. He'd been given a chance. He would not waste it.

Though he felt guilty about it, he had no trouble concealing his plans from his new teammates—as Gray had promised, the best in the state. Sacrifice would never occur to them. They were practical men, botanists and geologists and engineers. Clearwater was a work of love for them too, but also a work of politics.

There were so many politics, more than Rand's sixteen-year-old self could have ever conceived. When the head of the Clearwater Marsh Game Protective Association had wagged Rand's hand and quipped, "We should make every conservation project a war industry!" he had not at first understood. Manning had had to explain how Gray, armored with the authority of the Department of Agriculture, had strongarmed the Rock River Land Company, which owned thirty-five thousand acres of marsh, into selling it to the government as an essential war resource. In two weeks Rand's team had acquired rights for which the shooting clubs, university ecologists, and inhabitants of nearby towns had been agitating for a decade. They could dam the dredge-widened Rock River, plug the seventeen drainage ditches, bribe the muck farmers away from their peaty carrots.

As thanks, the sportsmen of the Clearwater Shooting Club had invited Rand's team to bunk in their clubhouse, sharing its sheds, barn, and milk house. The club's president had even pressed on Rand a new shotgun, promising to take him out for the first geese in March. When Rand had shuddered, he'd withdrawn the gun and grinned. "One of those, eh?"

From the tussocks the buntings lifted with dissatisfied *chiks*. He shook his head, noting the meadow's location. If he asked his team to reflood it, in time its cattails would rattle with foraging swamp sparrows and marsh wrens. He could not see them—his mind's eye still lay blank— but it was enough to know they would live on when he had gone. He turned back toward the clubhouse.

Holiday crepe still hung from the house's eaves. Rand lowered his eyes. On his way up the steps he passed Ned. With touching fidelity he'd followed Rand from Europe to Clearwater; the university was happy to let a graduate student go rather than loan out one of their professional botanists. He was kneeling on the porch atop a thankless spread of sedge spikes. As Rand touched the doorknob he asked him, "Shouldn't you identify those inside?"

"Light's terrible. Hey, you know your sister's here?"

Rand's breath caught. Then he laughed softly. He should not be surprised that Greta had surprised him. Ned continued, "We set her up in the lounge to warm. She can't stay long, she says. You better talk before Manning gets back from Kekoskee with the rye."

Rand was already scrabbling at his bootlaces. While his teammates usually forgot that he was serving a prison sentence, Manning would not. Nor would Greta, however she had managed to get here against his parents' orders.

He found her crouched before the iron stove, warming her hands. Her broad face was ruddy with cold. As he entered she turned to him, pale with a determination he recognized. A broad, square package of brown paper leaned against her chair. "Greta, you know I'm not allowed—" he began, but the next moment she had flung herself at him and he was burying his face in her hair.

He had to take several deep breaths before he could speak again. He had been trying to forget Christmas, where his brief supper visit had been supervised by a warrant officer, and they had not been allowed such open affection. His father had placed him at one end of the holiday table, drawing his sisters and mother to the other. "I do not disown my children, however disappointing they may be," he had declared in German. "But I did not raise a communist, or a liar, or a—fairy. Whatever has corrupted you, I won't let it hurt the girls." Behind him, his mother's face was bowed. When he'd tried to smile at Anna, she'd hidden her eyes.

Only once had he attempted to prepare them for what was coming. "My power is poorly understood," he'd said. "I can't predict what it will do to me." His mother had looked worried, his father confused. Saying more might betray the truth, so he stopped. He did not know if his parents would be proud when they learned he had died for Clearwater. He hoped so. He'd eaten quickly and tastelessly, and spent the rest of the meal silent, trying to drink in their features. On the train back to Clearwater he'd leaned his forehead against the window, eyes stinging, breath wordlessly fogging the cold glass.

"Happy New Year," Greta muttered against his neck. Her voice wavered. "Winter term begins next week. Of course I was going to see you."

"How long do you have?"

"The train for Madison leaves Chester at four. You'd better talk fast."

He pulled away and combed her hair back into the bun where his embrace had disarrayed it. They had not hugged at home, so he hadn't noticed how tall she'd grown. "About what?"

"To start, everything you left out of your letters." She laughed weakly, then waved out at the marsh. "Including this."

How strange it was hearing her demand his confidence, as if they were both fourteen again. For a vertiginous moment he felt younger than her, tongue-tied. He did not know how to explain Clearwater without giving himself away. Then remembering their woodlot tramps, he said, "Maybe it will help if I just show you. Hang on." He ducked out to the hall closet and removed a heavy coat and Ned's lined winter boots.

When he returned, she had resettled before the stove. She wore a sad, patient smile he had never seen before. He remembered that she was twenty-one, and had lived on her own at university for three years.

"I don't mean your swamp," she said. "I got that from the papers. I mean you. What has all this done to you?" She blinked hard. "At Christmas . . ."

Laying aside the coat and boots, he knelt before her. The stove washed his face with heat. "Greta. I'm sorry."

"No, you're not." Sighing, she lay her hand on his head, a gesture oddly like his mother's. "You know I don't care if you're a fairy, or a red, or even that you couldn't tell me you had a—magic plant power, or whatever it is. I care that I don't know who my brother is anymore."

He stared past her knees out of the window, at the long mudflats beneath their snow. She was wrong: he was sorry. Still, for his family's sake he would not have changed anything, what he'd hidden, whom he'd loved, his plans now. He had hurt Greta, and would hurt her again. He could not protect her from himself.

He fought the urge to force his hand against the iron screen. Even to his family, he gave nothing.

"Rand? Did you hear me?" She tugged his hair, and abruptly she was his little sister again, for whom he was responsible. "I wasn't kidding, about talking fast. You can start now."

He pulled away from her fingers. He looked at her face, quiet and trusting, his oldest confidant. Now he would never see her become a woman, graduate, marry. Inside him an ache crested, nearly broke into speech—then dissolved into foam and sank.

Retrieving the coat and boots, he laid them in her lap. "Come on, Gretchen. Let me show you the marsh."

Her eyes fell. For a moment he feared she would stand her ground. But the authority of birth order reasserted itself. She stood and followed him.

On the marsh, he talked. Omitting direct mention of his gift, he outlined his plans to restore Clearwater's reed stands and sedge meadows. He explained his disagreement with Clements's belief that a marsh could not be a stable climax community. He drew portraits of his teammates, Ned and his species lists, the engineers' plans to plug the ditches, the chemists calculating how much nitrogen and phosphorus would be required for twenty acres of bulrush and cattail. As Greta had requested, he spoke fast. He talked as Gabriel had danced in Paris, whirling across surfaces, keeping himself afloat. Trying to make her laugh, he conjured the release of the decoy ducks, who would help convince the native waterfowl to return. When she did not smile, he appealed to her philosophical side, trying to draw her into his developing ideas about wilderness. She nodded blandly and asked no questions. He did not know how to handle a Greta who asked no questions. He spoke faster.

At last they reached the end of the icy dike. He took her arm. "Let's go back. It's cold, and you have a train to catch." He had talked for forty minutes and said nothing of substance.

Though he avoided her eyes, he could feel them on his cheek, their strange new pity. But until they had reclimbed the steps to the clubhouse, she said nothing.

When she had shed Ned's coat, she picked up the package she'd left beside the chair. Beneath its twine he saw a folded paper affixed. Greta removed this and gave it to him. Her voice was subdued, with a maturity that sounded like either acceptance or defeat. "This is from Jonna," she said. "If you read it quickly, I can bring her a reply tonight. I'll stop by her apartment before going to my sorority."

His heart lifted a little. Though Jonna ignored the order denying him correspondence, it was a rare message that actually got through. He opened it.

Jonna wrote that she hoped he'd had a merry Christmas, that Marie disapproved of her pamphlets decrying Victor Berger's conviction for espionage, that the flu was all over Madison. She asked how the marsh looked, and when they'd send him south to grow wheat for the DOA. She sent her love. On the back of the letter she'd sketched the new capitol building, its dome wearing a thick cap of snow.

Gently he refolded it and tucked it in his shirt. "Tell her the marsh looks fine, March for the wheat, and to please take care of herself. They're raiding socialists in Milwaukee." He watched Greta commit the details to memory. Glancing over his shoulder, he drew a book from the club's tiny library and removed his own letter. Until the end he would reply as he could to Jonna. "If you could give this to her too."

"Nothing for Anna?" Greta asked.

Rand winced. "When you talk about me, does Anna still—?"

"She's young. She doesn't know any better. Though she'd probably understand if you had bothered to explain it to her." Greta's voice was tired. "Or me."

She did not need to say more, standing before him holding the letter he had written for the friend he really trusted. It was as close to an accusation as she would come. He wanted to tell her that the truth could only hurt her, that he had not even told it to Jonna. But his courage failed. He looked away and did not answer.

Into the ensuing silence she lifted the package. With forced cheer, she said, "Good thing I can still read you like a book. I think." As she handed it to him she added, "Since father wouldn't let us give you Christmas presents. I saw you staring at the advertisement for it in the Columbia catalog."

Before opening it, he knew. The twelve-inch record was entitled *Sarasate: Spanish Dances*. On the center's florid design, which resembled wrought iron, was stamped *Chicago Symphony Orchestra*.

Holding it, his hands felt numb. He crossed his arms over the sleeve, afraid he'd drop it. His heart beat against the cardboard. Greta said softly, in her older voice, "I thought so. Tell me the story sometime, all right?" He opened his mouth, then shut it.

She removed her own coat from the closet. "I'm sorry, but I do have to catch that train. Mr. Fawcett said he'd take me in the car because you're not allowed off the property."

He looked at her framed against the winter window, straight and uncomplaining, newly braced beneath the silent burden all women carried. His resolve cracked. He pitched forward to hug her again, the crush of his arms saying what he could not. Caught off guard, she hugged back, then pulled away. Her eyes were more worried than ever.

He flushed with shame and rose to retrieve his coat.

On the ride back he sat beside Ned in the front, the record across his lap. He stared out the window, too sapped for conversation. At the horizon, though it was not yet four o'clock, the eternal gray of Wisconsin winter was already darkening.

He had never thought Ned socially observant, but as they bumped over the frozen ground, he brought the car to a listing stop. When Rand turned to him, he was regarding him with the same attention he'd given the sedge spikes. "Remember my offer, all right?" he said. "For when this is all over."

He pushed the handbrake and the car shambled forward. Over, Rand thought. Above, a mocking wind clattered the bare trees.

At the clubhouse Manning was unloading crates of whiskey from the back of the one-horse sledge. As Rand slid down from the car, he tucked the record inside his coat. Manning frowned, but seemed to lack the energy for reprimand. Instead he rummaged inside his own coat and pulled out a booklet: *Wheat Production and Marketing, by C. R. Ball, Cerealist.*

"Read this through," said Manning, "especially the sections on dry farming. The men in Kekoskee say the thaw is coming, so in two weeks we'll head south and leave the engineers to their work. And reread your *Use Book*'s sections on range erosion. I've spoken to our contacts among the southwest's stockmen to see what we can offer them." He looked Rand up and down. "Some sunlight will do you good. You're looking peaky."

Rand took the book, nodding.

Returning to the lounge, he shed his coat and slipped the record from its jacket. The stippled shellac was cool under his fingers. He wound the old Victrola and placed the needle. Up leapt the music, scratchy but vital as a flame. The playing was unmistakable: light and dancing, like a fencer mocking the plod of the piano accompaniment.

He listened to each side once, flipped the record over, and listened again.

Stomping through on their way to the mess, the engineers gave him odd looks. Ned followed, pulling Manning after him. Over his shoulder he nodded a question. Rand answered with a shake of his head. As the smell of fried pork rose from the kitchen, he turned to face the window.

Outside, the gray marsh blurred into the dusk. South and west, shadows were blanketing the purple granite around Inselberg, and perhaps Ned's research station, wherever it lay. Rand's mother would be lighting the stove for supper. Greta's train would arrive in Madison long after dark. His mind strayed further south, over the plains, to the dagger of northeast New Mexico, where he was bound. As if blown by the relentless plains wind, it streamed east again, rippling over Clearwater's snow, dipping south to graze the cold towers of Chicago.

"O wild west wind," he remembered Thom quoting. He wondered what the poet had meant by *wild*. Spreading his hand on the record's sleeve, he stared down at his fingers. "Destroyer and preserver; hear, oh hear!"

He flipped the record over and played it again.

Chapter 17

The southwest was as beautiful as Gabriel had insisted, and much bigger. Driving across the plains toward the ridge of the Pecos, Rand felt as if the tall sky were pursuing him. The air was dry and sweet, the colors dull at a distance and fierce at close range. The clouds were so few he had to remind himself not to look at the sun.

The testing farm was tucked among the foothills along a tributary of the Sapello river, its green meanders as yet unswollen by spring melt. It was further west than he'd anticipated. New Mexico's wheatlands covered a northeast lobe of the state that ended, he'd thought, where the high plains did. "Why here?" he asked the district's ranger when he met Rand and Manning with horses in Las Vegas. "Is it for the water? I thought I was dry farming."

"You're *testing* dry farming," said Manning. "Which means we need something to mimic spring rains."

The ranger held out the reins of a squat pinto. "You ride, son?"

Rand did not query their location further. After the first day he was either too sore or too exhausted. The Office of Farm Management had requested he simulate a decade's worth of annual winter wheat in normal precipitation conditions. Spaced over two months, this meant slightly more than one crop per week, rotated with clover or legumes. *Normal precipitation* meant laboriously watering his field by hand with a can drawn from the creek. The silty bottomland from which he raised the wheat had to be harvested and tilled before each new crop could be seeded.

For these tasks the ranger supplied a farmhand who rode in from Las Vegas. His name was Joe. Rand liked him: he was older, short and broad and coated in dark hair, and his thick legs stirred a desire in Rand he had not expected to feel again, so close to the end. But with Manning present he could not try much. Besides, Joe only worked thrice weekly, and seemed dismissively bemused by the whole project. Rand promised himself to ask him why sometime.

The remaining labor fell to Rand and Manning. Given the isolation of the testing site—an abandoned farm, complete with a few desiccated fruit trees—they were also responsible for their own food and laundry. Unused to the dry work, Rand had no head for thinking. By each day's end he could barely concentrate long enough to record the required observations. If he finished before sunset he took a solitary walk in the foothills, or added lines to the letters he was secretly composing for Greta and Jonna, or ran his fingers along the grooves of the record, which, since they had no Victrola, he could not play. He rarely finished before sunset.

It was irritating how gamely Manning took to the work. Rand wanted no reason to temper his loathing, especially as their isolation had again eased Manning's disgust at him. Evenings, he let Rand ride out without supervision, perhaps knowing Rand had nowhere to run. At supper he even tried to make conversation. His comments were barbed, meant more to provoke than engage, like the schoolyard taunts of a bully. Rand answered him in monosyllables.

Out of boredom Manning kept trying, so Rand ate less and left faster.

Dusk in the desert swept the whole sky at once. The sun burned a red hole in its pale screen. Beneath, the mountains turned purple. Rand walked below light-headed, hazily contemplating death. He did not believe in heaven, the martyr's reward. But if he had, he could imagine it feeling something like this. The dry air had an astringent sweetness—manzanita, Joe had said. To Rand it smelled like carnations. When the wind fell, the air was so still he could hear a coyote's bark up the far canyons, or a solitaire fluting on some high pine. Watching the sun slip from the hills, he understood why Gabriel had grown up

believing in fate. He could feel his own here, not as an urgency cramp-
ing his chest but as a great, soft invitation. This desert was not Rand's
heart, but it held hearts gently. Nothing higher existed than to die for
a land someone could love as much as this.

He would give his all, and be satisfied.

Four weeks in, when May runoff was finally whitening the Sapello,
a Farm Management official, too leathery for a bureaucrat but too
pink for a cowboy, rode through on his way to Albuquerque. He collected Rand's reports on soil moisture, then asked to see the current
crop.

Rand led him to the field. The honey-colored wheat waved sparsely
in its loose earth. Red puffs of topsoil heaped against Rand's boots.

The official leaned over to brush the awns. "Remarkable—fully
grown." He rose and patted Rand's hair. "This is your fifth crop? My
boy, no one will care how red you are once they see your red fife!" He
chuckled at his own joke, though the variety was in fact Turkey.

"If you'll read my report," Rand said stonily, "you'll see that the
soil can't support successive wheat farming at this rain level, even with
nitrogen-fixing rotations." He thought of what Joe had told him when
he'd finally made time to ask, and wondered why the service was raising
such a thirsty crop without even installing an acequia, like all the local
farmers. "And we haven't accounted for the drought cycles."

The official nodded chummily. "You sound as if we've got no recourse.
Fertilizer does amazing things nowadays. Why, it might be traitorous
to say so, but have you seen the Germans' new synthetic ammonia?"

At Rand's side Manning, apparently continuing his effort at conversation, said, "It really is remarkable. Just think of what it could do in
your northern woods, Mr. Brandt." His mouth soured. "Not that those
farmers would use it properly. The service lets the Department of Immi-
gration advertise to settlers, and they pull in a bunch of atheists, fight-
ers, and Finns."

His offhandedness settled coldly in Rand's stomach. It took him a
second to understand why. "You talk as if that's all the service wants
for the northwoods."

Manning looked faintly confused. "Yes?"

"I thought we were planning a national forest," Rand said in a low voice. "That's what I was surveying for when I enlisted."

Manning blinked. Then a quiet, vicious smile crept across his face. "Well, Mr. Brandt," he said. "I'm so sorry. It seems they never told you. That survey of yours was the last gasp of a deal Gray was ordered to cut with your pit-bull senator, to tone down his objections to the war." He laughed. "But it seems Fighting Bob wouldn't grow a liver just to save some trees. A good thing, too. To think, a national forest among those degenerates! Well, of course you'd believe it, considering the company you keep."

Rand glared at Manning, trying to fasten fury over the pit of shame crumbling away beneath him. Again he'd been naïve; he had even wondered where all the other survey teams were, why his seemed the only one. With a little thought he could have worked it out. But he'd been too concerned with his own affairs. Doggedly he continued, "But we're not just going to keep luring settlers to the northwoods? It's poor farmland. What isn't bog is podzol filled with pine roots."

Manning's face creased with mock pity. "I *am* sorry. But if your Finnish friends bought themselves a lemon, that's their fault." His eyes flickered to the official, who was beginning to look bored, though as an OFM man he should have cared about the coming failure of thousands of ill-placed farms. Perhaps Joe was right to laugh off the service. They knew so little, still.

Setting his teeth against his own gullibility, Rand gave an icy bow. "Now that I've given my report, it seems you don't need me anymore. Suzy needs to be exercised."

Manning raised an eyebrow, triumphant. "You're excused, Mr. Brandt."

He could not find a clever retort, so he simply turned with a snap. He thought of how Gabriel would have made his disdain seem dashing.

Suzy whickered at him as he eased her down the streambed. Dwelling on his past foolishness would not help Clearwater, he told himself. He had a purpose; Manning's mockery could not divert it. Slowly he let his anger evaporate into the cooling dusk.

He was a better rider now. Often on these evenings he looped the reins about the saddle horn and let Suzy wander while he looked around, sometimes with binoculars, sometimes without. The steep sides of the wash relaxed as they neared the Sapello, whose banks were rocky, frilled in places with the upturned roots of willows. To an untrained eye, its barrenness would have seemed wild. But Rand could tell it was stripped. Nowhere did he see the diamond-shaped hoofprints indicating the area was still being actively grazed. The sheep had been thorough. Only a few tufts of grass remained. In the grass's absence manzanita and juniper had sprung up, weaving a tangle Suzy found vexing. He loosened the reins and let her nose downslope, toward the silt-choked ciénaga where the river flattened itself against the plain.

On his rides he had been trying to sherlock his way to a history of the area, based only on clues he could discover himself. It soothed his fears to put his ear to the land and listen. Understanding its voice required the same focus as his conversations over Jonna's drawing table or his nights with Gabriel. Still, he had known this wedge of New Mexico intimately for only two months. Compared to Joe, he was a novice in its character. Perhaps it took a lifetime to truly know a place, or a person.

But now he was thinking of Gabriel and Jonna again. He pulled his eyes up, to look at the marsh.

Though the migration was tapering, northbound birds still dipped toward the river's puddly meander to drink, bathe, and move on. Their number, too great for the available water, suggested that the marsh had shrunk recently enough that migration routes had not yet changed to accommodate it. Though livestock had grazed here since the seventeenth century, massive herds had only moved in after the Civil War, once the Indians had been driven off—cleaned out, as Ned would say. Cattle had torn away the grass cover, sheep throttled the streambed willows. In their wake, the Sapello had carved chunks from its denuded flanks and spat them into the ciénaga. In less than thirty years, the marsh had almost disappeared.

How long would it take to recover? Deserts healed more slowly, he had read. If he tried to die for this ciénaga, would his life be enough to save it? He had a hundred years to give, at best. Unclogging this marsh might take two. Miracles were not scientific, but such an exchange still seemed impossible.

Looking at the banks of dry silt, he thought of his rust-colored wheat-field, and of Whitesoil's bleached earth. Such ruined landscapes: what made him hope that any human life, however destined, could revive a spirit humans had destroyed? How could he breathe himself into a nature from which he should, by definition, be absent?

Upstream, a spotted sandpiper scrabbled its way up a steep bank. Below its track, silt sparkled in the green shallows.

But no, absent was not right. He thought of the Muir pages he'd sent to Jonna, their hymn to wild spring in the northwoods. Muir had met many people in that wild, fishing or tapping sap or snaring game. Some of them had been doing so for a very long time. Now that land was cutover, its people pressed north and west by lumbermen. Yet by Ned's logic, those dead woods were wilder, more natural now than they'd ever been.

Cleaned out, he thought again grimly, like a fish. The service had cleaned out other lives too: wolves from the north, grizzlies from the southwest. Rand must have known this, for neither predators nor people had ever featured in his daydreams of restoration, crouching among the fireweed in the Bitterroot, lodgepole pines emerging from the slash. Even Clearwater, which he knew the Indians had long harvested for wild rice, in his head stirred only with birds. His wilderness had always been cleaned out.

Stomach turning, he recalled the coppices at Gien. They too had been cleaned out—but not of people. They were loved, cared for. Yet they were not wild. While he had never seen the Cascades, he knew they must be wilder than Gien, if wilder meant healthier. Was one therefore more natural than the other? Manning's voice from Camp AU returned to him: "There is no wilderness, only forest, and we must manage it as carefully as we manage our populations." Did questioning nature cast him in with the eugenicists? Was his gift natural? Was he?

His heart skipped. Inside him, the pit he'd been skirting since Manning's revelation about the northwoods yawned. As he had at the court-martial, he felt himself tipping toward it. He caught Suzy's pommel for balance and clung there, reeling.

Perhaps he should refuse Clearwater, as he had first tried to in Paris. He had no proof that giving his life to the marsh would restore it or any nature. He could not even explain what restoring nature meant. He should give up, and abandon the promise he'd made to wilderness, since he could not possibly fulfill it.

At once he cringed away from the thought. No, he was shirking again, looking for a way out. These new fears were just another excuse to dodge pain. So many times he'd dreamed of wading into Clearwater's depths, his shoulders disappearing beneath the dark water. It was toward this climax his life had been directed. What else was he for, if not this?

He shook his head. Clearwater was not like Gien, or Whitesoil, or this gutted ciénaga. He loved the marsh. He had spent months preparing it alongside the best ecologists in the state, better men than Manning or the OFM bureaucrat, men who cared about wilderness as he did. He had spent months preparing to die. Crediting his reluctance to some philosophical quibbles about nature was merely cowardice. Clearwater was the best chance he would ever get.

At the bank's lip the sandpiper paused, lifted its wings, then vaulted into the air. He followed its stuttering circle over the ciénaga, its pivot north toward its breeding grounds.

Unlooping the reins, he turned Suzy west, back up the streambed. Night was drawing down its curtain of small noises. His heart pounded so loudly he could not hear them.

Two weeks later he was riding west again, trailing Manning over the Pecos toward Santa Fe through passes still treacherous with snow. Their contact among the stockmen did not travel for business, Manning had explained as they'd packed the horses. He was a wealthy man from an established family who owned a million acres on the New Mexico side of the Llano Estacado. "A Mr. Cedillo," Manning had added, lip curling, and thankfully not turning to see Rand go white.

In Santa Fe they took a room in a hotel. Rand scrubbed himself until his sunburn was raw. Manning laughed. "We're just going to the café across the street, Brandt."

The café was in fact a swishy new restaurant whose patio, built in the City Beautiful style, suspended a grape arbor on slender Doric columns. Rand felt like a bumpkin, despite the cleanliness of his hands.

He felt even more like one when a dark, neat man with silver hair wearing a tailored suit swept in and spoke peremptorily to a waiter, who scurried off for champagne. Two women followed, in red and yellow chiffon. Though their features were more delicate, Rand recognized the heavy curls, broad nose, and expression of cynical bemusement. Both seemed over twenty: Carmelita and Inés, probably.

If Manning saw the family resemblance, he did not say. Nor did Gabriel's father seem to recognize Manning. The discharge order must have been sent by an assistant, who did not notice or care that Gabriel had enlisted under his mother's name.

Rand sat, staring stupidly at the sisters, as Manning and Cedillo discussed range management. Normally he would have interjected: to help Manning nudge Cedillo away from his request that Rand regrass the Wool Growers' private lands so they could avoid applying for grazing permits in the national forests; or to smother Manning's suggestion that the Wool Growers expand by buying up local ejidos.

Instead he held his silence, wondering if Gabriel had given the idea of regrassing the Wool Growers' range to his father. Between polite reassurances that the service's forage fees were very reasonable, Manning glared at Rand for aid as he cited Mr. Potter's studies showing the impossibility of reseeding native grasses. Then he suggested alternate schemes for range restoration. All, Rand noted, were intended to stem erosion and so might work even if the plants died quickly: weaving willow baffles to induce meanders, threading cottonwood bundles beneath the ground to support failing banks.

Cedillo waved his hand. "So you can restore the watershed, fine. What about the grasslands?" He leveled his eyes at Rand, whose heart lurched at the familiar look of confident impatience. "I thought your magic power was growing wheat? Isn't that what you did in the war?"

He stared for a second, then said, "The war was different."

Cedillo snorted. "So my coward son insisted, before they kicked him out. With all respect, Mr. Manning, if the United States Forest Service is no more useful to our operation than he was, you are simply wasting my time."

He saw the color drain from Manning's face, but his warning glance at Rand came too late. Inside him something cracked, and he found himself facing Cedillo and saying with soft anger, "I was in the army with your son, and he was the bravest man I've ever known."

Silence swept the table. Rand saw the sisters catch each other's eyes.

Cedillo's face was startled. He allowed himself only a moment of discomposure, then leaned forward. "Is that so? That's not what his discharge papers said. I was told he deserted, among—other things."

Rand ignored Manning's glower. "Then you didn't get the full story." Whatever had snapped inside him was seeping through his chest. He could not control it as he continued, "It's my fault your son was discharged. He left his post to save my life after I went AWOL. I was captured by German spies and he shot them off me. The service needed a scapegoat for my desertion, so they picked him. You can guess why." He met Cedillo's eyes.

"Mr. Brandt, I will not have you spreading lies," Manning began. But Cedillo had leaned back, and the look he gave Manning was cold. Manning's knuckles whitened.

Rand saw that the impotent taunting was over, that he would pay for this later. A satisfied pain burned through him. "Perhaps you should take the ladies for a stroll," Manning said. It was not a suggestion. "Mr. Cedillo and I do not require your presence for our business."

Immediately the sister in yellow said, "Yes, let's walk." Rising, she plucked at Rand's collar. He started again at the gesture's familiarity. The sister in red moved to flank him. Taking his arms, they marched him out of the café.

Together they steered down the shady side of the street. Rand's fury was cooling, replaced by a spent lassitude. He was not sure what his outburst had achieved. Neither sister addressed him. Instead, swinging him to one side so she linked arms with her sister, the woman in the red dress burst out in a flurry of Spanish. Her sister replied, waving her free hand for emphasis. Though their accent was familiar, their speed was too great for him to pick out more than a few words. But those he did catch made him redden and hunch his shoulders.

The sister in the yellow dress raised an eyebrow. "Ah, so you talked some too," she said. "That's at least something."

"You're Inés?" he ventured.

She slowed their march a little. "Yes," she said. "More than some, then."

The second sister added, "I'm Carmelita. Thank you for saying that—we knew our brother couldn't have been discharged for cowardice. But father will only believe another man, and Gabo has been too proud to tell us anything. That bastard hasn't written us in eight months." A little tremor crossed her face. "How is he? Is he all right?"

The ache burrowed into his stomach, but the surprise was sharper. "Eight months? You mean he hasn't written since he left Europe? He said he wouldn't, but I always figured he'd come around."

"He's back in America?" said Carmelita.

"Yes. Chicago, I think."

She frowned. "You think? What, did you lose him?"

"We're not in touch just now." He strove to hold his face still. Though they'd never speak again, Gabriel would not hear that Rand had broken down before his sisters. He saw Inés touch Carmelita's arm. Instead of softening, Carmelita's scowl deepened. In another rush of Spanish, Rand caught the word *again*. He looked down.

"Well, we can't control his tastes," said Inés in English. Her face was milder, though not quite sympathetic. She turned to Rand. "When was the last time you spoke with him?"

"Last August," he said. "But I can tell you a little. He auditioned for the Chicago Symphony and got a position. He's going by Losada. You'd be proud of him."

"We always are. He's still a bastard," said Carmelita. Her frown eased. "I'm glad to know where he is. Now I can write him and tell him what I think of him for trying to shut us out. Maybe if we explain things well enough, Father will even let us visit." For a moment her face flickered toward pain, before Rand saw her catch and contain it. So stoicism was a family trait.

"I'm sorry," he said quietly. "It's true, what I said about his discharge. It really is my fault."

Inés said, "That may be, but it's Father's for disowning him." She sighed and detached herself from Rand's arm, then turned to her sister. "Maybe we shouldn't write. If he hasn't told us anything, he must have his reasons. This is the life he wanted. And that we wanted—don't look like that, you know Father only let you keep the books because he 'doesn't have a son.'"

Carmelita released Rand's other arm. "He would have given them to me anyway, after a few years of Gabo running us into the ground. You'd just let him abandon us? He's our only brother."

Inés replied tautly in Spanish, too quick for Rand to follow. Then they were arguing. He stepped backward, into the long shadow of the hotel across the street. Gabriel had said his enlistment had begun to soften his father. Rand saw now how his thoughtlessness had interrupted that softening, tainting all Gabriel's prior heroism. If Cedillo realized what Gabriel's sisters had about who he was, his defense would count for very little.

For another minute he watched the sisters argue. Then he turned and looked up, at the hotel's second-floor window. Probably he shouldn't meddle further. Nothing he might say could atone for Gabriel's discharge. But he thought of the square swaddle of blankets he had packed carefully in his saddlebag, which in two months he would no longer need.

When he reappeared five minutes later the sisters had stopped arguing. Inés watched him cross the street with raised brows.

"His name isn't on it," he said, handing her the record. "But the symphony's is, and it's clearly him."

"Sarasate," Inés said, turning it over. "Mother will appreciate that."

"I don't know what it will mean to your father. But it's proof of what I told you."

Carmelita asked, "You rode across the mountain with this?"

Instead of answering, he untucked two thick envelopes from his armpit. Handing them over with a few coins, he said, "I have a favor to ask of you both. Because of the conditions of my work with the service,

I'm not allowed correspondence. These are letters for my sisters and my best friend. If you could mail them, I'd be very grateful."

"Easy." Carmelita unsnapped her purse and slipped the letters inside. "Do you have anything for Gabriel? Or would you like us to give him a message?"

In the pause the temptation nearly overwhelmed him. He strangled it and gave the responsible answer.

Carmelita gazed at him then, as Inés already was. The pity in their eyes embarrassed him. "Let's go back to lunch," he said roughly. "I need to know what will be expected of me."

Inés pursed her lips, seemed about to speak, then decided against it. Linking one arm in Rand's and the other in her sister's, she walked them back to the café.

When, in early June, he reviewed those next weeks from the hot window of a train shuddering north, he found he could not remember much in detail. After that first lunch he had not seen the sisters again. For three days he'd paced behind Gabriel's scowling father up a tributary of the Pecos, demonstrating his ability to grow willow baffles. The next week he and Manning had returned over the mountains for the final four crops of wheat. On his back the mounting May sun had hammered. As the wheat rose, died, and rose again, he'd laughed with Joe at the futility of it all. Then he'd held his eyes. It only worked once, but that hasty evening beside the ciénaga fueled him for the remaining weeks. Otherwise, nights, he'd simply lain in his sweat, wondering if Greta and Jonna had received his letters. Or he'd woken panting from rougher dreams, his body heavy with desire. He'd buried his face in the blanket to scrub them away.

Always he saw Clearwater waiting in the distance. It shimmered before him like a mirage, a curtain of dark water into which he would wade and be transformed.

He unstuck his forehead from the warm glass. Outside, Kansas chugged by, dry and golden. He would return to Wisconsin having missed his favorite flowers of early spring, the easter-colored liverleaf beneath the naked branches, the furled cups of bloodroot. He would arrive in summer with the shade plants, cranesbill, waterleaf, white sweet cicely. A sudden violent grief closed his chest, followed quickly by reproach. He must not mourn. He had had enough springs, and through Clearwater would give back many more.

To staunch his self-pity, he turned his face back to the window. The yellow prairie waved in the wind like swells on the ocean, reeds on an endless marsh, the sides of a canvas tent where a poster flapped in the sun.

He would love one thing well.

Chapter 18

On Clearwater Marsh redwings screamed, hunching their red shoulders above trenchfuls of brown water.

The ditches were not nearly so visible now. A lake six inches deep lapped in a vast oblong from north to south along the Rock River's former course. Beneath, the charred peat had been churned with ammonia, phosphorus, and potash. The air smelled ripe. Ringing the marsh's dark pupil, ridges of June green rustled in the wind.

The eastern shore was lined with people in Sunday colors. From his station at the water's mucky edge, Rand scanned the crowd for his family but saw no one he recognized. Along the mud beside him, representatives of the Audubon Society and Sierra Club crouched in waders, releasing mallards and Canada geese to the cheers of children. A crew from RKO had wedged their camera between rocks. Nearby, Gray stood like a weary scarecrow, smoking and talking to two officials from the state conservation commission. Behind him, a banner flapped from the eaves of the shooting club's front porch: *Swamp Boy Comes Home.*

Under Manning's orders, at dinner the night before, Rand had eaten liver and drunk a lot of water. Later he had vomited it all into the bushes. He felt light-headed. Ned, standing beside him with the species lists, kept touching his elbow.

"Fifteen minutes until your debut," Ned said. "Do you want to go over grasses again?"

Rand did not answer. Beyond, the marsh waited.

It was now midmorning. The close gray sky was too dull to reflect from the water. Though he stood near the new lake's northeast corner, his mind's eye drew contours on its circumference: on this long fetch, a fleet of bulrushes; on that drumlin, an oak opening. Everything orderly, species progressing through their successions in correct relative relationship to one another. While he was sinking elodea and pondweed in the bare water he'd root oak grubs in the shrub-carr; while replacing the pondweed with wild rice, he'd raise sedge tussocks among the reeds.

The images flickered through his brain, slides under pale light. He wanted to ache for them, as he had once ached at the memory of dawn flaring pink between Clearwater's cattails. He could not. No longing stirred his heart, only a chill submission, a numbness cold as deep water. He was no longer troubled by this lack of feeling. He knew that it was only the marsh granting him its own wild dispassion—pledging him to itself, as women tie scarves on a beloved's arm as he goes off to war.

As he stared over the brown water, at the edge of his mind a small voice rippled: he should stop; his life was not enough to restore the marsh's; his gift would never serve preservation, not because of what he wasn't but because of what it was—only he had never really understood it, and might never understand, in the same way he might never understand the marsh itself, its hundreds of animals and plants in their endless, interwoven relation.

The voice was cowardly and selfish, and he silenced it.

"I'm ready," he told Ned.

Then without waiting for an answer, he pushed his boat out onto the marsh.

Behind him he heard Gray's call and Manning's hoarse reprimand. The glee band sputtered prematurely into "America the Beautiful." As he poled, these shore sounds dropped away. Before him Clearwater lay in silence, its water slick as an old burn.

He landed on a low island, where he could no longer see the clubhouse. Placing the pole in the boat's bottom, he pushed it back onto the water. No frogs leapt in protest at the disturbance; no turtles slid. The marsh lay lifeless in its bed of brown mud. But he would heal it.

Somewhere to the east, he thought he heard the squeal of a starling.

He knelt at the water's margin and worked his hands into the muck. One last time he thumbed his mind along the diagram he'd created from Ned's species lists. Murmuring their major genuses, he conjured their roles in the picture: for the reed marsh, *Cyperus*, *Eleocharis*, *Typha*, and *Zizania*; for the sedge meadow, four types of *Carex*, *Calamagrostis*, and *Angelica*; for the shrub-carr, *Cornus*, *Sambucus*, and *Salix* of several species. Then he worked his way through the minor parts, the arrowheads and bladderworts, apple moss and duckweed. In his mind's eye he blocked each species into place, like a director shuffling actors over their marks.

Finally, closing his eyes, he reached out with his gift. As he had in the alders at Verdun, he let his senses soak into the earth, feeling his way as if with fingers. The cattails' foot-long rhizomes tickled him; the scars in the scorched peat scraped his palms. He reached deeper. This time he sought not seeds and tubers but the marsh's vital spirit: the web that shimmered between species, holding the whole organism together. He listened for the note that had rung him when he'd first seen the silver mist lift, all those years ago.

When he found it, or thought he had, its pulse beat feebly, a bare flutter beneath his fingers. The silver net was faint, but it lived.

He braced himself. Then he opened his chest to touch the answering flutter there.

For a fish to walk, it must forsake its tail. For a lover to deserve love, first he must give it. He stared down at his wrists, flexed like roots in the mud. He would not be afraid.

Shaking, he dipped his gift like a pen into his thudding heartbeat. He drew, filling it. Then he reached back deep into the marsh.

As his senses threaded through the burnt peat, down to the glacial till and up past the brown water, rhizomes flared along them like nerves. Each flare sparked an image that he clasped around himself—circles of bulrush spreading clonally through a mat of cattail; cottonwoods thickening on slopes; green whorls of water dock browning to drop their seeds.

He reached deeper. The dark curtain of the present tore, and a blade of light rent him with illuminating pain. In some sunlit past or future, he saw damselflies resting on the pickerelweed, coots chugging toward the eelgrass beds, muskrats cropping the cattail for lodges. The pictures spooled through him like film reel, their backlight the bright lamp of his own blood.

At last, when he was furled so thoroughly in the marsh he could no longer tell where it ended and he began, when his pulse was dissolved and the pain a high distant whisper like a heron passing above, he opened his eyes and looked down into the brown water, into the heart of Clearwater, which he had loved since he was a boy.

He gave.

~

Summer dawn on the great marsh. The sun has risen in cloud, and the fog that rolls over the open water is still white and opaque. Beneath it a float of teals skims the duckweed. In the meadow, a field mouse shakes dew from its fur.

Presently the clouds unclump and a lance of sun sets fire to the mist. Over the next few hours it burns off. In the opened sky a harrier rises. Below, a fleet of goslings paddle behind their flagship parents.

By noon it is hot enough for the turtles to haul themselves out and sit smiling on logs. Metallic dragonflies perch horizontally on twigs. From an oak along the ridge, a vireo calls lazily into the still air.

As the falling sun draws shadows over the water, the water lilies reclose, as do the wings of the basking cormorants. The muskrat's wake is golden. Evening goes purple between the cattails.

In summer, dusk is long, night never quite black. Some ducks lie nested, beaks tucked; others forage in the quiet. Raccoons shuffle toward their nightly buffet. Everywhere, rest precipitates in cool dew.

The marsh sleeps with one eye open, waiting for the dawn.

~

He woke to white light and a great thirst.

He had not expected to wake. The light was painful, artificial. Flinching into it he tried to shift his body, only to find his muscles shudder with weakness. The air smelled sterile. At his motion the weight at the end of his bed—it was a bed—shifted.

"You're up?" said Jonna's voice. "Thank god."

He forced his eyes wider. She was sitting cross-legged at the foot, book in her lap. Behind her the white wall's gleam was bisected by a brown hospital door.

"Madison General," she said, watching his face. "Your family insisted, because it was closer than Milwaukee. Don't talk. I'll get you some water."

She left and returned. In the interim his head began to clear. He was not supposed to have woken. If he had, it meant something of his had been left over. And that meant—Jonna pressed a glass to his lips and he drank mechanically. Dimly he heard her explaining that he'd been out for three weeks; that his parents had visited every week, and Greta every day; that Jonna herself had begun sneaking in after a week, when Manning wasn't around.

"Clearwater," he said. She stopped. His voice rasped. "The marsh, Jonna. How is it?"

She looked at him, and he knew.

"How bad?" he whispered.

"We shouldn't talk about this yet," she said, but he saw her brace herself. Neither of them had ever been able to forestall a truly important conversation.

More firmly he asked, "How bad?"

"I can't say for sure. I'm not one of your naturalists, and I haven't been back for two weeks." She looked down. "But when I left, the water was bright green. A lot of dead things had floated to the surface."

His stomach pitched. "Algae? How would a bloom that big—no, no. Did anything eat it? The geese?"

"Some survived. But the ducks they released . . ."

He clutched at his thigh below the blanket. His fingers were so weak, he barely felt the pinch. "The flora. Did you see it?"

"Maybe?"

"How were the cattails? The rushes? What about the flowers, the spatterdock and the pickerelweed? What color were the dogwoods? Or the willow thickets? Did the damage reach up into the oak barrens? Were the tussocks in the meadows—"

She was rising to his panic. "I don't know! I didn't see everything. I was only there a day! Your trees always died slowly. I couldn't tell. The grass looked dry, I guess? The water lilies all sank."

She kept talking, but he could no longer see the white room. In the dusk he slogged through green muck, the bloated bellies of fish bumping on his boots. On the hill the oaks were naked sticks, the willows below gone gray and brittle. A flock of geese lay together, bodies still as stones. As he watched, over the marsh a fog unrolled itself, a white pall. The fog became ice, still and pure.

He had killed it. He imagined the marsh as a maiden whisking her token away, replacing it with a white feather.

All the warnings he had ignored crowded icily in his chest, hardening to a grim, airless fury. His life had not been enough; or he had been wrong; or something else. It did not matter. He had killed it. For such betrayal he must be punished. Since he had tied his fate to the marsh's, it was unjust that he should survive it. He was a coward, but he could be loyal at the last. Perhaps that might finally prove he'd really loved Clearwater—

"You were right." Jonna's voice jarred him. "We really don't know enough to use your gift well. I'm so sorry the service put you up to this."

Through the fury trapping him like river ice, he looked up at her. The water was cold and deep, and he did not want to surface.

Then he thought of the marsh, green with death under its shroud of mud. Despite his love, no sacrifice had saved it. And despite his guilt now, no pain would restore it. He could sink forever into the sickly water, never surfacing, his remorse joining the other scorched and sunken things among the peat. Yet no new reeds would ever rise from such a poisoned body.

Underwater, something shifted. "They didn't force me," he said slowly. "I wanted to. Even though I knew it wouldn't work."

Jonna's brows creased. "What do you mean, you knew? Then why didn't you back out?"

"Because I wanted—even more than I wanted to save the marsh—" The ice heaved, flashing darkness beneath. He could not say it, even to her. He knew nothing of himself or nature, of love or death or sacrifice. But he lacked the strength to swim down anymore.

Inside he seized, split, and something warm and weak broke free.

He looked at Jonna and said very calmly, "I need to go."

She frowned. "You're still a prisoner. I haven't even called a nurse because they'd have to bring your guards. Where would you go?"

"Anywhere. Away from the service. I don't care." Muscles shaking, he began to climb out of the bed. The hot air spun around him. From somewhere the dizzy thought came that birds did not desert, when they fled the cold; they only flew to where they needed to be. Steadying himself on the bedpost, he looked again at Jonna. "You should leave now, so you're not an accomplice."

She rolled her eyes, then wedged a shoulder under his arm. "Come on, I'll get us some clothes from the laundry. Marie gave me her keys."

As the nurse and her patient, masked for the flu, limped slowly through the hospital and out into Madison's thick heat, no one stopped them. At their passage he saw a few heads shake, heard whispers, *shell shock*. Distantly he noticed he was crying.

Jonna's shoulder trembled beneath him. Her mouth was set in iron. They were halfway toward the flat she shared with Marie when he realized they had not sought her in the hospital. His suspicions were confirmed when not an hour after they'd arrived Marie whirled in, slamming the door behind her. She nodded at Rand with cold unsurprise, then flung her mask into the corner and snapped at Jonna,

"For god's sake, love! I fudged the discharge records to give us a few more hours, but this is still the first place they'll look."

Jonna bristled. "Where else were we supposed to go?"

"If you'd only told me, we could have planned something! This is just like your Berger pamphlets, all that work thrown away on a dangerous stunt. What are you trying to prove?"

"He asked for help! And publicity isn't a stunt—"

Rand rose, cutting Jonna off. "Marie's right. I can find somewhere else."

With a hard palm Marie tipped him back into his chair. "Sit. Your legs have atrophied. If you make it out of this alive, look me up in three months and I'll sock you." She rubbed her face with the heel of her hand. In a controlled voice she said, "Jonna, let's continue this in the other room. Rand: by the time we're back you will have come up with a different place to stay. You're sensible. You understand why we can't have the police here."

"Yes," he said as she stalked toward the bedroom. Jonna followed, her face stormy. Though Marie closed the door, he could still hear their raised voices. Foggily he tried to recall what Jonna had said in her last letter. She had not mentioned any fighting. She and Marie had been living in Madison for months now. He'd thought they were happy.

For a minute he simply sagged in the chair, his head heavy with green water. Yet the clarity that had cracked him open in the hospital remained. He prodded his heart like a scientist, watching it jerk with the urge to scourge himself for the danger he'd brought to this house. But punishment, observed the scientist, would not help Jonna and Marie.

He cinched a tourniquet around his guilt, and thought.

The flat had two windows. One of these faced southwest, where Madison's smaller lake spread its shield against gold farmland. The fields' gentle undulations wavered in the heat. He imagined the smells rising off them, sweet hay, heady yarrow, the richness of compass plants in first flower. The raspberries would be ripening behind his parents' house. If only he could disappear into the summer, touching nothing, hurting nothing, just opening his notebooks to record the land conversing with the season.

His notebooks—he sat up. North through the other window, the university's distant red-brick halls rose against the sky.

The flat had a telephone for when the hospital wanted Marie. As he addressed the operator he prayed Ned was the sort of man who worked from his office.

Ned sounded nervous. "I offered to make you a research assistant, not help you flee prison."

"Please." Rand grit his teeth, ignored his pride. "You won't have to feed me. I'll snare my own game."

"The facilities are very rustic."

"So I'll camp! You don't even have to drive me, just give me the coordinates. It's north of Inselberg? A long day's walk."

A beat of silence; he could almost hear him brooding. Then: "Well, hell. If you're going to be there you might as well make observations. I'll get the equipment. Be outside the Capitol, north side, in thirty minutes." The line clicked.

He looked up from the receiver to find Jonna and Marie watching him.

"I'm going to Ned's cabin. The university owns it."

"For how long?" Marie asked. Beside her, Jonna wiped her eyes.

"I don't know. I'm meeting him in a half hour. Do you have any clothes?"

For the next fifteen minutes the women bustled silently, filling one of Jonna's large canvas totes with supplies: pan, knives, coffeepot, razor, blankets. They spoke little to each other. Given Marie's earlier anger, he was surprised at her generosity. He helped as much as his weakness permitted, allowing the mild work to absorb his concentration. Like a kestrel he floated above his grief, refusing to let himself stoop to the green water.

When he noticed Jonna folding clothes and layering them with her sketchpad in a second bag, he paused and looked at her.

She returned a wincing smile. "If it's a cabin, you're going to need help. You could barely pump water in your state."

"Are you sure that's all right? What does Marie think?"

"Marie thinks it's a good idea," Jonna said quickly.

"Oh, Jonna. I'm sorry."

"We're fine," she muttered. "It's just for a few weeks, so I can figure some things out. We're fine." Her voice was uneven.

Not knowing what else to do, he took her hand and squeezed it.

Marie walked with them to the Capitol. The saplings on its lawn were still propped with sticks. Ned and his car waited beside a line of them, tapping his foot. He helped Rand lift his bags into the back seat. When he saw Jonna add her luggage to its trunk, he frowned. "I thought you were fleeing the law, not going on your honeymoon." When Marie caught Jonna's hands and they held one another just a bit too close before she climbed in, his nose wrinkled. He gave Rand an even stranger frown. But he said nothing until well after they'd left the city.

"I'll visit you once a week to check in and ensure Miss Larson is well accommodated," he said awkwardly. He had to shout over the engine's roar. "It is very, very rustic, miss. I hope you're prepared." Jonna still had enough spark to scowl.

On the way, they formulated a cover story for Manning that would conceal Ned and Marie's involvement. Ned also explained Rand's duties. "There's a photometer, thermometer, flora, and bird guide, plus cages and nest box traps for banding. You're trained, I trust? Good. Also three new notebooks. I figured they didn't let you keep yours, after."

Rand remembered suddenly that Ned had seen everything. He could explain it as Jonna couldn't. "How bad was it?" he asked.

Ned did not answer at once. At last he said, "Glad you're out of that business."

"Ned." He ignored Jonna's warning headshake. "I woke up this morning. I haven't even seen the papers. At least tell me if you think the marsh will recover."

He saw Ned's arms stiffen. "You know better than to ask that," he said. "Of course it will recover. Into what? I don't know. Will it take longer than it would have if we'd just let it be? Don't know that either. All I can say is, you won't have the Sierra Club knocking on your door anytime soon."

"That's a relief," said Jonna. "Then maybe the service won't be looking either."

Rand barely heard her. His heart felt ashen. To distract himself he stared out the window. They were nearing the river, where the fields rippled into hills mounted with red, conifer-topped sea stacks. Little bogs were tucked about their necks like napkins. Among the hollows nested the stumpy remains of old farms. He'd once dreamed of restoring these hills, their wet maple-basswood valleys, dry crests of red oak. He would have died for them, if he could.

"I wish I'd never been given this power," he said. "I wish Gray had never recruited me."

Jonna patted him on the shoulder. She'd never quite known how to handle his self-pity. But Ned's brows rose. "I thought you'd volunteered," he said.

"Not exactly. Gray's my chief. He ordered me to war. What else could I have said?"

On his shoulder Jonna's hand tightened. "But you signed your card," she said. "You mean they never drew your number?"

"No, or Gabriel's, or anyone's in the survey team." His fists balled in his lap. "You think I should have fought back. You're right. I was stupid."

"That's not what I meant," Jonna began, but he waved her off.

"It doesn't matter."

They dropped the conversation. But for the rest of the ride, Jonna's frown remained.

After another bumpy hour, Ned turned off onto a dirt track that hugged the south side of the river, just before its long loop west toward Devil's Lake.

The research station had once been a farm. Its cabin remained, weather-beaten, with a cracked hearth and gaps in the roof. Its trees were gone, save a windbreak of oaks and a small woodlot that sloped downhill toward a floodplain of silver maple. Sliding out of the Ford's metallic rattle to stand on the warm ground was startling, like wading into a deep pool of quiet. The old fields, long fallow, were weedy with yellow sandbur and campion. It was very hot and still.

Rand took a deep breath of the warmth and let it fill his lungs. As Ned was unloading the bags, he snapped off a red hawkweed and tucked it behind Jonna's ear.

"You're calm, for a fugitive," she said.

"I feel calm," he replied, surprising himself. Standing on the poor sandy soil, its heat radiating up his legs, felt like thawing. The relief was unearned, but recrimination was hard to sustain in the quiet sunlight.

"I suppose you did grow up here," she said.

But it wasn't that. He did not know what it was. The farm was shabby, not wild. It was no longer even fertile: little whorls of sand showed its last farmer had stripped it badly. He could not see why Ned wanted data from such a wounded place. Yet it drew him.

Though his muscles were still slack, he took a brush and began cleaning the hearth. Ned leaned through the door to wave goodbye. "I'll be by every Tuesday to drop off supplies and collect your data. Decide soon how long you'll be here, all right? I can't nanny you through winter."

When he was gone, Jonna slid down with her back against the chimney. Her face was taut. Rand brushed old soot from his knees. "Are you all right?" he asked.

Since Madison she had held her composure. Now her cheeks scrunched. He wanted to hug her, but held back. He wondered how Marie felt, alone in their flat; perhaps as drowned as he had, alone in France.

Jonna was crying, trying to hide it.

He said, "Do you want to take a walk before we unpack? There's some oaks out there that would make a good picture."

She gave a choking laugh. "That line of broccoli?" But she stood and retrieved her sketchpad.

As they walked slowly toward the windbreak, Rand leaning on Jonna's arm, she echoed, "Are you all right?"

He tilted his head up. The sun pressed on his face like a heavy palm. He was too tired to feel. Below the warm air his soil lay, and like the farm's, it was blasted. Tomorrow he would have to dig. But for now, he listened.

From the oaks an indigo bunting called, bird of woodlot margins, half-wild. It said everything twice: *What what? Where where? See it! See it!*

"Not yet," he said.

Chapter 19

FARM JOURNAL: JULY 15, 1919

Dawn chorus: fd. sparrow 3.36, oriole 3.40, house wren 3.46, robin 3.51 . . .

On the flat bottomland near the river, night brought little relief from the heat. By three thirty Rand was awake, the roll of shirts he used for a pillow itchy on his cheek. He lay with his eyes closed until he heard the first birdsong: the dropped marble of a field sparrow, north toward the jack pines.

He rose and crept to the door, trying not to creak the floorboards. He failed; Jonna turned on her cot. But she would not rise until daylight.

Once outside, he leaned his back against the cabin's weathered doorframe. The fading night was blue and fragrant. The door faced the weedy yard, ghostly with the faint candles of wild white indigo. Beyond the yard lay the dirt road, which four miles down joined the levee built twenty years before to protect nearby towns from the river. If he strained his eyes north he could just see the dim marsh, where a meadow of pale green darkened to circles of rushes.

On his lap he propped open his latest notebook, then fished for a pencil. At the edge of the yard, an oriole, clear and musical as a flute, whistled from above its swinging nest on the elm. Next the house wren in the old woodpile struck up; then the robin in the oak snag (late this morning); then the yellowthroats, towhees, and cardinals. He wrote quickly, squinting at his watch. Ned had said he'd take any useful data.

Rand hoped this gave him license to include the sort he found most soothing.

By four the chorus was a cacophony, an orchestra tuning. By five it had settled into a steadier rhythm. The blue night was watery with dawn. Jonna would rise soon. Closing his pencil into his book, he stood and removed the looped wire from its hanger and walked toward the jack pine copse to check the snares.

He returned a half hour later with a fat buck rabbit, to the smell of woodsmoke. Jonna was stoking the fire. As he reentered the cabin, he handed her the buck, then took the jar of flour from the shelf and set a pan to heat. Jonna's knifework was neater, his biscuits more edible. It was how she'd split things with Marie, she'd explained on the first day, before looking away.

Jonna granted Rand his mornings with the birds as she granted him his silence. Two weeks into their stay at the farm, he had not yet been able to talk to her about anything. It still felt too heavy to say: I gave myself and was rejected. His waterlogged heart had lost the pressure necessary to confession. The panic of his first day after Clearwater had drained off into the sandy soil. Below, the water table rose only slowly.

Nor had he been able to draw much from Jonna. What she had told him was little more than he'd already guessed. Her return to Madison with Marie had first elated her, as had her small job writing features for *La Follette's Weekly*. Then spring came, with its mail bombs and imprisonments, and summer with its strikes; and what Jonna suddenly found urgent Marie found dangerous. "We live in Madison," she'd sighed, as if the problem were self-evident.

"I thought you were happy to be back?" he'd asked.

"Yes, but—it may be the capital, but it's so out of the way. I have to shout so much louder to be heard."

"And Marie?"

"She doesn't want me to shout at all."

Whether her reticence to say more was fear or shame, he could not tell. Like wounded dancers in a pas de deux, they minded each other's injuries. Jonna watched Rand's eyes as he read the newspapers he'd begged from Ned documenting the Clearwater disaster. He asked nothing when she wrote her daily letters to Marie, which Ned retrieved when he visited to drop off supplies. They circled one another, and waited.

Now as he slopped the dough in the spitting lard, she placed the tray of meat on the table. He heard her unscrew the flour jar, then ducked aside to let her drop two coated legs beside the frying biscuits. "Work on the roof today?" he asked. On some afternoons they did dilatory repairs on the cabin.

"If I finish the piece on the Local 8." The ironworkers' union had helped raise the capital building's dome, and she had spent May interviewing members by letter.

"Sure. I'm going to the prairie today. Is there anything I can bring you for a still life?"

"Some of those little roses."

"Sure."

They ate quickly, in silence. Jonna seemed preoccupied. When he rose, however, she touched his arm. "Swim today, after lunch?"

He found it odd that she wanted to confirm their usual routine, but nodded anyway. As he packed his bag, he saw her reach beneath the cot and withdraw not the stack of ironworkers' letters but her sketchbook, filled with drawings from Madison.

To reach the floodplain prairie—a remnant of a landscape that had once hugged long swaths of the river—he had to walk east through the yard and old cornfield, a decade fallow and filled with red sorrel and panic grass. The route led him past most of the sites he'd chosen for observations. He visited each twice daily: mornings, for flowers and fruits, and to check on the nighttime activity of animals; afternoons, for those blooms that opened with full sun, and for the best light to determine leaf color.

Along the road, the weedy gnarls of smartweed were blossoming, and the speedwell's purple wicks lit. The yard was sticky with the smell of milkweed. A hothouse could not have been more vividly perfumed. In his notebook he scribbled: *First bloom: smartweed, Veronica sp. Full bloom: yarrow, common milkweed, bl. eyed Susan, bindweed, fleabane.* The weeds' whites and pinks and violets waved above the pale, tired dirt.

Agriculturally considered, the whole area was impoverished. Its remaining farmers grew hay and corn, but their yields could not compete with those of the fertile south. The abandoned farm's poverty was typical. The sandy glacial plains along the river contained a moth-eaten quilt of similar empty lots. This one had been cleared before the Civil War, based on the size of the two white pines planted on either side of the cabin. Whoever cleared it had probably tried wheat first, as had many homesteaders in the middle of the last century. He had given it up sooner than the state's other farmers, who, though they'd eroded their hillsides, had at least started with good soil.

Nor could the area fit anyone's definition of wild. Dotted with gravel quarries and river towns, its few unpeopled spaces were so only because their timber or soil had been exhausted. This stretch of river was a waste margin. Like an empty lot or a rail embankment, its barren edges bordered richer lands.

Yet at eight o'clock on a Wednesday morning, the farm was cheery with life. The cicadas' background buzz was like the din of a funfair. A red-bellied woodpecker drilled for grubs with the energy of a girl bobbing apples. The yellow coreopsis and black-eyed Susans smelled chocolatey, adding to the effect. In a neighbor's hayfield Michigan lilies were exploding their orange sparklers. Rand had spent his first week exploring the farm and its surroundings. By the second, he no longer wondered why Ned valued its data.

Walking along the road, he was suddenly reminded of his first excursions as a boy in Inselberg. He had spent hours crouched in his family's woodlot, marveling at the spring pool's spread of yellow crowfoot. In the little hollow behind the neighbor's farm he'd lost himself tracking phoebes to their nests on granite overhangs. These tamed remnants had been vital to him, their wilderness irrelevant.

He thought of the plantation at Gien. Barren and regulated, it had still soothed him to lie beneath its branches. He flinched but followed the memory: under those trees he'd told Gabriel that Clearwater was his heart, though at that point he'd spent only a handful of days there. He'd built the marsh's shrine from silver mist and longing.

A smaller shadow cut across his own like a thrown spear. He looked up to see a Cooper's hawk land in the elbow of an elm. Clutched in one claw was a downy squab. The mourning doves in the cabin's eaves would earn their name today. It was the funfair's first tragedy, a reminder that life paid no heed to boundaries of mood or definition.

He stopped and watched it eat.

Birds: r.b. woodpecker on hickory; Cooper's hawk, 1.

He returned from the prairie bug-eaten. The dwarf roses were nearly blown, but he had found two with petals still firm enough to snip.

When he arrived at the cabin, Jonna was sitting on a stump at the doorway, chewing a rabbit sandwich. She kept her eyes down as he placed the roses in a bowl of water. The swimming bag lay packed beside her.

"I'll eat quickly," he said.

Their afternoon swim spanned the hot hours from one to four o'clock. Their spot was a grassy lip on an oxbow, shaded by silver maples. Several uprooted trees, perhaps a decade fallen, served as benches. Across the river, a red sandbar curved from a tall island of pines. They often swam out to it and sat talking. The sand was more pleasant than the muck of the floodplain forest, which was soft as pudding and stitched with tracks: raccoons returning from a night's clamming, turtle slides, the strut of a curious catbird.

Usually before swimming Rand would record the tracks, but that day he simply shucked his shirt and paddled toward the sandbar. He'd seen Jonna's face.

As he watched her dark head bob across the river, his nerves embarrassed him. To distract from his own griefs, he had spent too much time imagining what had gone wrong between Jonna and Marie. He worried he had not read Jonna correctly. As far as he could tell, she was not callous to Marie's concerns. Rather something else in her, something deeper, would not budge. He did not know how to ask what it was.

The intensity of his hope that the girls would reconcile was also too obviously a proxy. This mortified him. He swore to focus on Jonna and not let his own regrets interfere.

Once on the sandbar, Jonna lay for a moment panting, then hurled herself back into the water. She swam hard for another ten minutes.

When she beached herself again, ribs heaving, she lay her forearm over her eyes.

"Marie would say that swimming in this current is too dangerous." Her tone was slightly aggressive.

Rand waited.

"She always begs me to be cautious," she continued. "Whenever I do anything for the cause."

"You mean your articles?" he asked.

"No, the real things. Stuffing ballot boxes with suffrage leaflets, tarring and feathering a Loyalty Legion office. She thinks I'm a child, that she has to protect me."

His shoulders shivered. He'd known about the leaflets but not the feathering. He wondered if Jonna courted danger for the same reasons he had. Then, wincing, he recognized her resentment at being patronized. "So she hides things from you? Tries to decide things for you?" He thought of Gabriel's frown at Gien and set his teeth. "She avoids you, to keep you safe?"

"What? No." Jonna's laugh surprised him. "No, she never wants to stop talking about it. She keeps trying to find a compromise."

He reddened a little, but she didn't notice. "And that's the problem?"

"How can I claim to be a comrade if I dilute my actions for 'personal reasons'? You're either a supporter or you're not." She sat up, digging her heels into the sand. "I've already compromised so much. Taking that job for Gray, leaving Paris." Cradling her chin on her knees, she stared across the river. Rand followed her eyes to the bank, where the silver maples clung to their waste margin. The light beneath their canopy was sea green, and very beautiful.

"Have you told Marie how you feel about this?" He faltered. "Sorry, of course you have. I suppose that's why she turned you out. Forget it. I don't know what I'm saying."

Jonna did not answer. He felt foolish, insulting her by presuming she shared his errors. But her silence grew so long he leaned over to see her face. It was dark red, and her stare of inward anger was so familiar it stopped his breath.

She sat up and said stiffly, "She didn't turn me out. I left."

"What? You were so—"

"I know. But coming here was my idea. I suggested it because I was angry. And then she agreed, so I had to say yes." Her voice was miserable. "I was afraid."

His heart twisted. He'd thought Jonna wiser than he; her blunders somehow made his own worse. Despite his vow to suppress his feelings, he could not hold back. "Afraid of what? Talking? At least Marie tries. I could never even do that."

At once he regretted speaking, but Jonna cocked her head at him.

"Yes, I remember. It wasn't like you at all. Why?"

"I didn't think he needed to know—certain things."

The old skepticism flashed across Jonna's face. He was grateful to see it, despite the pain it concealed. "No wonder you fought," she said. "But Marie isn't like that. She never babies me, just frets. I don't know how to make her see how important it all is."

She trailed off. On the opposite shore, a turtle clambered onto a log and lay there, gleaming.

He said, "You know, she once told me she's afraid of dirtying you."

"Dirtying?"

"Your ideals. With her—she called it selfishness."

Jonna's voice lowered. "She said that?"

"Yes."

"Well."

For a time she said nothing else, but wriggled her feet in the sand. Beneath her boy's hair, which she'd kept short since Paris, her eyes were thoughtful. She looked like a young knight in a painting: silent in the green cathedral, quest complete, wondering where to go next.

Then, standing, she waded out and dove.

Rand watched her shake her reddened neck beneath the current. Below this oxbow the Wisconsin flowed west to the Mississippi. So too did the Rock River, further south. Even Clearwater eventually gave itself to the sea. He had hoped to be the marsh's knight, wear its favor. Where did that favor stop—Iowa, the Atlantic? Land was never just one place. Unlike a quest, it never ended.

Jonna was far out now, drifting in the olive-green current. On his own back the sweat was running in rivulets.

He stood up, shook out his arms, and joined her.

Back at the cabin, he compiled his notebooks for the afternoon's phenological rounds. Jonna sat down at the table and drew out the letter she had been reading that morning. As he walked out, she placed a sheet of paper before her and a pencil at the corner of her mouth.

On his return she was still inside. Reluctant to disturb her, he loitered in the garden he'd optimistically begun in the hope of having vegetables by August. The rocket had sprouted, and the radishes were half an inch tall. He marveled at their small life, nurtured by his hands. At that moment they seemed more remarkable than his gift. In a long box below the window, the California poppies he'd seeded were just nosing from the dirt.

Dinner was perch from the bottle trap below the oxbow. Jonna had finished her letter and stowed it. He did not ask what it contained. She'd tell him, if she chose.

As night fell, they sat on the floor with their backs against the doorframe, its mosquito net drawn. In the summer twilight, they read. Jonna had brought her own books and requested a few from Ned, mostly novels and poetry. One German volume called *New Poems* she'd handed to Rand with a smile. "I'd meant to give you this in Paris, but forgot. Marie swears he's good." At university he had read little poetry; he'd skipped those classes to go birding. He was surprised how many pages of the Rilke he'd already dog-eared.

> But when you went, a streak of reality
> broke in upon the stage through that fissure
> where you'd left: green of real green,
> real sunshine, real forest . . .

When it finally grew too dark to read, he lay the book on his lap. Above the trees, Venus was milky in the blue. "Wir spielen—we go on acting," he quoted.

"Mostly without knowing it," Jonna replied. She stretched her hand before her as she did when judging proportions for a painting. It looked as if she were sieving the stars. "You have to get off the stage, first. This is as offstage a place as I've ever been."

She seemed calmer, if not content. In a rush of feeling he recalled their rambling, night-long talks at university, when the world was still.

The effort reminded him of the date. "It's been a year since I grew that wheat in no-man's-land."

Jonna continued to examine her fingers. "The wheat that won the war. They didn't even give you a medal."

"I didn't want one."

"Really."

He flushed. "Well, not the kind the service wanted to give me." He raised his eyes to the yard, its pale weeds shining in the dusk. A year ago he would have dreamed of wading through it, red pines crackling up behind him. "Though they almost convinced me."

"The lure of the stage," said Jonna. Then, kindly: "So what kind of hero did you want to be, Swamp Boy?"

A last tan cloud hung low in the blue. He thought of the poster, flapping, then of the endless poppies he'd grown among endless white crosses. He'd had nothing to give in the end. Beneath his ribs the dark water rippled.

"It seems to me you wanted to be the dead kind," said Jonna.

Her words hit him keenly, but without surprise. He must have been silent for a long time. He looked up. She stared back, unflinching. Jonna could always read him better than he read her.

"Maybe." She would never know how close she'd come to his real theory. He could not tell what he thought of it now; that place in him still lay too deep. Instead he said, "I thought that because I loved Clearwater, I would be able to save it."

Jonna nodded. "You had that look, when you woke up."

"I even told Gabriel that Clearwater was my center." He shook his head. "But you know what? I barely thought about it when I wasn't there."

"Because people aren't paintings, with focal points." Her tone was wry. "They don't have a single purpose."

"Weren't you just complaining that you've compromised yours?"

"No, I said I have several purposes, and I've compromised them all. Pay attention." She laughed softly, and a little bitterly. "You're no savior.

Don't balk, I mean that as a compliment. I've seen you sit for hours in that yard, identifying weeds. That's what you love."

"Weeds?"

"It's a metaphor," she said, though it wasn't, entirely.

He was about to object, then paused. Gingerly he thumbed through the events of the past two years. What rose first to his heart were not the wheat at Reims or Clearwater's cattails but their brushy margins: the pitching deck of the *Carpathia*, long strolls in Paris, his rides to the ciénaga. His grand dreams seemed transparent by comparison, bled of their energetic agony. It was as if his memory were a map on which only the waste spaces had been colored. Jonna was right. Like the farm itself, he cherished no wilderness, no greatness.

He blushed again. "It's true. For everything I've done, all I seem to care about are the in-between times, when I wasn't doing anything useful, just listening, or talking." As he said it, he raised his eyes to the yard, from whose tired soil rose constellations of fleabane, white as stars.

Jonna said angrily, "No, that's not that I meant at all. You sound just like the Loyalty Legion, calling us the weaker sex because we don't get shot for Uncle Sam. We just listen and talk." Startled, Rand looked at her. She'd curled her arms around her knees. "As if those things were nothing. As if they were easy."

He remembered her tense silence as she'd packed for the cabin, the misunderstanding she could not bring herself to correct. He touched her shoulder. "I'm sorry."

She stilled. Then as if remembering something, she glanced up at him over her crossed arms. "Ha. Soft."

Fearing he'd embarrassed her, he began to withdraw his hand. But she caught it and squeezed.

From the old cornfield a night wind blew, momentarily flushing the mosquitos. Overhead in the eaves, he imagined the doves curled around their broken nest. Though he could not see them, he knew the deer were making their silent rounds, and the raccoon waddling toward the river. Everywhere along the farm's waste margin, night rustled with life.

As if he were illustrating one of his old letters to her, he raised Jonna's hand and pointed toward a soprano buzz at the edge of the yard. "That's a nighthawk," he said. "You have those up north, yes?" Then he lowered the hand at a whistling bobwhite. "You probably don't have those."

She shook off his hand. "I know what a quail is, dope." In the dark he saw her cheek curve in a smile. She waved at the woodlot to their left, where a gray treefrog was singing its flapping trill. "Tell me about that."

He did.

Chapter 20

Big lightning storm last night. Returned from visit to Madison
to find the old oak split . . .

Early Monday morning Ned dropped them off at the end of the dirt road
to the farm. Its bed was rutted from Saturday's storm, so their walk
took longer than usual. As they rounded the final corner, he saw the
black oak's charred V, the clatter of branches barring the road like wire.

He examined the wilted leaves. "It won't recover. Will you help me
fell it? We should get it away from the road so it won't fall across. In a
year it will make good firewood."

"A year," Jonna said. "How long are you planning to stay here?"

It was the question he wanted to ask her. Since coming to the farm
they'd made three weekend visits to Ned's house in Madison. Marie
had attended the last two. Whatever Ned guessed, he did not ask questions, and each weekend tractably let Rand maneuver him outside for
conversations about the news—the lynchings in Chicago, whose casu-
alty lists Rand scanned with his heart in his mouth; Palmer's red raids;
the rumors of strikes in coal and steel. Ned also updated him on the
Forest Service's manhunt, which remained oddly scattershot, and Clearwater's conservationists, who were now fighting to set aside the refilled
marsh as a refuge to which wildlife might someday return.

Though these talks were for Jonna's benefit, their length was genu-
ine. Rand felt isolated at the cabin. It was a fraught feeling. While he

was grateful to be out of the spotlight, neither Swamp Boy nor Forest Service hero, the urgency of each week's news still seemed to demand immediate response. By retreating to the cabin, he had forsaken speed. He wondered if all shelters were like this, eddies in time's stream, and what would happen when he stepped back into the current.

At least his conversations with Ned gave Jonna enough time. When they came back inside, her face was always brighter. But both Sundays she'd still waved Marie goodbye at the door.

"You're not staying through winter?" Jonna prompted, reminding him he had not yet answered her.

"I'll leave before the first snow," he said. "Probably."

He had given Greta the same reassurance when she appeared un-invited at this last visit. Neither he nor Ned knew how she'd found out. He would have been more worried had Greta not greeted him with her adult eyes.

Shaking slightly, he'd drawn her aside and told her everything— except the one thing he could not, which would only hurt her to learn. When he'd finished, she'd held him at arm's length, as if appraising him. She'd said, "I won't tell, because that farm seems to agree with you. The second it doesn't, I'm writing Mama. May I visit you and Jonna some time?" Yes, he'd replied.

She'd smiled then, and asked him if Jonna was really responsible for wrecking the Loyalty Legion offices. Then she'd asked if she was a real socialist, and which papers she wrote for, so she might take them for her sorority. After ten more minutes of this he'd laughed and said, "But you came to see your brother, right?" She'd shrugged and smiled again.

Later, walking her to the door, he'd glanced at himself in Ned's mir-ror. The man in the reflection had fuller cheeks and shoulders, browner skin, and bleached hair. Perhaps the farm did agree with him.

Now walking back to the oak from the cabin, he whistled, gripping one handle of the crosscut saw. Carrying the other, Jonna held her silence. Her face was pensive and slightly pained.

The oak had split unevenly down its trunk and listed away from the road. He stood beneath to judge the line of its fall, then took several minutes to notch it. As he shook out his arms, he said in what he hoped was a casual voice, "Do you want to take an early swim today? We'll want it, this is dusty work."

She gave her wry smile. "At least you didn't try to have this talk while we were cutting the tree."

"So, yes?"

"Just tell me how to saw."

After coaching her in the proper technique, he knelt on the opposite side of the notch and laid the crosscut's teeth to the base. They sawed for three minutes, stopped to pant, then sawed again. The pale wood oozed. After a quarter hour, the trunk groaned. Shouting, he yanked Jonna back in time to watch the oak lean forward, snap, and slide free.

A minute later he was kneeling over the stump. The cut showed the rings clearly, bright bands of yellow sapwood surrounding the tea-colored heartwood. Pricking the lopsided pith with his knife, he began counting: eighty rings, give or take a few years. Twenty rings out, a wider set of bands showed the oak had buttressed itself against pressure, perhaps a leaning tree cracked by the bad winters in the '80s that had defeated the old wheat farmer. A thinner band ten years on told of drought, ironically in the same decade the levee had gone up. Fifteen years later the rings thinned again, in one place bulging to a black scar. He remembered those fires. At eleven he'd climbed the bluffs at Devil's Lake to watch them burn. This fit the evidence of the old cornfield, whose mix of grasses, a slow succession on poor soil, was not twenty years old. For the last ten years the farm had lain fallow, tranquil save for the occasional storm. A recent scar in the sapwood could have been made by the same blue norther that, he suspected, had in 1911 upended the maples near their swimming spot.

"Look," he said, sitting back on his heels. "The farm's whole history is here. You can see the Snow Winter, and the droughts in the '90s, and the fires in the middle of the last decade." As it had on his first day here, the ground's warmth hummed through him, a strange, joyful gravity. "Jonna?"

She was lying with his hat over her face. Touching his hand to his neck, he found it raw with sunburn. "Oh."

They left the oak where it lay. On the short walk back to the cabin, each familiar tree rang him like a bell.

By the time they had eaten and changed for swimming, the afternoon had passed zenith. Groggy with sun, Rand did not try for the sandbar but settled on the muck at river's edge, propping his back against the slimy bark of a drowned maple.

Jonna did not swim. She perched above on a ledge of turf, dabbling her feet in the water.

He did not have to wait long this time. "She asked me to come back," she said. "I said no. Why did I say no?"

He looked up at her. Sleep and heat had sapped the edge from her voice. In her rapt posture the puzzled young knight had returned, who having found the grail did not know what to do with it.

"You could go tomorrow," he said. "The farmer down the road has a car. We could walk there in the morning."

Her voice was distant. "She said she loves me for myself. How can I return until I'm sure who that is?"

"Jonna." He could not address the logic of her question, only its emotion. "Do you hold anyone else to these standards?"

"I know who I'm supposed to be: a sophisticated city girl, a comrade, a decent lover . . ."

Her eyes were fixed on the sky, which August's wet heat had turned nearly gray. Rand recalled Gien, his daydreams of the future self who would achieve all he hadn't, who he did not trust himself to become. He said gently: "I thought you came back here because you weren't happy in Paris. As for the other things—aren't you fighting with your girl because you're so red she's worried for your safety? I don't understand what you're not sure of."

"You wouldn't." Her voice was too soft for a retort. "You've always been exactly who you are. You've just decided you hate him."

He sat up straight, his stomach cold. "That's unfair."

"Says the man who tried to die for a swamp."

There was no irony in her voice now. For the first time he under-stood how badly he must have scared her. He winced, but refused to be distracted.

"Jonna." To face her he twisted, bracing himself on the tree. "You saw Greta. You're the most sophisticated person she's ever met. I swear you've inspired her to unionize her sorority." She snorted and turned away. He continued to her back, "What I mean is, you're the only per-son who doesn't think you're enough."

"I'm the only person whose opinion counts."

"That's true. But . . ." Sinking back into the muck, he stared across at the big island. The elderberry blooms had passed, and the far bank was dark and quiet, satiate with green. "It just seems to me you're spending all your energy trying to trellis a vine that doesn't need it."

"Trying to trellis?"

"I mean you stand on your own."

"That gift's infected your brain," she said. But she drew her knees to her chest and tucked her chin against them. Her narrow face was vul-nerable; he sensed she did not want to be watched. Turning his head, he obliged.

A long silence fell. Behind them, among the maples, wind jangled the beds of whorled loosestrife and flapped the leaves of the swamp oak grubs. Further up the bank, a young hickory had been bent nearly double from its knobby bole. Its bowing crown, like everything in the understory, was gray brown with silt. Had this floodplain been drier, it would have made rich farmland.

"I'm sorry I wrote you that speech," Jonna said abruptly. He turned. Her gaze seemed focused on something far off. "I did it for me, not you."

"It worked for me."

"No, it gave you another whip to lash yourself with. And it didn't prove what I wanted it to. A vine. Ha ha." She finally turned to pat him on the shoulder. Her eyes were wet but clear. "I need to be alone for a little, Swamp Boy."

He teetered up, feet sinking in the muck. Soft, he thought reflexively. "Sure. I'll go see how the prairie fared after the storm."

As he rubbed his legs dry in a clump of wild rye, he glanced over his shoulder. Jonna sat on the bank, curled around herself, her eyes following the moving water.

The fastest way to the prairie was back south through the maples, then east again past the marsh. On the road he stepped over the oak they'd sawn that morning. He paused to run his fingers over its rings. Through them he could almost feel the slow years of sun transforming into yellow wood. Though he had read some of their histories, others—whole decades—remained obscure. They were as dark as the seasons he did not know in Jonna's life, whose vast outlines he was only now beginning to see.

Lifting his fingers, he walked on. To his right the marsh spread its circles of sedge and bulrush, as deep a mystery as the oak's illegible rings. What did he know of it? Only that in past Augusts haymakers had come to reap it, skirmishing with the cranes who now guided their red colts unchallenged through the grass. How little he still understood this farm. It was strange to think he knew it more intimately than he'd ever known Clearwater.

In the grass the cranes raised their heads, then lowered them.

Clearwater, he thought again, as they bugled his departure. The thought hurt less this time. Tentatively he pursued it. He surveyed his last four months at the marsh. He'd walked its dikes end to end, made species lists, imported waterfowl. He'd spent hours inside his own memories, playing the same silver reel of mist and cattail. Yet for all his obsession, he had left every two weeks. He'd missed the spring peepers, the summer's first goslings, the poplars' fall gold. He had not lived on the marsh for even a full season. Because he loved Clearwater, he thought he'd understood it. But his memories were as far from the real marsh as the adult Greta was from the girl he remembered, or Jonna from her own reproachful self-portrait.

On his left the levee rose, his signal to turn in through the shrubby black oaks toward the prairie. His legs followed the path like a marionette's, barely feeling the earth beneath.

It was the task of ideals to recede, he supposed. But if Clearwater was an ideal, he could never step inside it. For all his lofty talk about organism and community, he'd approached the marsh not as its fellow but as its deliverer—bearing his gift as Saint Sebastian's body, shot with arrows. He had not listened to it. He'd assumed his sacrifice would be enough.

He grit his teeth. He was a scientist; he should have known conservation was not accomplished deus ex machina. Jonna was right. Selfish fool, wanting to die for a marsh.

Without noticing, he'd passed through the black oaks. Before him the prairie opened. Bluejoint and wild timothy reached past his hips. He waded out, stepping carefully around the fruiting dwarf roses. This prairie had survived plow and hoof only because it was too wet. Had the levee not been built, it would have perished from overgrazing.

The image of herds recalled the southwest and his first, failed promise. Like Clearwater, Gabriel had never demanded sacrifice. What he had wanted Rand could not at once name. Urgently, as if his notebook lay before him, he flicked through his memories for an answer. They returned what they always had: Gabriel's face, easy in sleep; their long talks in the darkness; his smile as Rand strung sheet music on clothespins. The nothing moments, the waste margins, the weeds.

He had not listened. He had not thought he needed to.

His legs went fluid, and he bent into the grass. Under his knees the prairie felt bottomless. Jonna might try to placate him, but his self-hatred was justified. What other response could such stupidity warrant? His fists balled against his thigh, and he imagined the grass's green tangle as dark waves, rising. Closing his eyes, he punched, until the world went as numb as cold water.

When it was over, he looked up.

Around him day had closed like an aperture. The quaking aspen did not clatter their leaves; the yellow warblers did not dart between islands of willow. The prairie's bright, hazy landscape had disappeared into the darkness of the bruises on his legs. In the remaining light all he could see was himself. He unclenched his fist, then combed his fingers through a tuft of bluejoint. They caught, as if in a lover's hair.

What did the saint hear, fixed with arrows? Very little, probably. His own pain was too loud.

He sat up slowly. When he had knelt, his notebook had slipped from his breast pocket into the grass. Retrieving it, he opened a new page. Then he looked around.

Wild bergamot was bursting on the prairie's low ridges with its smell of dry spice. On the roses the hips hung heavy. Tall sawtooth sunflowers turned new blooms to the sky. From the thicket of pin cherry, cedar waxwings' cries needled the air. Though August seemed still, the prairie paced steadily through it, its species laced together like fingers.

He looked down at his hand, quelled of his gift. On the prairie, the only idol before which he might fall was himself. He did not want to stand outside anymore.

Pressing his palm to his knees, he stood. Grasshoppers sprung away at the motion. His thigh throbbed. When he returned to the cabin he'd dip it in the river to cool the bruises.

Then limping a little, notebook open, he made his way back along his path through the black oaks.

He listened.

As he went, he paused at familiar spots as if they were the porches of neighbors on an evening walk. Here was the sandblow made by the corn farmer in the hole of an uprooted birch; there the red-bellies' and orioles' nests; here the patch of crimson cardinal flowers and its attendant hummingbirds. Since July the flora had turned over, and the midsummer blooms were giving way to autumn's asters and gentians. Already the barn swallows were massing in the sedges.

He looked down at his rolled sleeves and imagined himself as he hoped an observer might see him: a short, sunburnt farmer, marveling anew at a field he'd known all his life.

When he reached the cabin, evening was violet in the air.

Jonna sat outside, cross-legged, a plate of fried perch on her lap. Beside her lay a packed suitcase.

"I speared one for you," she said, holding out a second plate. He took it and looked at the suitcase. "Can you buck that oak by yourself?"

"I'd be a poor forester if I couldn't." He sat beside her. "You're leaving."

"Tomorrow, with the farmer, like you suggested."

"I'm glad," he said, with a small, bright pain. "Does this mean you're—?"

"No. But I'm not sure we get that kind of proof." She smiled. "So there's no point in waiting any longer. What about you? You won't stay through winter?"

At his back the cabin's weathered wood creaked. He thought of August's feeling of suspension, how soon it would tip and plummet into fall. He had lived inside his sacrifice for so long, he did not know what grew beyond it.

"I'll know when it's time," he said doubtfully. Jonna did not look like she believed him.

Early the next morning, they walked through the neighbor's hay-field, passing the wiry seedpods of the Michigan lilies. Jonna seemed resigned but peaceful. When he asked her what her plans were, she raised an eyebrow and said, "Putting down roots." He smiled, knowing she would never let him live down his sappy metaphor. But she had remembered it.

When they reached the truck, the neighbor chivalrously lifted Jonna's luggage to the trunk while she bit her tongue. Before climbing the carriage, she closed her arms about Rand's chest. "You're all right," she said. He did not know how to respond.

Then she was up, and the neighbor's car sputtered to life, drowning all words. He watched the pale oval of her face at the back window as the car trundled off, until the pluming dust hid it.

On the walk back, in the rising heat, he imagined their reconciliation in Madison. Jonna would be embarrassed but make amends with her usual directness. How Marie would reply he did not know, though he could picture, vividly, the relief on both their faces. He hoped his envy had not been too obvious. His own chance at reconciliation was long past.

In the sedge meadow to his left, the crane family was marching toward breakfast. From the willows a yellowthroat piped, G, G flat. A wave of fresh pain swept him. He bowed his head. One could make amends without seeking reconciliation. If he used no return address, if he asked for nothing, it would not be an appeal, only what he owed.

He passed the old cornfield, its grass spangled with purple asters. Once its dry soil had held red and white pine. The first farmers had cut those pines for barns, perhaps, and they'd never regrown. Though the university owned the farm now, they had not tried to restore its forest. The land was poor. To replant its trees would take patience, and a deep knowledge of the farm's community. It must be done from the inside.

He stopped and studied the cornfield. For every fifty saplings, perhaps two would live. Over many years, if he watched and listened, he might learn which survived and why. That Tuesday when Ned visited, he would ask him for a bed of seedlings for fall planting.

He did not know what would happen to him once he returned to the world. Certainly the service would exact its punishment. It might take years. But when it was over, maybe he could return here. Restoring the farm would be slow, unglamorous work, requiring no gifts—only care and open ears.

He could learn to love it very well.

Dear G,

I am writing to you through the symphony, as I know from your recordings you are a soloist there. I want to congratulate you, and to apologize. The orchestra is very lucky, as I'm sure they know.

I am so sorry I treated you how I did. I lied to you, didn't trust you. I had no excuse.

I know you'll have a brilliant career. I wish you all the best at it, and hope you love every minute. You've earned it.

R

Chapter 21

Tamaracks yellowing. First bloom: turtlehead sp. Full bloom: milkwort, closed gentian . . .

One month later he awoke in the cool dark, to silence. Dawns were quieter now, and the dew on the morning grass chilly. In the window box, the poppies were in bud.

In his notebooks the entries for new blooms had declined, replaced by detailed accounts of leaf color: the black oaks' burnt gold, copper elms, purple viburnum, everything turning later than it should after the summer drought. Yesterday he'd seen the first junco chipping from a fencepost.

Every morning now resembled the last. He rose, recorded whatever desultory birdsong remained, then at six checked the photometer behind the woodshed. Because of the shortening daylight, his two phenological walks had contracted to one, which he made in the early afternoon, before his solitary swim.

Despite the failing season, his notebook entries lengthened. Each day he noticed something new. A squirrel was slowly stripping the poison ivy behind the woodpile of its pale fruits, apparently no worse for the wear. At the edge of the marsh the rabbits girdled red dogwood, but only those plants whose bark was infected by scale insects. Other members of the farm's community had grown almost predictable. The woodcock spent noons in the prickly ash thicket below the ridge. The silver maples near the swimming spot turned steadily more yellow than their red counterparts up the bank.

He took a settled joy in these observations. Some part of him now felt rooted in the farm, though he knew he was an itinerant bird who would fly before winter. Still, catching a glimpse of himself in the river was like touching a limb he hadn't realized he'd lost. His heart, like the season, was warm and quiet. One day in late September, as he returned to the cabin through the golden autumn afternoon, he realized he hadn't thought about his gift in days.

His forest helped. In the old cornfield, messy rows of white and red pine seedlings waved their thin fingers. At Ned's first visit after Jonna's departure, Rand had convinced him that an experimental forest might be a valuable addition to his research. Surprisingly, the university had agreed.

The following weekend Ned had driven a flatbed truck filled with a hundred seedlings to the edge of the field. They'd borrowed a plow and team from another neighbor and dug long furrows. "Not too neat," Rand said, thinking of Gien. Ned helped him plant the first batch, then wiped his brow and asked how many more he'd need. "As many as possible," Rand replied. "Most of these will die." For the next two weekends Ned brought two more beds of seedlings. Those Rand could not plant at once he stored in the cabin's old root cellar.

After Ned's final delivery, he'd leaned against the truck and gazed at the little plantation. "I'll be checking on these over the winter, but I told you I can't keep hiding you here," Ned said. "When will you leave?"

Rand had prepared for the question. "By the end of October."

"Where will you go? To Milwaukee, with your, ah, lady friends?" Ned still did not know what to do with Jonna and Marie, especially after their last visit, when Jonna had announced that they were moving to Milwaukee. Marie would take up a post at the surgical hospital and Jonna try to write for the *Leader*. She'd seemed slightly dazed by the news, though it was her own.

"I don't know," Rand told Ned. "They've risked enough for me as it is." Before Ned could reply, he continued, "You too. You won't have to worry about keeping me in a cupboard at Christmas. I owe you for this." Over the last weeks he had realized that his data, covering only a single summer, would be phenologically useless. Ned's motives were pure charity; he too was softer than he seemed. "Whenever I'm free for calling in debts, I hope you ring."

"Well, thanks," Ned replied. Then he climbed in the truck, and left.

Rand was grateful he had not asked when he would be free, or from what. The Forest Service's manhunt remained idle. Rand was no seasoned fugitive; with a little scratching the farm should have been easy to unearth. His continued freedom was therefore deliberate. While he could imagine Gray wanted him back—the chief was a meticulous man who hated loose ends—he guessed his reappearance would mean work and trouble. Gray was likely so spent from cleaning up after the demobilization that he had no energy to spend on an extra nuisance. So he took his time.

If Rand wanted, he could probably run forever. He'd spent September considering how he might do it. There were so many places a man could disappear: the west coast of Canada, the deep Rockies, Mexico. But every time he considered running, his heart snagged. He squirmed and felt the hooks in it, the wide mesh to which the lines ran.

He had tried to describe the feeling to Jonna at their last meeting in Madison. When he finished, she nodded. Her fingers drummed the letter of introduction she'd written to Meta Berger, wife of the *Leader*'s editor. She seemed proud of the opportunity, and a little embarrassed. "No one chooses all their allegiances," she said.

Now he looked out over his infant forest, frail in the mellow sunlight. This duty he had chosen. The pride he took in it differed from what he'd once felt toward his gift. That had been compulsive. This was receptive and steady, more like belonging than honor.

As he knelt to check the soil about the seedlings, he realized he preferred the man who was proud of the forest. Remembering the poppies in the window, he suddenly wondered if Gabriel had too.

He leaned away from the thought. Reaching down, he tamped the earth around a red pine that had been knocked off-kilter by wind or rabbits. Loose soil created air pockets that would draw water from the roots, desiccating the little tree. Though it and its fellows would probably die anyway, he would try to preserve them as long as possible. This grove was his first contribution to the farm's community. He was, as much as he could be, responsible for it.

He watched his fingers press the dry land, and thought of October.

The new month arrived in rains. Driving, unseasonal thunderstorms broke coldly over the river, churning its brown foam into the maples. The muck of the swimming spot became an iron-colored soup skinned with red leaves.

Rain or sun, Rand still completed his phenological rounds. The downpours curtained his mind. Sometimes a shape like the future rose in the red lantern of a raspberry bush or the arrow of southering geese overhead. Then the rain swept in and hid it again.

On the month's first weekend, Ned handed him the first clutch of letters from Milwaukee. Jonna and Marie had set up in a little apartment on Juneau street, north of the hospital. Jonna's tone was uncharacteristically peppy. *We've found some friends here*, she wrote. *In Milwaukee, who would have thought! We have dinner sometimes. You should visit.* She did not mention how her appeal to the *Leader* had gone.

Sitting at the table, rain hushing outside, he debated whether to ask her. Undecided, he finally put down the pencil. He stared out the gray window and thought about allegiances.

By the second weekend, the last sapling was planted. He stood back to survey the field, combing damp from his hair. Before him, the sodden mud was a bald pate screwed with wires. Though he had striven for a natural distribution, the lines of the plow still ridged its skin. Squinting, he imagined how the trees would look grown: tall, regular pines, their trunks shading a lush understory. Even if most of them lived, they would all be the same age, instantly recognizable as unnatural, a plantation rather than wilderness.

He was surprised at how little it troubled him. His woods, with their congenial dominants and light management, would one day grow more vigorous than Gien, whose single species sprouted only to be logged. Yet his woods were still sicklier than the old-growth mountainsides of the Cascades—at least, until those were logged too. In a hundred years, which landscape would seem more natural, more wild? He could not tell. Health was tangible in a way wilderness and nature were not.

A grumble on the horizon alerted him to a thunderhead banking behind the scraps of rain. Stretching, he balanced the shovel on his shoulder and turned toward the cabin. He felt heretical, and wondered what Muir would make of him, though Muir, too, had loved a farm.

What he loved about this farm was not wild: the wren in the wood-pile, the woodcock in the prickly ash, the summer smells of yarrow and milkweed. He thought of Clearwater. What if he had considered its health rather than its wilderness? Watching the farm's marsh rise to his left, he pictured himself thin with zealotry, standing before the banner: *Swamp Boy Comes Home*. For an instant, shame raked him. But then he recalled the shooting club, the conservationists, the crowd craning its neck at the decoy ducks. They had believed in the marsh's wilderness as strongly as he had. If they hadn't, they would not have come.

His steps slowed. An older memory surfaced: Gray's haggard voice, explaining the importance of publicity to a large organization. Gray had never needed him to be a hero, merely to seem like one. Maybe wilderness was more about the seeming, too. No one could define it, but faith in it was sometimes useful. He would not have cared what he called Clearwater, if he'd been able to save it.

He remembered how fervidly he'd followed the Hetch Hetchy campaign, rehearsed Muir's reverent defenses in *Century* and the *Atlantic*. Had Muir sensed, in his odes to the valley's wilds, that he was painting a flag to defend rather than recording a truth about the land? It was a cynical idea. But then—he thought of Jonna—idealism was not always truth, either.

He laughed at his thoughts, and how strange they would have seemed to him just a year ago. Gray should have simply shipped him to this farm, rather than try to tempt him with what he'd thought he'd wanted.

Beneath the shame still lifting from his skin, the hooks tugged. Hesitantly he touched a string. If he was part of the farm now and thereby responsible for it, that logic extended to other communities. He had not chosen his allegiance to the Forest Service. It remained regardless, lodged in his bones with the tenacity of the prairie tallgrass, whose roots run deep.

He was before the cabin now. The light had slid from its wet roof, and the boughs of the white pines on either side creaked in the rising wind. Shivering, he raised the woodpile's tarp and gathered logs mindlessly.

Certainly, Gray would court-martial him again. He'd be put to work for the service with a longer prison term. But if it was work like this, slow and attentive, he could do some good. And though wilderness might be show, he would not be anymore. Before he turned himself in, he'd find a newspaper and tell the truth, all of it. He would raise no fleet of pitch pines, restore no parks. He would never use his gift again. It was too lethal.

A red flurry broke his thoughts. From the poison ivy patch the squirrel had launched, trampolining itself from the tarp to the elm overhead. In its wake the ivy's crimson leaves roiled.

He stopped and looked at them. At his arrival in July, he'd meant to clear the patch, but had put it off. In the interim, he'd seen deer browse the ivy's leaves, rabbits gnaw its twigs, and dozens of birds, catbirds and bluebirds and waxwings, crop its pale fruits. In September its color had deepened so that in the morning mist it shone like a fringe of rubies.

Once he would have thought it a noxious plant, or at best useless. But it too was a member, however minor, of the farm's community. It did its small job quietly and well.

His laugh was gentler this time. Refusing to play the hero, he still thought like one. As if his gift were useless because it could not restore whole biota—could not heal the realm, like Percival. He thought of Ned's research. One of his colleagues was studying the growth patterns in taproots. How simple it would be for Rand to grow a batch of specimens for dissection or fill a seedbank.

As he stood over the ivy's rubies in the hardening rain, the smell of daffodils, out of place in a summer city, returned to him. If nothing else—if Gray rejected these small uses—in the meantime, he might grow flowers.

With a violent jerk the wind yanked back the tarp. Lunging forward, he cinched it down. The rain was gusting now. Against the darkening sky the trees' silhouettes blurred their gray heads. He retrieved the photometer and cage traps and unhooked the thermometer from the cabin's back wall. He bolted the door to the cabin, hooked the shutters, then for good measure nailed a board across the window.

The sky was black, not deep olive, and it was October. He would not worry about the cabin yet. But his chest tightened for his saplings. The old field, like the rest of the farm, was below the levee.

To distract himself he sat down to compose a letter to Jonna. She would have good advice on which papers he might approach with his story. As the drumming on the roof became a roar, he explained his plans for after his sentence: joining the Clearwater restoration campaign, taking some minor university position. He asked what articles she was working on and if Marie's hospital was still full of flu patients. He described the farm, his saplings. He filled four pages, cross-written on both sides. Still the rain drummed. Withdrawing another sheaf of paper, he began a second letter to Greta, filled with much the same information.

Two hours later the sky had grown no lighter. A corner of the roof was dripping. He strained his ears north toward the river, but the wind's roar flattened all other noise.

He lay his letters in a neat pile, then rose to check his stores. Three jugs of well water, a bag of flour, some salt and lard, and a bucket of apples from the neighbor. He hadn't visited the snares that morning.

Returning to his seat, he began the final, much harder letter. *Dear Mother and Father . . .*

Outside, the rain fell. When he gave up outwaiting the storm and curled up on the cot, he expected to wake to a floor of water. But at dawn the swept dirt was dry and the light weak beyond the jamb. He cracked the door.

The downpour fuzzed his view, shrouding the trees' tops in gray. Below, a brown monster rolled between their trunks. It stretched its fluid limbs into the yard, whose ground lay only slightly higher than the old field and his saplings.

His heart dropped away, into the water. Though he no longer believed in his own destiny, Gabriel was right about fate's lessons. Perhaps he'd been too quick to recover his pride in himself. He watched the flood's arms grapple the elms at the yard's edge. Or maybe this was a test. With what he'd learned about erosion control in the southwest, he could wade out, lash himself to a trunk, and grow a wall of cottonwood baffles as a levee. His saplings might be saved. His own death would be incidental.

Yet behind the idea he felt the blurry halo of glory, and behind that, the comforting shadow of the raised lash. He froze at the jamb. How to purify his intentions, to know that he gave not to martyr himself but to preserve what he loved? He tried to rake back the layers of his heart, but it was saturated with fear. At the edge of the woodpile he could just see a faint patch of red, the ivy, drowning. Beside it, the gentians' blue bottles lay broken on the swimming dirt. Their muted colors were eerily beautiful. He imagined how the oaks' fallen coppers must be gilding the levee, a mile off behind the rain's gray curtain. That levee had been built because the Wisconsin had flooded before; because those who built it knew their river and its storms.

He drew a long breath. Then, slowly, he shut the door. Floods were what storms did. No matter his intentions, to second-guess them was its own conceit. To listen meant also listening to the thunder.

Returning to the table, he sat and put his head in his hands. He asked himself the question again and again, but the storm's steady roar contained no answer.

The next morning, the rain stopped.

He cracked the door. The exhausted light fell shadowlessly on a seasick corona of brown water. It had swallowed the yard and the woodpile, and its shallow embrace lapped nearly to his doorstep. He had been spared by the cabin's position on the swell of the old gravel ridge. Craning his neck, he saw that the river had leapt its banks and linked hands with the marsh. The cranes' meadow was now a pool staked with brown spikes. From the flow of the water he judged that it would take a few days to recede.

His saplings were certainly dead. Squelching a log into the muck against the cabin wall, he sat down to watch the water. He was not sure what lesson, if any, he'd learned.

The flood took three days to ebb. He spent them clean-copying his letters, rationing his water, and reading Rilke. *All the things to which I give myself grow rich and spend me.*

On the third day the ground was firm enough to venture out. He packed a knapsack with his letters, notebooks, and equipment, then swept the cabin and arranged it. Before he left, he laid his fingers to the budding poppies. A thread of warmth seeped up their heads, which burst into orange petals. These dropped, and the slender pods swelled like green flames. It was the first time since Clearwater he'd used his gift.

Snapping the pods and slipping them into his pocket, he began down the miry road toward the neighbor's.

Passing his little forest, he paused. The water had drained slowly from the field. Over its recession a thick pad of silt had been swept like a rug. Through it poked the snagged nails of his remaining seedlings. His hands shook as he knelt down to dig around an upturned root. Not one tree had survived. In three days, all evidence of his care had been swept away.

Dully he stared at the waterlogged soil. The silt was fine and heavy, a swirl of black and warm brown. Its color was deeper than the sandy, sterile ground in which he'd originally planted. It resembled the rich soil at the swimming spot.

Straightening, he looked around. Over the road and field, the same dark silt had been heaped. Once dry, and turned into the soil, it would be thick and fertile. In a year or two, trees seeded here would grow easier, stronger—healthier than they would have grown, if planted before the flood. The downpour had killed his saplings but enriched the land.

Staring down at his muddy knees, he laughed aloud. He did not know how long he would be away from the farm. In his absence, how many floods might deposit fresh silt on the old cornfield? Would the elms at its edge spread to take root in the new earth? Or would a prairie grow here, a sea of bluejoint shoaled with roses? How rich this waste margin might be when he returned.

He looked up at the trees' limbs, undressed by the storm. It was October now, too late for new plantings. He thought of his family, and Clearwater, and Jonna. Whatever his obligations to this place, others were now more pressing.

He would walk to meet them, and trust whatever rains came.

He was still smiling in the mud when he heard the horn. Ned waved from the side of his car, far down the road where the silt ended.

"Glad you made it," he said as Rand rolled his wet pant cuffs and climbed in beside him. "This was the first day the water was low enough for me to come out here. I worried you'd drowned. Why don't you come back to Madison for a week? It's not as if the service will be looking. They're tied up doing flood control at the Dells."

"Just a day," Rand said. "Then I'm going to Washington, to turn myself in to Gray."

Ned whistled through his teeth. Rand sensed his irritation. "Really. Well, you won't have to go so far. In a week Gray's headed to Chicago to commemorate the forestry Engineers. The last battalion to return home was mostly middle-westerners. They only arrived in September." He whistled again. "After all this time"—*after all my effort*, Rand thought—"you're just giving up." He was almost charmed that Ned had become so invested in his charity project. Lab work must have been slow that fall.

"Once my sentence is complete, I'll come back to Madison and the farm," he said. "All my seedlings died. I mean to replant them, and more if I can. When I do, whatever my gift or I can do for your research, it's yours."

A grunt of amusement softened Ned's ire. "Sure. No free lodging this time, though." He adjusted his hands on the wheel. "You'll need to get a proper job."

"I'll open a florist's," Rand said. "Grown-to-order."

It took Ned a moment to laugh.

Rand turned to the window. On either side of the road, waterlogged fields flashed gray in the cloudy light. Like a stone giant the storm system was stamping slowly east. He gazed across the glacial plain at its broad receding back, and thought, Chicago.

Chapter 22

Even the muskrats have abandoned their lodges. Deer still present & in rut: rubbed-off bark on ridge oaks (not my oaks—those all died).

On Clearwater Marsh, ice plated the new mudflats. From the channel of the Rock River, once fringed with bulrushes, these bald areas had spread like a rash. Rand could only walk them because freezing had firmed the mud. Its chill sponginess was wormed with nets of dead reeds, some still snaring fishbones. In the sedge meadows, the tussocks he'd raised lay flattened. Grown too tall too fast, their roots could not sustain their tops. Beyond, the willow thickets had browned and dropped their leaves. A smell of plant rot wavered warmly over the frost.

Above, the October air was silent. Rand heard only half of what the conservation officer beside him said, his ear turned to the empty sky. The marsh had once been a fall flyway. Now not even the hardy over-winterers, the scaups and goldeneyes, stopped here on their way east to the lake.

Clearwater was a ruin. No wonder Ned had been reluctant with details.

At least it put the ruin he'd left at home into perspective. His visit to Inselberg had been brief and formal, one day of the seven before he must entrain for Chicago. His father had spent it silent; whatever else they disagreed on, Rand had lied to his parents and could not expect sympathy. Still, their disappointment hurt less than he feared. Perhaps they would not have been as proud as he'd believed, had he succeeded at Clearwater. He might have shamed them, but they preferred him alive. So did most parents of most sons, despite what the posters said.

Greta, for her part, performed her surprise well. "Write me," she told him, meaning write me properly, as a friend. He promised. She must have spoken to Anna too, because his little sister had hugged him before he'd swung up onto the local southbound for Madison.

Leaning out the window, he'd watched his family shrink on the platform. His mother's face was red.

"Mr. Brandt, are you listening?" The officer's voice was terse. It had been terse since that morning, when Rand had appeared on the doorstep of the conservation commission's tiny office in Chester. "If you have a problem with taking a lesser part in the restoration, I'm afraid we can't accommodate you. You must understand why few so men in our organization trust you. Frankly, I'm not even sure I believe you really are on your way to Chief Gray."

"I'm sorry." Rand shook his head clear. "I understand. Please believe me when I say I'd prefer a minor role. I can be a typist, or record data, or . . ." He could not think of anything else. "Whatever's needed, once my sentence is up." The officer's face remained skeptical, but he nodded. Rand guessed the prospect of his jail time rendered all his promises more palatable, as the conservation commission did not have to worry about them for several years. "Thank you."

A faint echo overhead startled them both. The officer craned his neck, raising his binoculars. Rand followed his eyes. Far above, at the eastern fringe of the marsh, arrows of geese were flying. Their formations overlapped like scales. There must have been hundreds. Their great bow wavered, dipping toward Clearwater then faltering up again, as if the geese had sought something below and, perplexed at not finding it, struggled to move on.

In Rand's chest the dark water rippled. He breathed to still it. Whatever he deserved, he would not mistake punishment for reparation. One could not apologize to geese, only build them a new marsh.

At his side the officer whistled. "Lots of migration patterns are going to change now," he said. "Maybe we'll put you to work studying that."

Rand nodded. In his pocket, the poppy pods rattled.

The next day, Jonna met him at the station in Milwaukee. He would spend two days with her before continuing to Chicago. She was dressed smartly in trousers and held a case of papers beneath one arm. Her eyes and jaw were set, as if she were aiming through the world about her at a distant target.

When he'd stepped off the train, after a tight hug, she examined his face. "You're sure this is what you want?"

"Wanting is complicated," he said.

On their walk back to her apartment, they stopped in at the *Leader*'s office on Seventh Street. "I'm still writing for commission," she explained when she returned. "They liked my piece for *La Follette's* on the Local 8, and want more exclusives. Berger hopes they'll increase subscribers within the city, since we lost national circulation to the war hawks. I hope I can get a good enough scoop to be hired on staff." Though her tone was slightly embarrassed, her face was animated. "There's so much to be done! Organizing all our new voters, making sure the Party hears their voices."

The talk continued that night at dinner. Marie had taken the evening off, and invited another pair of women, steel-colored and middle-aged, whose '90s dress belied their up-to-date conversation. As he watched them debate the Whites' losses in Russia, Jonna nudged him with her elbow. "It's not like Paris," she said quietly. "But it is like us."

Later, elbow-deep in dish suds, he detailed his plan to take his confession to the press. Though he tried not to ask in a leading way, when he finished she still lay the dishrag down with pained eyes.

"I've already written you one self-serving character assassination."

"But isn't this the kind of feature the *Leader* is looking for? I'm even a homegrown story. And though I'm not a member of the Party, they know my sympathies."

She shook her head. "I won't use you to boost my confidence again." From the dining room came a burst of laughter. Her face softened. "I'm trying to do that on my own."

"That's why I'm asking you. I would trust you more than any reporter to do the truth justice." He looked down at his hands, buried in the foaming water. "Either way, I'm not going to walk into Gray's arms without having spoken to a paper. If you aren't interested, I'll go to the *Journal*'s offices tomorrow morning."

He felt the dishrag bounce wetly from his cheek. "The *Journal*!" Jonna cried. "They're no better than an arm of the Defense League. Fine, you manipulative bastard. I'll let you crucify yourself in our pages."

Stiffly he said, "It's just the truth."

"I know your motives."

"Jonna, please. They're different now. Or not exactly—I mean, they're better." He caught her eyes. She held them, and he endured the familiar lancet of her scrutiny. Its keenness was comforting; he would miss it.

After what seemed like a long time she nodded. "All right." She knelt to retrieve the dishrag. "Anyway, I'm the writer. If you do try to nail yourself to anything, I'll strike it." He did not know whether he should laugh.

They spent most of the next morning over Jonna's desk. Rand told the story slowly, starting from the beginning and omitting nothing, even the parts that made him blush, which he knew would never make it into the *Leader*. From Jonna's professional nods and grunts, the metronomic precision of her shorthand, he could not tell if anything surprised her. Perhaps she'd guessed it all already.

When he finished, she leaned back and flexed her cramped fingers like a bow-hand stretch.

"Will it make a good story?" he asked.

"A story! More like a tall tale. I'll have to tone it down to make it believable." Her satisfaction as she patted her notes reminded him of a farmer squeezing a tomato. He felt relief, then noticed she was watching him.

"So Gray is in Chicago," she said, "and you're going there tomorrow."

"Yes."

"Yes? That's it?"

"Yes," he repeated, more firmly than he felt. He saw Jonna shrug. She knew better than to press him.

"Do you have any money?"

"Fifty cents. The service froze my pay after the court-martial."

"It's a start." Opening a drawer on the desk, she rummaged, then handed him another fifty. "It's not very much, but—"

He pushed it back. "I'm just going to prison, probably. All I need is train fare and a sandwich."

"If you're going to prison, you should enjoy your last chance to be free and in a new city." Her smile was faintly sour. "Have a last supper, on us."

Shamed, he took the money.

But by the following afternoon on the rail platform, her disapproval had faded to what simply seemed like sorrow. Her doubts meant less to both of them than that they might not meet again for years. When they did, they would have different lives. Rand ached thinking of it, as if he'd lost her friendship already, though it would never be loss, just change.

That morning at the turnoff toward the hospital, Marie had pressed Jonna's arm, tipped her chin, then professionally tightened her scarf. Earlier that morning she had produced a suit of obscure provenance for Rand, with a wool coat to match. They both fit uncannily well; one did not question doctors. Otherwise he took little with him, only a knapsack with his notebooks, papers, and Rilke.

Down the rail corridor a cold wind blew, stinging both their faces. Autumn fog had risen from the lake. The wind bored a tunnel in it, through which he'd disappear toward Chicago.

He hugged Jonna close, as if the pressure could close the hollow in his chest. "I'll write as often as they let me," he said. "Will you? And send drawings?"

Sure," she said, rubbing her wrist across her eyes. "Sure."

With a screech and stench of oil, the engine arrived. He boarded. Again he leaned out the window to wave, watching Jonna's small, straight figure diminish in the fog. Then a second train passed, and he had to pull his head inside.

Chicago was cold. The wind's blade was honed by tall whetstones of buildings. Beneath, the din was another sort of weather. The rattle of tram and horse-cart, the flinty clang of construction, the bawl of boats in the harbor and the softer bawl of human voices: all echoed against the high, gray sky like approaching thunder. In the city's unease, also like thunder's, he heard the memory of its bloody summer. As he bent into the wind toward the service's memorial, he wondered how many of those returning regiments were colored men from this city. Then he thought of Manning, and sickened at the hands into which he was giving himself.

The commemoration was scheduled to last three days. Today was the first, and the only part of the ceremony open to the public. To host it the service had booked a banquet hall at the Chicago Club, in the old art museum. According to the station's map, he had to walk east, then turn south just before the railway and the lake. He followed the directions mechanically, head down, mind cold with fog.

He hadn't visited Chicago since before university. So as he turned on to Michigan Avenue, he did not remember where Orchestra Hall stood until he looked up and there it was. Red-brick, iced in creamy sandstone, its facade boasted a fleet of chiseled German names: Bach, Beethoven, Schubert.

For a moment he struggled, then helplessly followed his feet beneath the marquee. Posters flanking the doors advertised that night's performances. *4 & 8 p.m.: Sibelius, Violin Concerto; Rachmaninoff, Symphony No. 2. G. Losada, violin.*

He felt the door he'd closed so carefully straining at its hinges. That Gabriel was listed as a soloist was astonishing, even given his record work. Violinists usually worked years toward concertmaster. If Gabriel had achieved the position already—light-headed, he had to reread the second poster, promoting a summer solo tour: *The New Spanish Sensation! A Second Sarasate!* His joy contracted, knowing how Gabriel must have fought *Spanish*. Would they advertise him like that in Santa Fe, where people knew better? Though perhaps then his family could see him play.

Catching himself, he shouldered frantically against the door. But the lock had broken. Pictures poured into the breach: Gabriel in uniform, whistling and twisting the pegs; in shirtsleeves restringing, his forearms taut; in less than that, hands opening. Yet the image that finally shamed him enough to drive his feet forward was the one he'd never seen: Gabriel in a dark suit on a bright stage, lowering his bow, and his face as the applause rose to meet him.

His head still rang as he turned into the Chicago Club, where the hum of the crowd submerged him. He was surprised to see such public enthusiasm for the service's role in the war. Few men from the 10th Engineers had died, and so, as Jonna would have said, the crowd's patriotism had less to justify. He had to shoulder his way to the front of the hall, and could only manage it by explaining that he was a veteran.

He placed himself squarely before the podium, just in time. A moment later the crowd hushed. Gray climbed the platform. Behind him on a banner, a row of pale, blank faces stared out from below the words *They Gave Their All*. There were more faces than Rand had expected.

Gray's voice fit his name now. As he began his speech, Rand heard a deadening in his tone that sounded like disgust. He did not seem to be trying to believe himself, or to convince the crowd he did.

They believed anyway. Around Rand eyes softened, mouths pursed. He recalled the unusual cynicism of the company he'd kept during the war. Looking around, he wondered if his own were visible.

When his eyes wandered back to Gray, he forgot the thought. Gray was glaring, not in anger but fatigue, as if he were the camel and Rand the straw. Rand met his eyes and nodded his question. Gray tipped his head toward a small side door near the podium. Nodding again, Rand threaded toward it through the crowd. He was grateful he'd been so rattled by the symphony. Now his fear roared only dully, a muffled engine.

Gray met him when the speech ended, deflecting a flock of hands held out to shake. "I'm taking you to a private office," he said, gripping Rand's shoulder. Rand let himself be steered.

When Gray left the room again, he did not lock the door. He made a deliberate show of it, catching Rand's eye as he turned the knob.

Rand considered obliging him and fleeing. Instead he sank into a chair and drew the poppy pods from his pocket. He jingled their slender forms, thinking of the farm to quiet himself. Over its darkening fields autumn wind arced, a high, clear song.

After ten minutes Gray pushed the door. Rand had hoped he would come alone, but Manning strode in after. Farm and music fell away. Rand stood.

"I'm here to turn myself in," he said before Gray could speak.

Gray rubbed his temples. "Yes, Mr. Brandt, I know. Go ahead, say your piece."

Rand almost felt sorry for him. "You can do whatever you like with me, but I won't use my gift for conservation, or lie about it for publicity." He saw Manning begin to bristle and pushed on: "Later this week the Milwaukee *Leader* will publish the truth about me. I expect the national papers to pick up the story soon." He paused. Gray's exhaustion looked self-aware, even a bit bemused. "I guess you don't really want me back."

A thin smile wrinkled Gray's mouth. "So being a fugitive has finally wised you up. Why did you return? You saw we weren't trying very hard to find you."

Rand nodded at the question he had endlessly asked himself. His only answer was that the hooks ran deep, and he had nowhere else to go. But he doubted Gray would care for this reply. He said, "Because I'm still a member of the service."

Gray snorted. "How dutiful. Well, you'll be one longer than me. I'm retiring at the end of this year. In January Major Grawley—you'll remember him from Gien—will become chief. I was hoping you'd have the grace to stay lost until then." He sighed. "I'm tired, Brandt. I dislike propaganda as much as you do, you know. I just understand why it's necessary."

Rand fumbled for a reply. He'd always known Gray as private and dogged, and was unsettled by this frank admission of weakness. "I do understand," he said uncertainly. "If I don't have to lie, I guess you could still publicize me. Back in France, Jonna Larson told me that the public doesn't care if my trees die. She's probably right. Though I would rather work in research."

Manning's lip curled. "You would *rather*! Sir, why do you always let him negotiate?" Rand reflected that Manning might have lobbied to find him, since losing him had probably wounded his pride. "He's tarred the service, personally embarrassed you—"

"A man can stand a little embarrassment." Gray cut him off with an irritation Rand found quietly satisfying. "In this case Mr. Brandt is correct. His gift would be valuable in the laboratory, though it might not save him. It all depends on the jury at his second trial."

"My second trial." Rand tried to keep his tone steady. "When will that be?"

"The doctor and I leave for Washington tomorrow. I was only here to give the opening speech. You'll come with us. Grawley will be your judge. He'll be sympathetic, but you might still be assigned a few years of hard labor. I hope your sense of duty is ready for it." Gray's smile was bitter; for a bewildering second he reminded Rand of Jonna. "It will not be pleasant."

In his ears the blood thundered, and he felt the lure of its flood voice, inviting him to submerge himself. Then he remembered the old cornfield, north and west in the quiet afternoon. A few years was an elm sapling, one heavy oak mast, ten litters of rabbits.

He said, "I'm ready, sir."

"Fine. You'll meet me at 9 a.m. tomorrow, at the Union Station." Gray rubbed his face again. "You have a free evening. Make the most of it."

"How can you trust him?" Manning demanded. "What if he runs again?"

"He won't." Gray pushed himself up from the table where he'd been leaning. He did not look at Rand. "Unfortunately for us, Mr. Brandt is the sort of man who keeps his promises." He waved his hand again. "You're dismissed. See you tomorrow."

Numbly Rand turned. At the door he glanced back over his shoulder. "Sir, how likely is it that Grawley will assign me to research afterward?"

Gray's gray face did not shift. "We'll see."

Outside, evening had fallen in the fog. People bumped through the colorless streets, their bodies saturated with nightfall. Rand wandered along Michigan Avenue, jingling the poppy pods in his coat. His own body was opaque to him. He felt relief, if not peace. He had done what was necessary. Not all ties were as gracious as his friendship with Jonna, or the farm.

He thought of both now deliberately. Jonna would want to know the outcome of his capitulation, as she'd called it. He might find a diner and write to her over supper. Or he could ask Ned if he knew any researchers in Washington who could use a living seedbank. One evening was not much time. Perhaps it would be best if he simply found a hotel and went to bed.

He looked up and found himself before the symphony.

The performance began in one hour. With fifty cents he could buy a cheap balcony ticket. Standing before the door he struggled, already knowing he was too tired to resist. It was just one evening, and his last free one. If he did not disturb Gabriel, there was no reason to deny himself.

He entered the bright lobby and bought the best seat he could afford. "Do you know of a florist still open?" he asked the attendant.

As he paced up Adams Street, he felt slightly unhinged. He would give the bouquet to a well-dressed lady at the end of the performance, explaining that it was imparted to him by an apologetic music lover, one Miss Williams—boring, forgettable—who regretted her early departure. Then he would regret his own. It was an absurd plan, melodramatic, like something from a novel. His laughter stung his chest.

The florist's was closing. Its remaining bouquets were pale and ugly. "October," the cashier explained, shrugging. With the last of his money, Rand bought a small spray of white chrysanthemums. As he exited the shop the night quickly grayed them.

His heart faltered, until he turned back onto Michigan and saw the trees of the art museum's park.

He ducked across the road. Kneeling to feel the soil, he thanked the lake effect: it was still soft enough. From his coat he drew the poppy pods. Peeling each slim pod apart, he scattered the seeds within. Then he laid his fingers to the grass.

When he walked through the lobby again his knees were wet. But a splash of orange summer nestled in his arm. He smiled, shaken by his own indulgence.

He folded Marie's wool coat beneath him as he took his seat in the balcony. Below, the orchestra was warming up, a rich confusion reminiscent of the dawn chorus. Many chairs stood empty.

Presently the players settled. Silence rippled outward. The lights dimmed, and on cue the orchestra stood.

A short, dark figure strode across the stage, as poised as if he'd done so every night for his whole life. He wore a tailored suit that hugged the places his body had filled out after the privations of army life. His hair was brilliantined to gleaming. His hands were the same, though, and as he lifted them to invoke the oboe, Rand felt them again on his neck, trailing down his stomach. Inside him something burst, more vital than any organ. He should leave at once.

He remained. The conductor, a stocky man with a German mustache, mounted the podium and apologized for the absence of so many players, including the concertmaster and his assistant. The flu had made a late attack in August. Luckily, he said, the orchestra had recently gained a truly virtuosic talent.

Coolly professional, Gabriel did not even nod. He kept one eye on the conductor and the other on his section. When the baton fell, he lifted his bow. Rand watched, breath held. Then the music began, and he was drowned.

At intermission, the woman next to him lay her handkerchief discreetly on his knee. "Sir, do you need—?" He mumbled some answer. To stretch, he stumbled to the lobby, saw night black beyond the doors, knew again that he should leave, and returned to his seat.

He sat through the second half of the program as if underwater. He knew only when it ended, and the vision he'd seen standing outside the orchestra became real. Gabriel lowered his bow, stepped to the front of the stage, and bowed into the applause. In the footlights Rand could see his face clearly for the first time. It was young with joy.

He had to leave now. Turning to the woman who'd offered him the handkerchief, he pressed the bouquet into her hands. From a music lover—a Miss Something—for the concertmaster, in appreciation; his regrets. Reeling out and down the stairs, he gained the wide dark doors.

No place in the city remained in his mind. The buildings were tall and faceless, the streets anonymous. He remembered that he needed to be at the train the next morning, and that the station, different from the one where he'd arrived, lay a straight walk away from the lake.

His stupefied body turned east. Its legs worked.

When the fog burst over the scaffolding and sagged into the orange construction holes, he knew he'd reached it. Slipping inside the makeshift waiting area, he sank onto the first bench he saw. He set his knapsack beside him, then drew his knees to his chin.

At least he had escaped unnoticed, and without doing harm. His money was gone, so he might as well spend the night here.

His knees smelled of the blunt city grass. To slow his breathing, he imagined the farm's night air, mulchy with wet leaves. At this hour the deer would be nibbling the remaining ivy. Three fawns had been born to the farm's herd that year, and they were stripping whatever they could in advance of the coming cold. The grief in his heart warmed, stilled. Because he'd spared the ivy, an extra fawn might live an extra week.

"Hello, Ernest. Thanks for the flowers."

He raised his face from his knees. Gabriel's cheeks glistened with sweat above his coat's high collar. His eyes were defensive and a bit amused. In his arms lay a pile of bouquets. Rand's flashed orange at their top. "How did you know?" he asked.

"California poppies, in Chicago, in October? You might as well have left your card."

"Oh. Yes."

They stared at one another.

The farm's night was still in Rand's mouth, a cool pebble. Holding it there like a talisman, he stretched his legs and stood. "You played beautifully tonight."

"I got your letter," Gabriel said.

Rand swallowed several times before he could speak. "I'm glad. I meant it," he said finally. "I really am sorry. And happy for you. You're a natural concertmaster."

"It's only for a few weeks. The flu took out so many of our principals that Stock had to hold auditions while they recover." Gabriel smiled faintly. "But thanks."

Rand could not understand the rules of this conversation, or why Gabriel was continuing it. "It seems you've made an impression," he ventured. "'A Second Sarasate?'"

"Oh, that. It's just propaganda, to sell records. Stupid stuff, but at least my sisters find it amusing." Something hard passed across Gabriel's face. "You know, all four of them came up to see me in July. They attended my rehearsals, even sat in when the Columbia people came to record." Rand tensed, knowing what was next. "Inés told me that you'd met her in Santa Fe, that you told my father that I was up here with the symphony. And made me out to be some kind of hero."

"You saved my life," Rand said quietly.

"Lousy flatterer." Gabriel flushed and waved his hand. "Anyhow, after my father heard that, my sisters worked on him until he let them visit. So I have you partially to thank for siccing Carmelita on me."

Rand bit his lip. "Did she really sock you?"

"Yes. But it was worth it, to see her and Inés, and the girls. When I accepted this position I swore I wouldn't write, because I figured that was the choice I'd made. I thought I'd never be able to . . ." Abruptly Gabriel turned away, the muscles about his eyes tightening. Rand waited until he'd composed himself. "So, what brings you to Chicago? I'd say it was me, but you ran away from my concert without even saying hello." His voice was brittle.

At his side Rand's hands curled. All the panicked impulses of habit tugged at his heart, commanding him to prostrate himself, promise sacrificial impossibilities. Instead he thought of the farm, cool in the moonlight. "You're right," he said. "It was thoughtless of me. I'm sorry." He met his eyes, held them. "So I'll say it now. Hello, Gabriel. It's good to see you."

Gabriel's brows lifted. Rand continued quickly, "You're not wrong, though. I'm here to turn myself in to the Forest Service. I fled my sentence for a few months after I destroyed that marsh I told you about."

"Clearwater. Yes." Gabriel frowned. "I was relieved to get your letter. The last I'd heard you were in a coma. When the news stopped, I thought—"

"You were following the story?"

Gabriel gave him a small, wry smile. "Inés told me you were lugging a record you couldn't play around the Pecos."

"Yes." He rubbed his hand across his neck, feeling sheepish; he almost said, touché. Then he shook his head. If he did not ask now, he never would. "But I'd rather not waste time talking about that. How have you been, since—Paris?"

Gabriel's eyes hardened again. "That's a long conversation. When does your train leave?"

"Tomorrow morning."

"What, were you planning to sleep in the station?"

"Plenty of men do. It's cheap, and I'm a little hard up."

Gabriel glanced at the bouquet in his arms, then back at Rand. His mouth pursed. "Have you eaten?"

"No."

"Would you like to?"

Rand felt lifted, suspended. "What I said about being broke . . ."

"I have some cold beef at my apartment. It's not as if we could go to a restaurant anyway. Especially me. The suit and violin are a decent protection during the day, but at night . . ." His voice lowered, and Rand felt a spike of fear. "This summer I always took a cab after our evening performances."

"Where do you need to go tonight?" Rand asked. "I'll walk with you." He stopped, realizing he might have shamed him. "I'm not implying you can't handle yourself. I know you can. I only meant—"

"I know what you meant." Gabriel laughed. "And the only place I'm going is home. So how about it?"

He looked at Gabriel. The yellow light of the waiting area smoothed his dark coat and hair, burnishing him like a statue. Even surprised, annoyed, he seemed more complete now, as if he'd settled into the mold life had cast for him. His offer was a gift. Rand's first urge was to fear he did not deserve it.

Then he looked harder. Gabriel's neck was damp, his eyes keen. He was not charity, or a sacrifice. He was only himself.

Rand's eyes sought the poppies in Gabriel's bouquet, bright against the line of his jaw. He remembered the warmth in his fingers as they'd sprung up through them in the dark. An answering warmth climbed his stomach.

"Yes," he said. "If you're sure."

"I'm sure. You never ate enough anyway. Though it looks like that's changed lately. Sleeping, too." Rand saw his hand lift toward his face, before he remembered their location, and jerked it back. "What time in the morning does your train leave?"

"Nine." Rand stooped to retrieve his coat and knapsack. When he straightened again, Gabriel had turned his face to the light. The glow sharpened his thick lashes, slight stubble, the neat line where his mustache met his lips. "Ah," Rand said. He watched the lips bow into a smirk.

"I'll try have you back by nine," Gabriel said. He turned toward the doors.

As they walked out into the fog-draped darkness, Rand said, "I know I said I didn't want to talk about it, but you should know they could commute my sentence, or extend it. I might not return for a few weeks— or years."

"Don't get ahead of yourself." Gabriel's shoes clicked on the pavement. "I invited you over for one night."

Chastened, Rand said, "Of course. And if my sentence is shorter, and I come from DC by train?"

He saw Gabriel's shoulders shift in the fog. "We'll see."

The next day was bright and icy, the late October cold snap that precedes an early middle-western winter. Through the windows of the PPR train, Rand watched bars of pale afternoon sunlight slant down the fulcrum of the Appalachian hills.

In the seat across from him, Gray was dozing against the plush seat. Beside Gray, Manning glanced up occasionally from Galton's *Hereditary Genius* to scowl. He had not forgiven Rand for defying his predictions that morning by arriving on time. Gray had merely nodded, yawning, and told him he hoped he'd tied up all his loose ends.

He'd said goodbye to Gabriel at dawn, after a night that was not as easy as both of them had seemed to want, and had involved more talking than, by admission, either had expected. Yet Gabriel had still walked him to the train station as the sun rose. He'd even removed his gloves to press Rand's hands before departing. His fingers were warm. When Rand asked if he could write, he had smiled and said, "If you like."

Now he was writing. With his new trial so close, Gray had not cared to uphold the old rules of his sentence. He would get as many letters out as he could before their arrival in DC. Thankfully he'd had the foresight to bring paper. He braced the letters against Rilke, whom he leafed occasionally, thinking of Jonna. He would write her first, because it was easiest, and because no matter what happened to him, they would understand each other. His parents would be next—short and matter-of-fact—then, longer, Greta. Gabriel's letter he saved for last, when his heart was more settled. *Across what instrument are we stretched taut?* asked Rilke.

The train jolted. He lay down the pen to gaze out the window. The red hills of southwestern Pennsylvania rolled past, maybe the same hills he'd seen two years ago on the train to Camp AU, when he dreamed he'd fill their wounds with chestnuts.

In his letters, he would not outline any hopes for the future. These were promises. He'd make them to no one but himself. But indulging them as daydreams could not hurt. He might even come to need those dreams, if Grawley did give him a stint in a labor camp.

He thought of Ned's research, what small truths his gift might help ecology uncover. While he had never pictured himself in a lab, nature rarely did what was expected of it, and his gift was as natural as anything else. Besides, if it did prove scientifically useless, he could always open a greengrocer's in Chicago. This last idea he heard in Gabriel's voice, since he had offered it the night before, laughing into a pillow. He heard too Jonna's hum of approval, since his living in Strike Town USA would give her an excuse to visit often.

Next he thought of himself at Clearwater, counting migrating cranes through his binoculars. He did not know what the marsh would look like in a decade. Never again would it be what it was; never wild in the way Muir would have meant it. But then, it had not been that for years. He could only hope it might grow back healthier than it had been.

The farm was easier to picture. Of all his promises it felt most like the pith, the first ring laid down, though it was the last. Even if Rand did not return for a decade, Ned would continue the experimental forest he'd begun. In thirty years the saplings would rise into a dry pine wood, its needled floor shading mayflower and pipsissewa. More native flowers would fill the wet prairie, attracting tiger moths and fritillaries; more cranes would come to breed in the sedge meadows. In fifty years his pines would match those beside the cabin, and in a hundred, tower above their fallen snags. Whenever he returned, he would repair the leaky cabin and live there, or at least visit on weekends, so that for life he would remain a member of the farm's community. That community would outlive him, as it would outlive all its members—its always changing parts neither deserving nor undeserving, but merely present.

He thought then in the shorter term, of the farm through this fall and winter. Now, as he rode east, noon light was falling over the flood-plastered leaves, the new silt laid down by water. In his field of saplings squirrels were busy depositing hickory nuts. Snow would cover their hiding places and stop the sap in the elms at the field's edge. In the long dark, chickadees would peck the elms for frozen insects, then roost in the yellow birches near the slough. The seeds would lie cold and quiet. In March, their owners would return to dig them up.

But squirrels were forgetful. Some seed—a pine scale, an acorn— would be left. And this season or next, in April as the thaw bled through the soil, its radicle would nose out and down, toward the water.

Acknowledgments

Look closely at any book, like any tree, and you'll see how it's not a single thing but a network. *Dry Land* owes so much to so many people.

Thank you to the Milwaukee Public Library, Marquette University Library, and the University of Wisconsin library system for their rich collections of Wisconsin history materials, especially early forestry manuals. Please keep these old books in the system; you never know who might want them. Thank you to the archivists at the Chicago Symphony Orchestra's Rosenthal Archives for their lightning-fast responses. And especial thanks to the back catalog of the University of Wisconsin Press. *Dry Land* found the perfect home here, because without UW Press books—from John T. Curtis's magisterial *Vegetation of Wisconsin* to Curt Meine's insightful biography of Aldo Leopold to field guides on flowers, grasses, and trees—this novel would not exist.

Many thanks to my agent, Brenna English-Loeb, for her enthusiastic advocacy and editing suggestions that made my final round of revisions click. Thanks to the great team at UW Press, especially Dennis Lloyd, Alison Shay, Sheila McMahon, Jennifer Conn, Jacqueline Krass, and copyeditor Michelle Wing. As a writer with an academic day job, it was both strange and familiar to have a novel put through peer review, and my thanks to my two careful anonymous readers, whose feedback greatly improved the book. Thank you to *Lackington's*, the wonderful magazine that first published the story that was its seed, and to Karen Joy Fowler, who first suggested I turn the story into a novel.

Thank you to friends in Marquette's English department who encouraged me to write what brought me joy, especially my then chair, Leah Flack, and my colleagues Jason Farr, Liza Strakhov, Lilly Campbell, Gerry

Canavan, Liz Angeli, and Angela Sorby. The university might be (perpetually) in ruins, but I work with awesome people.

My deepest thanks to my amazing Clarion West classmates. I wouldn't have written a word of this without your friendship and daily encouragement, especially on our Slack channel, which was a lifeline for me during the pandemic and a season of great change in my own life. Natalia Theodoridou, Isabel Cañas, Ewen Ma, E.C. Barrett, Ash Beker, Dora Klindžić, Natasha C. Calder, Rafeeat Aliyu, Woody Dismukes, Jen Sexton-Riley, Dennis Staples: you're all the best. Especial thanks to Isabel for invaluable advice on Gabriel; Dora and Natasha for perceptive edit letters; and Natalia, Isabel, and E.C. for conversations about character building, self-building, life building. Thanks to all the other friends whose talks kept me afloat from 2019 through 2022, especially Joel Rodgers, Morgan Vanek, and Allie Kilmer. Thanks to Mom, Dad, and my sister, Kelsey, for believing in my writing and sharing virtual hugs and cat pictures throughout the pandemic.

Finally, endless thanks to Jonathan, my co-adventurer in reading and hiking and life, for always being there and for being proud of me even when I couldn't be; and to Lucy for warm purrs.

Note. The translations of Rilke in this book come from Edward Snow's beautiful *The Poetry of Rilke* (North Point Press, 2009).

B. PLADEK is associate professor of literature at Marquette University in Milwaukee, Wisconsin, where he teaches Romantic literature, literature and medicine, and creative writing. He's published short fiction in *Strange Horizons*, *The Offing*, *Slate Future Tense Fiction*, and elsewhere. His academic monograph, *The Poetics of Palliation: Romantic Literary Therapy, 1790–1850*, appeared in 2019 from Liverpool University Press. *Dry Land* is his first novel.